Deandre asked, "You don't ha[ve a problem] working with me?"

Sheri's eyes narrowed slightly as she asked hesitantly, "Why would I? Because you're a cop?"

He chuckled softly. "Because I'm the cop that arrested you a few years back."

She flinched, closed her eyes and let out a heavy breath. "Damn, I thought you didn't recognize me." She laughed and waved a hand. "My baseball bat days are over. No, I don't mind working with you—if you don't mind working with me."

Her baseball bat days might be over, but her fiery personality was still there. He needed her fire to bring the community together, but not in any other way. He'd always told his son to stay away from women with drama. Sheri was drama.

He lifted his coffee mug and saluted her. "I don't mind working with you at all. How about we meet up later and talk about some things?"

"Your place or mine?" She cocked a brow.

Deandre choked on his coffee. Did she have to sound so sexy saying that? "Excuse me?"

"Where do you want to meet and plan?" She spoke slowly as if he were having a hard time comprehending.

Hell, he was having a hard time. He'd gone too long without sex. Now his brain was finding innuendos where there were none.

Dear Reader,

I knew I wanted to write Sheri "Li'l Bit" Thomas's story from the moment I thought up the character in *Summoning Up Love*. Maybe it's because I'm messy. Maybe it's because I love Jazmine Sullivan's "Bust Your Windows" and Carrie Underwood's "Before He Cheats." Either way, I wanted to write a story about a woman who'd been at her lowest in romance but didn't give up her dream of finding love. I also knew from the start that I wanted her to find love where she least expected it—with the man who arrested her after she busted a window. Many of us have experienced heartbreak, and sometimes when it hurts, it's hard to imagine being in love again. This story is about rebuilding, finding peace with life and learning to be honest about what you want in a relationship. I hope you enjoy Li'l Bit and Deandre's road to happily-ever-after. And listen to the songs I mentioned, but don't bust any windows!

Happy reading,

Synithia

A LITTLE BIT OF LOVE

SYNITHIA WILLIAMS

HARLEQUIN
SPECIAL
EDITION

HARLEQUIN®
SPECIAL
EDITION™

Recycling programs
for this product may
not exist in your area.

ISBN-13: 978-1-335-59469-3

A Little Bit of Love
Copyright © 2024 by Synithia R. Williams

About Last Night
Copyright © 2023 by Synithia R. Williams

Harlequin Enterprises ULC
22 Adelaide St. West, 41st Floor
Toronto, Ontario M5H 4E3, Canada
www.Harlequin.com

Printed in Lithuania

MIX
Paper | Supporting
responsible forestry
FSC® C021394

Synithia Williams has published over twenty-five novels since 2012. Her novel *A Malibu Kind of Romance* was a 2017 RITA® Award finalist, and she is a 2018 and 2019 African American Literary Awards Show nominee in Romance. Her books have been listed as Amazon Editors' "Best Book of the Month" in Romance. Reviews of Synithia's books can be found in *Publishers Weekly*, *Library Journal*, *Woman's World*, *Kirkus Reviews* and *Entertainment Weekly*. Synithia lives in Columbia, South Carolina, with her husband and two kids.

Also by Synithia Williams

Jackson Falls

Forbidden Promises
The Promise of a Kiss
Scandalous Secrets
Careless Whispers
Foolish Hearts

For additional books by Synithia Williams, visit her website, synithiawilliams.com.

To the ladies looking for love. It's out there.
You deserve it.

CONTENTS

A LITTLE BIT OF LOVE

Chapter One

Sheri "Lil Bit" Thomas squinted at the back door of her restaurant. She couldn't be seeing what she thought she was seeing. The dim lights in the back parking area and the waning 4:00 a.m. moonlight had to be playing tricks with her eyes. She shuffled around in the canvas bag she carried instead of a purse, pushing aside her wallet, multiple lipsticks, old receipts and other random items until her hand finally settled around her cell phone. Pulling it out, she turned on the flashlight and beamed the bright light on the back door.

"Well, damn," she muttered to herself.

Her eyes weren't playing tricks on her. There were scratches around the lock. Scratches and a dent in the metal door as if someone had taken a crowbar to it and tried to pry their way in. Sheri glanced up and down the alley that separated the back doors of the row of businesses on the south end of the strip in Sunshine Beach and the chain-link fence of a parking lot behind another row of buildings. No one and nothing was there. Whoever had tried to break into her restaurant was long gone.

Cursing to herself, she cut off the flashlight and dialed her mom's number. She balanced the phone between her ear and shoulder, while she reached into her bag and felt around for the keys to the building.

"Lil Bit, what's wrong?" Dorothy Jean's voice was scratchy, as if she'd just woken up, and filled with concern.

"Why does something have to be wrong?"

"Because you only call me this early when there's a problem. What's wrong?"

Her mom was right. Sheri didn't call this early unless something was going on. Her mom helped in the restaurant, but she didn't come in until right before they opened at seven. Sheri knew her mom was not about to get out of bed before 5:00 a.m. so she tried to reserve her calls for help at the restaurant before opening for when she was desperate.

"I think someone tried to break into the restaurant."

A heartbeat passed as if the words had to sink in before her mom shrieked, "What? Are you sure? Are they still there?"

Sheri shook her head even though her mom couldn't see. "I don't think they got inside. Scratches on the door. That's why I'm calling. Did you see scratches yesterday?"

"Scratches? There weren't any scratches. Did you call the police?"

"Not yet. Like I said, I don't think they got past the dead bolt, but still."

"Girl, if you don't get your narrow behind off this phone with me and call the police, I'm getting dressed and coming." Her mom's voice was breathless and a little muffled. She'd probably jumped out of bed and was scrambling around her room. "Is JD there?" JD was their main line cook.

"Not yet, but he should be here soon," Sheri answered. "He's usually right after me." She looked down the alley again as if he might magically materialize.

"Goodness, you're there alone. Call the cops. Now. I'm on my way."

"Yes, ma'am." Sheri hung up and then dialed 911.

JD arrived right before the cops did. Tall and stout with golden brown skin, JD had an ever-present scowl on his face, unless he was listening to old-school jams. Then he grinned and crooned out the hits with a surprisingly mellow voice.

When Sheri left her job waiting tables at the Waffle House to open her own restaurant, JD was the first person she'd thought of asking to help her. He'd been the best line cook at Waffle House. She hadn't wasted any time calling and begging JD to come work for her when she'd received a grant from the town of Sunshine Beach for small business owners willing to open in south end—an area the town was desperate to revitalize. To her surprise and excitement, he'd immediately said yes.

"What happened to the door?" he asked. His yellow T-shirt had The Breakfast Nook, the restaurant's name, across the front and he'd matched it with a pair of gray sweats and a pair of white New Balance sneakers.

Sheri was in the kitchen waiting for the cops to arrive. She'd already pulled out the ingredients needed for the buttermilk biscuits and pancake mix and slipped a red apron over her own yellow The Breakfast Nook T-shirt and jeans. The person hadn't succeeded in breaking in, so she'd had no good reason to at least get started pulling together what they'd need to start breakfast.

"I think someone tried to break in," she said.

JD's scowl deepened. He crossed his arms and looked around the room as if wishing the would-be robber would pop out so he could jump them. "When?"

Sheri shrugged. "Last night. I didn't notice scratches on the door when I left yesterday. Did you?"

He shook his head. "I would have noticed scratches. Who would break in here?"

"I don't know, but I don't like it," she muttered.

The reflection of blue lights flashing in the dining area caught her attention. "The cops are here."

JD recoiled. "You called the cops?"

"That is what you do when someone tries to break into your place of business."

JD waved a hand. "You don't need a cop to tell you what happened."

"What happened?" Sheri headed to the front door.

He wagged a finger toward the front of the restaurant toward the street. "Probably one of those kids hanging around on the corner. They see you doing well and think there's money up in here."

"It might not be the kids," Sheri replied, but JD only grunted.

Sheri didn't want to immediately blame the teens who hung out along the strip. She used to be one of those kids. The south end of the beach was where most teenagers hung out. When she was younger, the south end was the area with the record and video game stores, an arcade and restaurants with the kind of cheap, delicious foods a teenager could afford on a budget. Many of those same hangout spots had closed over the past fifteen or so years, but the few remaining places were enough to still make the south end a popular hangout spot.

The town wanted to revitalize not just because of empty storefronts bringing down the property value at the beach but also because of the number of young people who loitered in the area. Sheri, who'd grown up loving that part of the beach, had jumped at the chance to open her breakfast and brunch spot in the area where she'd spent so much time in her youth. She wanted the area to get back to the thriving center it had once been but wasn't convinced revitalization had to come at the cost of kicking out all the teens. Sunshine Beach wasn't as lively as Myrtle Beach and didn't lean into the Southern charm like Charleston. The town was trying to find a way to get more tourists to visit.

"Probably one of those kids hanging out on the corner," Officer Duncan said after looking at her back door and checking to make sure nothing else was damaged or taken. "We've had a string of break-ins and vandalism. Most coming from a young group that's calling themselves a gang."

JD snorted. "Gangs, in Sunshine Beach? What are they representing? Whose subdivision is harder than the other?"

Officer Duncan gave a half smile. "You'd think we wouldn't have that problem here, but unfortunately, we do. Even for a small town we've got young people who think being in a gang is cool."

Sheri crossed her arms. "Well, what is the town doing to give these kids other alternatives? Most of the places that kept them busy on this end of the beach are shut down. The town cut the budget for the after-school programs at the community center. They have nowhere to turn to."

Officer Duncan tore a sheet of paper from his notebook and held it out toward her. "Talk about the town's budget is above my pay grade," he said. "This is a copy of the report I'm going to file. I recommend you keep that dead bolt on the back door, but also put in some cameras in the back just in case they come back. We'll increase patrols over the next few days."

"Increased patrols won't make the kids hanging out feel more comfortable." If anything, increased patrols might cause anxiety for the kids.

Officer Duncan winked. "Exactly."

Sheri pulled back and frowned. "Look, I don't want my business broken into or anything, but I don't think scaring the kids is the answer. There has to be something else we can do."

He looked exasperated with her plea but thankfully, no signs of frustration came through in his voice. "Look, if you want to get involved, the man who owns the burger shop asked us to start a neighborhood watch after his place was broken into the other week."

"There's a neighborhood watch?" That was the first she'd heard, and she'd been open for just over a year.

Officer Duncan nodded while adjusting the belt around his hips. "The next meeting is in the old Kings Clothing store building on Wednesday evening. Maybe come and learn more about the problems these kids are causing before you start worrying about police presence making them uncomfortable."

Sheri lifted her chin. "I will."

Her mom rushed in just as Officer Duncan was leaving. Like a hurricane, Dorothy Jean Thomas flew through the back door and surveyed everything. Seeing her mom move with such efficiency through the building was something Sheri wouldn't have thought she'd see when she'd come home years ago to help her recover from a stroke. Seeing her mom up and thriving, something she couldn't have imagined even three years ago, made giving up the job in Charlotte and starting over worth it.

"Oh my word, what happened?" Dorothy Jean said, examining Sheri from head to toe. She'd put her short, pixie-cut-style wig on crooked and her yellow The Breakfast Nook T-shirt was on backward. "Are you okay? Did they take anything? Who broke in here? I'm going take a switch to their behind."

JD waved off her mom's words. "Just some kids, Dorothy Jean. They didn't even get in here."

Her mom pressed a hand to her ample chest. Sheri and her mom had the same shape, top-heavy with not much to brag about in the hip and thighs department. "Thank goodness. You sure nothing is taken?"

Sheri reached out and straightened her mom's wig. "Nothing was taken. They didn't even get in the back door."

Her mom raised a hand. "Praise Jesus." She slapped Sheri's hand away. "Are you okay?"

Satisfied that her mom's wig was correct, she stepped back to avoid being swatted at again. She'd deal with the backward shirt later. "Other than being annoyed that the police want to scare the teenagers away and being aggravated that we didn't get the chance to start on the biscuits yet, I'm good."

"You don't worry about those kids. Especially if they're trying to break in. If they are trying to break in it's only because they've got nothing to do. An idle mind is the devil's playground." She pointed at Sheri. "As for the biscuits, I can help you and JD get them started."

JD grunted and nodded in agreement with her mom. He turned away from them and started grabbing the ingredients needed for the biscuits.

"I can't help but care about the kids in the area," Sheri said. "I used to hang out down here. Every kid who's down here isn't a juvenile delinquent. There just isn't much to do in Sunshine Beach for teenagers."

"That's not your problem to solve." Dorothy Jean glanced at the clock on the wall and threw up her hands. "Goodness, look at the time. JD, when do your helpers get here? We got to get the biscuits made and someone needs to start getting the chicken battered and ready for the fryer for the chicken and waffles."

"They'll be here in a second," JD grumbled. Typically, he'd already be complaining about the kitchen crew not being there by now, but as much as he complained he also was protective of the people he worked with. Because her mom asked, he wasn't going to throw them under the bus.

"I'll start the chicken if you help with the biscuits," Sheri said.

They split up and began preparations for their breakfast offerings. The rest of the kitchen staff arrived a few minutes later. Despite being busy with the prep work, Sheri couldn't get her mind off the way JD, her mom and Officer Duncan were so eager to accuse the teens in the area of the break-in. Just another reason to push the kids off the strip like they'd tried to do when she was younger. A curfew and increased police patrols had resulted in what they wanted. Sheri and her friends found other places to hang out and the south end of the beach had lost a lot of business. By the time they'd lifted the curfew and put the police in other areas, the south end businesses had declined. Now, they wanted revitalization without considering every part of the population who used the area.

Not if she had anything to do with it. She was going to the neighborhood watch meeting and instead of complaining, she was going to demand that the Sunshine Beach Police Department do something to help the teenagers in the area instead of just trying to scare them off.

Chapter Two

Sheri stood outside the old storefront that used to be a popular clothing store. Now the vacant building was being used as the location for the neighborhood watch meeting, the place where she would make her case that the new businesses and the teens who hung out in the area could find a way to coincide. She'd never really gotten involved with community issues, but that didn't mean she couldn't start now. Everyone had to start somewhere. She took a fortifying breath and nodded firmly.

A folding table stood inside the door. Multiple papers and flyers covered the tabletop. A young white woman Sheri didn't recognize sat behind the table and greeted Sheri just as she entered. She wore a dark blue shirt with the Sunshine Beach PD seal on the chest.

"Hi, I'm Rebecca. I'm a community liaison with the Sunshine Beach Police Department," she said cheerfully. "Sign in here, please."

Sheri returned Rebecca's smile before scribbling her name, business and contact information on the sign in sheet. "I own The Breakfast Nook. This is my first meeting."

"That's great and welcome!" Rebecca said shaking Sheri's hand. "The neighborhood watch only recently started as part of the department's efforts to become more involved in the community. This is just the second time we've pulled the group together. Thank you for coming by tonight." Rebecca handed Sheri a few sheets of paper. "Here's your agenda and information on the latest crime report."

"The latest crime report? Why do I need that?" Sheri quickly scanned the paper and saw the attempted break-in at her restaurant listed near the top.

"We go over what's been happening in the neighborhood. This keeps everyone in the loop so they know what to be on the lookout for."

Sheri nodded, even though seeing the list of recent crimes in the area made her stomach twist. Sheri folded the paper in half as she went farther into the building. Metal chairs were set up in neat rows facing the back wall. A podium with a microphone attached to it stood in front of the chairs. Several people already mingled around the refreshment table set up in the left corner or sat in the chairs reviewing the same information Sheri had been given.

She recognized a few of the other shop owners. When she'd been setting up her restaurant, she'd made a point to go by and introduce herself to the other owners on the block. There was Ivy, who owned the tattoo and piercing parlor. She was curvy, with honey gold skin, a wide afro of reddish-brown curls and beautiful tattoos of flowers and the African goddess Oshun on her right arm. Then she saw Jared, the owner of the CDB oil shop. She remembered the tall, lanky white guy with curly brown hair from high school. He'd been cool back when they were in school and he'd been just as laid-back and welcoming when she'd reintroduced herself after opening her restaurant. She also recognized Mr. Lee and his wife, a sweet Korean couple who'd run the souvenir shop for as long as Sheri could remember.

Some of the newer owners who'd taken advantage of the grants from the town were also in attendance. She'd met Kelly, a mahogany-skinned self-proclaimed geek taking her chance on her love of comics by opening her own comic book shop, at the orientation meeting for people interested in the revitalization grants. Her eyes met with Belinda, someone else Sheri remembered from high school, though they'd run in opposite groups. While Sheri hung out in the south end of Sunshine Beach, Belinda had attended ballet lessons and cotillions. Sheri hadn't believed her eyes when she'd visited the new yoga studio and discovered Belinda was the owner. In high school Belinda belittled the kids hanging out at the south end of the beach.

Sheri tried not to hold Belinda's attitude in high school against her. People could change. Lord knew she'd gone through a rough patch that some people still judged her for. One that she couldn't even blame on youth. She'd vandalized the car of her ex, Tyrone Livingston, thanks to too much tequila, her cousin's bad influence and a bruised ego. So, she would not judge Belinda because the woman had come across as stuck-up when they were teens.

Sheri went around and spoke to everyone she knew and introduced herself to a few people she didn't. Surprisingly, many of the residents in the surrounding neighborhoods were also in attendance. She'd assumed the meeting was focused on the commercial area, but the crime watch zone extended into the residential district.

A few minutes after she'd made her way around the room and gotten a plate of cookies and a cup of lemonade, the door opened and the officer who'd responded to her attempted break-in entered, followed by another man. Sheri's brows rose as she took in the tall, handsome Black man behind Officer Duncan. He wasn't in uniform like Officer Duncan, but his commanding presence and quick, efficient scan of the room gave her a "he's in law enforcement" vibe.

He looked familiar, but she couldn't place where she knew him from. His chin was free of a beard, and his dark hair was cut in a neat fade. His broad shoulders filled the dark blue T-shirt he wore, and his tan slacks fitted just enough to show off strong legs.

Sheri quickly made her way to one of the seats near the front of the room next to Ivy. She leaned over and asked, "Who's the guy with Officer Duncan?"

Ivy glanced over her shoulder. Her curly red hair made a halo around her face and a nose ring stud was the only visible piercing outside of the three in both ears.

"Oh, that's Lieutenant King. He's the head of the community outreach team at the Sunshine Beach Police Department and the one who started up the crime watch for our neighborhood."

The cookie in Sheri's hand dropped into her lap and her heart slapped against her rib cage. "Lieutenant King?"

Ivy raised a brow and nodded. "Yeah, why?"

Sheri closed her eyes and cursed. Recognition slammed into her hard and fast. He was the same officer who'd arrested her when she'd decided to channel Jasmine Sullivan and bust the windows out of Tyrone Livingston's car.

Lieutenant King and Officer Duncan moved from speaking to Rebecca to join the rest of the group. He seemed to know everyone there and asked about their business. When his eyes scanned the front row, they skimmed over her before jerking back. Sheri stopped chewing the cookie. She waited for recognition to brighten his eyes. For a frown to cross his handsome face before he lectured her again on how *"a guy isn't worth catching a charge"* as he'd done the night Tyrone's neighbors called the cops.

He didn't do either. A heart-stopping second after his eyes met hers, he gave a brief nod of acknowledgment before glancing away and continuing his conversation with Mr. Lee. Sheri let out a sigh of relief. Then she frowned. Did he recognize her, or was he pretending he didn't to be polite? Not like he had a reason to be polite and act like he didn't remember. Unlike her family, who loved to remind her of her moment of stupidity.

His conversation with Mr. Lee wound down and then Lieutenant King's deep, rumbling voice called out to get everyone's attention before he started the meeting. He was quick and efficient as he went over the crime report: three break-ins, five attempted break-ins, two reports of stolen items from unlocked vehicles, numerous calls of loitering and one public drunkenness.

Even though she had a copy of the crime report, hearing the listing of all the activity in the area was surprising. She knew that end of Sunshine Beach had its challenges, but she'd considered them limited to the lack of investment in the shops over the years and the need for renovations. She had not considered that crime was truly a problem.

"With the increase in activity lately, the Sunshine Beach Community Outreach Unit would like to host an outreach event in the area," Lieutenant King said after completing the report. "This will also give us an opportunity to learn more about what's happening in the area and help you come up with solutions to improve the situation."

"Please do," Belinda said in an exasperated voice one row behind Sheri. "These kids in the neighborhood and their antics are scaring away my clients. No one wants to finish a yoga class only to go out and find a bunch of delinquents hanging out around their car." The slightly fake, welcoming tone Belinda had used when Sheri had greeted her was gone, replaced with one of disdain and irritation. So much for not judging too early.

Sheri spun around in her seat and scowled at Belinda. "They aren't delinquents."

Belinda raised a brow. "Then what do you call them? I didn't want to go so far as to say *thugs*, but if the shoe fits..." Belinda waved a hand.

Sheri stood up and placed a hand on her hip. "They aren't thugs, either. They're just kids."

"Kids who like to break into cars and take whatever they see," Belinda continued. A few other people in the room made sounds of agreement. "As far as I'm concerned, if the city really wants to revitalize this part of town they'd do something about these delinquents."

Sheri opened her mouth to shoot back, but Lieutenant King spoke before she could go off. "The city *is* doing something. It's engaging with you all who are invested in the community like we're doing tonight and finding ways to reduce crime while also not displacing the kids who just want to come out and enjoy the beach."

Sheri spun toward him, pleasantly surprised he hadn't immediately agreed with Belinda. "Thank you. Just because some kids are making trouble doesn't mean they all need to be treated like criminals."

"I agree," he said evenly.

"I used to be one of those kids," Sheri said. "I loved hanging out on the south end because this was the end that had stuff for teenagers to do. I chose to open a restaurant at this end because of those memories. I want to achieve my dream here but also keep some of the things that made the south end special."

Lieutenant King nodded and smiled. "I couldn't agree with you more."

His smile was like sunshine on a cold day, warming Sheri's insides in a way that she wasn't quite prepared for.

Her cheeks prickled with embarrassment from her reaction, and she nodded. "Thank you." She looked away quickly before he noticed she wanted to grin back at him and gave Belinda a triumphant look.

"Which is why I think you'll make the perfect head of our neighborhood outreach committee."

Sheri blinked and she looked back at him. "Say what now?"

Lieutenant King placed his hands on his hips and stared at her with confidence and authority. "Congratulations on being appointed as the head of the South End Community Outreach Committee."

Chapter Three

Deandre King stared at the front door of The Breakfast Nook. The words were painted in a gold script across the door and a sign emblazoned with the same words hung above the door. He remembered when the restaurant opened. Once he'd taken over as the head of the department's Community Outreach Division he'd kept up with the people using the grants given out by the city to support new businesses along the south end of the beach. In the year since The Breakfast Nook opened there'd been a steady stream of people coming in and out, but this was his first visit. Breakfast might be the most important meal of the day, but Deandre didn't make breakfast a priority. He wasn't a big fan of what was considered breakfast food, so he hadn't thought of visiting a restaurant focused on breakfast and brunch.

Maybe that's why he hadn't realized that the Sheri Thomas who opened the place was the same woman he'd arrested when he'd first moved to Sunshine Beach and taken the job with the police department. He'd forgotten all about her after she'd been bailed out and the charges dropped. Well, mostly forgotten. The guy she'd been so angry with that she'd thought taking a bat to his car was worth it had gone on to get a television show investigating ghosts with his brothers and was engaged to someone else now. Deandre had thought about Sheri when he heard that bit of news. He'd wondered what happened to her and if she'd moved on.

Now he knew. She had moved on. Started a business. And, apparently, was going to be working with him to plan a community outreach event in the area. A community event he'd championed to have so he could prove the area could be restored without the heavy hand of law enforcement. The way she'd championed for the area the night before had made him quickly pick her to help, but was she really the right person to help him, or had he been blinded by her enthusiasm and made a knee-jerk decision?

"One way to find out," he muttered before opening the door.

The smell of food and coffee greeted him. Despite forcing himself to eat a banana that morning with his coffee to get something in his stomach and avoid not eating anything until lunch, his stomach rumbled, and his mouth watered. He might not be a fan of breakfast, but whatever they were cooking sure as hell smelled good.

A young girl at the front greeted him. She looked to be in her early twenties, had dark brown skin and long braids that fell past her waist. "Welcome to The Breakfast Nook. Did you place a carryout order?"

He shook his head. "No, I'd like to speak with Sheri Thomas if she's available."

The girl frowned. "Sheri is in the back and helping wait tables. I can sit you in her section if you'd like."

"That's fine."

She nodded, grabbed a set of silverware rolled up in a napkin and took him to one of the empty seats near the back of the restaurant. Once he sat down, she pointed to a QR code on the table. "You can scan that for the menu."

"I'll just have some coffee," he said.

She raised a brow. "You sure? We have great chicken and waffles. Plus, our pancakes are delicious."

He shook his head. "Just coffee. Pancakes aren't my thing."

"That's because you haven't had my pancakes," a woman's husky voice came from his side.

He turned away from the hostess and met Sheri's big, brown eyes. She was attractive; he'd noticed that the night he'd arrested her. Slim, but curvy enough to make his eyes want to linger on her full breasts and pert ass. He'd wondered why a woman as good-looking as her would even bother with vandalizing some guy's car. She could easily find someone else who'd appreciate her...unless she made busting taillights a habit.

She sashayed over to stand next to the hostess. *Sashay* was the only word that came to his mind watching her walk. "Go back to the front, D'asa, I've got him."

D'asa walked away and Sheri focused back on him. The lights in the restaurant glowed off her dark brown skin, and she'd pulled her thick, black hair into a ponytail that stopped just past her shoulders. All hers or a weave? he wondered. Didn't matter. Either way she looked good.

The wariness that had been on Sheri's face when she'd first seen him at the neighborhood watch meeting was gone. At first, he'd chalked up her hesitancy to unease from meeting a cop. He understood caution and mistrust was some people's initial reaction. Later, when she'd stood up and confronted Belinda from the yoga studio, he'd recognized her voice and realized who she was. Her hesitancy made even more sense then.

"You sure you don't want any pancakes with the coffee?" She leaned a hip against the chair across from him.

"I don't like pancakes."

Her eyes widened as if he'd declared that he hated sunshine. "Who doesn't like pancakes?"

He lifted a shoulder. "A person who prefers waffles when he does decide to eat breakfast."

She chuckled, and her laugh was like her voice, husky, throaty, and both brushed over him like an unexpected caress. Heat flared in his midsection along with a spark of arousal. He shifted in his seat. It had taken two years after losing his wife to accept that his heart might be broken but his body still had sexual urges. He'd needed another year to be open to the idea of possibly dating again. But this was the first time in the six years since she'd passed that he'd had a strong reaction to someone. He frowned, not liking the idea of Sheri causing the reaction. He'd arrested her before, for goodness' sake.

Sheri cocked her head to the side. "No need to get upset. I can make waffles if you want. Though, after working at the Waffle House for years I'm kind of tired of them."

He relaxed his features, not wanting to explain that his frown was caused by his body's reaction to her and not because of his aversion to pancakes over waffles. "Coffee is fine. I actually came by to talk to you about the community outreach event."

"I figured as much." She glanced around the room as if judging the level of activity before looking back at him. "I can talk for a few minutes. I'll get you some coffee and be right back."

A few minutes later, she came back and set a cup of coffee in front of him along with a plate with a biscuit on it and a selection of jams and honey.

He raised a brow as he watched her settle across from him. "I didn't need a biscuit."

"You look like you need something in your stomach. Go ahead, try it."

"This wasn't necessary."

She slid the plate closer to him. "I know, but I can't help it. My mom likes to feed people and I do, too."

"I guess that's why you opened a restaurant." He sliced the biscuit in half and reached for the grape jelly. Not because he wanted it, but because it would be rude to continue to reject her offering.

"One of the reasons. I worked at an expensive steak house when I lived in Charlotte after graduating from the University of South Carolina with a degree in hospitality. I was the business manager there but came back home when my mom got sick. I took the first job I could find, which was at the Waffle House."

"That's a lot different than a steak house." The biscuit smelled delicious and when he took a bite, it nearly melted in his mouth. "Damn, this is good."

Her full lips spread in a triumphant smile. "I knew you'd like it. And, yeah, Waffle House is a lot different, but they pay decent, the tips are good and I needed the flexibility to work early in the morning or late at night so I could take Mom to her appointments during the day. That taught me how to be quick on the go. When Mom got better, and I heard about the city wanting to revitalize what used to be my favorite hangout in town, I decided to give opening my own place a try."

He looked around the restaurant and back at her. "Looks like you're doing pretty good."

She shrugged. "I'm doing okay. I survived my first year, so that's worth celebrating. My customers are mostly locals, but I'm trying to get those people visiting the bougie north end of the beach to come on down to the south side and give my place a try."

"But you don't want to kick out the teenagers like some of the other shop owners."

She shook her head, the smile on her face disappearing. "I don't. I used to be one of those kids. I loved hanging out down here. We don't have to displace the people who live in Sunshine Beach just to draw in the visitors looking for a quaint beach experience. We can make it work."

"How?"

Her bright eyes widened, and she threw up her hands in a "Who knows?" fashion. "I don't know, but that's what we're figuring out together, right?"

He took another bite of the biscuit and nodded slowly while he considered her words. After he washed it down with the coffee, he studied her. "You don't have a problem working with me?"

She hesitated a second before shaking her head. Her eyes narrowed slightly as she asked hesitantly, "Why would I? Because you're a cop?"

He chuckled softly. She was willing to play dumb if he was. But playing dumb wasn't his style. "Because I'm the cop that arrested you a few years back."

She flinched, closed her eyes and let out a heavy breath. "Damn, I thought you didn't recognize me."

"I didn't at first."

She opened her eyes. "What gave me away?"

"I thought you'd take a baseball bat to Belinda's head like you did that car." He softened his words with a smile.

She laughed and waved a hand. "My baseball bat days are over. Belinda is bougie as hell, but not worth catching a charge over."

"Neither was Tyrone Livingston."

She sighed and crossed her arms on the table. She sat forward and met his eye. "Neither was he, but that's over and done with now. No, I don't mind working with you. If you don't mind working with me."

He wanted to know more about why she'd done what she did. Had she and Tyrone been serious? Was she still interested in Tyrone? He cut those thoughts short. Her baseball bat days may be over, but her fiery personality was still there. He needed her fire to bring the community together, but not in any other way. He'd always told his son to stay away from women with drama. Sheri was drama.

He lifted his coffee mug and saluted her. "I don't mind working with you at all."

She uncrossed her arms and slapped her hand on the table. "Good. Glad that's out of the way. So what do we do next?"

He looked up as another person entered. "How about we meet up tomorrow afternoon, when you're not working, and talk about some things."

"Works for me. Your place or mine?" She cocked a brow.

Deandre choked on his coffee. Sheri's eyes widened and she handed him a napkin. He took it and wiped his mouth. Did she have to sound so sexy saying that? "Excuse me?"

"Where do you want to meet and plan?" She spoke slowly as if he were having a hard time comprehending.

Considering where his mind had gone, he was having a hard time. Too much time had passed since he'd had sex. Now his brain was finding innuendos where there were none. "My bad. I can come back here after you close. Or we can use the Kings store again. It's become the spot for the Community Outreach Division's work on the south end. The city is thinking of setting it up as a visitor center later."

She sat up straight. "I like that idea. Yes, let's meet at

Kings. We close at two and it takes some time to clean up. How about three? That work for you?"

He thought about his day. DJ, his son, had wrestling practice until six. He'd still have time to get home and get dinner together before he got home. "That works."

Sheri beamed. "Good. Enjoy your biscuit. It's on the house, partner." She winked and he sucked in a breath. "It's about time for the late morning rush. Let me finish helping out but stay as long as you need."

Just like that she got up and walked away, oblivious to the way he'd reacted to her. He watched her greet the guy who'd sat down at the table next to him. Deandre tried not to focus on Sheri as he finished his biscuit and coffee. His efforts were in vain. He was aware of her movements. Her husky laugh with customers, the friendly greeting she gave them all, the way her hand touched the shoulders of some regulars when she chatted them up. He quickly downed his coffee, dropped a ten-dollar bill on the table despite her saying not to pay and got out of there before he became even more rattled than he already was.

Chapter Four

Sheri went out the front of the restaurant to bring in the sign with the specials handwritten in chalk from the walkway. It had been a busy day. Her shoulders ached and her feet were tired, but she wouldn't trade the feeling for anything else. She loved that the restaurant was doing well. She'd worried so much and prayed so hard that stepping away from a steady paycheck to open her own place would be worth the fear and uncertainty. So far, it had been. So, she would accept every ache, pain and fatigue that came after a busy day.

The sound of a catcall whistle from her left caught her attention. She looked up and sighed after spotting the group of boys standing a few doors down from her restaurant. She'd seen the boys before. Teenagers, who roamed up and down the strip after school and on weekends. She'd never witnessed them doing anything wrong, but she knew their hanging around outside the businesses was part of the reason some other shop owners wanted something done to keep the kids out of the area.

One of the boys stood in the middle. His mouth spread in a wide grin as he eyed her from head to toe. He rubbed his hands together and tried, she assumed, to look interesting.

"Hey lady, can I get your number?"

Sheri couldn't help herself, she laughed. Did this little

boy really think she was about to give him her number? "Young man, you don't want my number. I've got shoes older than you."

He lifted a thin shoulder. "I like my women seasoned."

"Seasoned? Lord, child, get out of here with that nonsense. Go try that mess with a girl your own age."

His friends laughed. Sheri shook her head and picked up her sign. She headed back inside. But she heard him grumble, "I didn't like her old ass anyway," before the door closed.

Sheri scowled. "Old?" she mumbled to herself. She was older than him, but she wasn't old. She locked the door with a flip of her wrist before heading to the back of the restaurant.

The "old ass" comment irritated her all the way from the restaurant to her mom's house. It was the first time she'd been referred to as *old*, within earshot at least. She knew the kid was just trying to save face after she'd shot him down, but the words had hit a mark. Sheri was, indeed, getting older. She would be forty in a couple of years. While her life was good, she still wasn't where she'd thought she'd be at this age. She'd expected to still be living in Charlotte, or maybe to have moved to Atlanta or even New York. She'd be working for a high-end restaurant, married to, or at least dating, the perfect man and on the road to having the two beautiful kids she'd always wanted. She never would have imagined she'd be back home in Sunshine Beach, living in a house next to her mom's, still single with no prospects.

She pulled into her mom's driveway and let out a sigh. Even though she wasn't where she thought she would be, she wasn't in a bad place, either. She constantly focused on that. She owned her own business, and her restaurant was successful. She'd inherited her grandmother's home next to her mom's, so she didn't have to worry about a mortgage, and she'd finally shaken off the stigma of taking a baseball bat to her former lover's car. All in all, her life could be worse. She wouldn't let a kid calling her an "old ass" make her start to doubt herself.

Internal pep talk complete, she went inside to check on her mom. It was part of her daily routine. Leave the restaurant, check in at her mom's house to make sure she was still feeling good, taking her meds, and maybe grab a meal if her mom had cooked. She knocked on the screen door before opening.

"Ma, it's me," she called out.

"In the kitchen," her mom called back.

Sure enough, the house smelled divine. The familiar smell of her mom's fried chicken filled the air. Sheri's stomach grumbled. She'd been so busy today she barely had time to eat. She wondered if Lieutenant Deandre King had eaten later in the day. The thought made her frown. She did not need to worry about whether or not he ate. The man was grown and could find his own meals. She blamed her mom. Her mom couldn't stand to see people not eating when there was plenty of food around. It was why Sheri had brought him the biscuit with his coffee. She'd caught the way his eyes had lingered on some of the plates on the tables. She hadn't been able to help herself. Her need to feed people kicked in, and she'd brought him food.

Her mom stood in front of the fridge, and pulled out two cans of Pepsi in her hands as she headed toward the door that led to the back patio. "I'm sitting out back with your aunt."

"Aunt Gwen's here?"

"Yeah, she stopped by after she got off work. Come on out back."

Sheri quickly moved to the back door and opened it for

her mom. Her mom's sister Gwen sat under the umbrella connected to her mom's patio table. It was a warm and humid afternoon, so an oscillating fan was plugged up to speed along the intermittent breeze. Despite the heat, her mom and aunt loved sitting on the back porch.

"Hey, Auntie." Sheri went over and gave her aunt a hug.

"Hey, Sheri, your mom said you would be here in a little bit." She was still in the dark blue uniform she wore as part of the custodial crew for the city of Sunshine Beach. She wore wire-framed glasses and her salt-and-pepper hair was pulled back into a ponytail.

Sheri pulled out a chair and sat around the round, glass patio table. "Did you need to see me?"

Her aunt took the Pepsi from her sister with one hand and pointed at Sheri with the other. "Why didn't you tell me someone tried to break into the restaurant?"

Sheri gave her mom a look. But her mom just shrugged. "What? You thought I wasn't going to tell her?"

"It wasn't that big of a deal. They didn't get in. I went to the neighborhood watch meeting, and they're already working on plans to try and help the south end."

Her aunt nodded. "They need to do something. The south end of the strip used to be a nice, safe place to go. Now, it's full of kids doing God knows what."

Sheri shifted her chair to try and get in the direct aim of the fan when it turned her way. "The kids are doing the same thing I did as a kid. Hanging out and looking for something to do."

"Well, I don't like it," Gwen said with a frown.

Her mom nodded. "Me, either. I'm glad the city is trying to make the south end better, but I need them to do something about the crime. How can your business stay successful if they're breaking in all the time?"

Sheri held up a finger. "First of all, it was one attempted break-in." She lifted another finger. "Second, we're looking at solutions."

Her mom's eyes narrowed. "That's why you were talking to that cop earlier today."

Sheri didn't bother to ask how her mom knew even though she hadn't come in this morning. JD probably called and told her mom the second Sheri had sat down at the table.

"Yes, that's why he was there. He's in charge of the new community outreach division. They want to create a better relationship between the department and the citizens. He wants to get my ideas."

Her aunt grunted and shook her head. "I don't trust cops."

Her mom nodded. "Me, either."

Sheri understood where they were coming from. She remembered the way her family and neighbors hadn't trusted law enforcement in and around Sunshine Beach when she was a kid. The delayed response to calls, the lack of engagement in their community, the harassment by the less-than-stellar cops. The mistrust ran deep and over generations.

"I get it," Sheri said. "And I'm not saying I'm going to marry him, I'm saying he wants to help the community, so I'll work with him and see if he's for real."

Gwen leaned forward with a skeptical look in her dark eyes. "What if he's not?"

Sheri shrugged. "Then, I'll find another way to help the community. I want the south end to be like it used to be. Working with the police is just one way to get there, but not the only way."

Her mom nodded. "Well, I hope he turns out to be okay. I would hate for a man that fine to be dirty."

Gwen sat up straight. "How do you know he's fine?"

"D'asa told me," her mom said. She looked at Sheri with a raised brow. "Is he?"

Fine wasn't enough to describe that man. Intense, good-looking, sexy, commanding. All of that and she still didn't think she'd accurately captured everything appealing about Deandre King.

Sheri waved a hand. "I mean, he's alright. I don't care about that. I'm just trying to help the neighborhood."

Her aunt waved a finger at Sheri. "Well, don't think about that. Even if he is fine. It's hard enough to trust a man, but if he's a cop." She sucked her teeth and shook her head. "No telling what he'll do."

"What's he gonna do, Gwen?" her mom asked laughing.

"I don't know, but I don't trust men and I don't trust cops, so obviously, you can't trust a man cop."

If Sheri were honest, she didn't trust herself more than she didn't trust men in general. Her judgment and track record when it came to guys wasn't great. She didn't have a hard time finding a guy. It was just that the type of guys she was typically attracted to turned out to be the worst kind of guy for her. Men like Deandre wouldn't usually cross her radar. Sure, he was good-looking, but he was a "nice" guy. Sheri had to admit she always went for a hint of bad boy with her good looks.

But bad boys, playboys and wanna-be thugs had given her nothing but a world of disappointment and embarrassment. Maybe she needed a nice guy like Deandre in her life. It wasn't as if he would give her a chance. He'd arrested her when she was at her worst. Nope, no need to focus on how sexy Deandre King was. That ship wasn't sailing.

Sheri sighed and patted her aunt's hand. "Don't worry. I'm not trying to do anything with Lieutenant King but help the community. No matter how cute he may be."

* * *

Deandre did everything he could to leave work on time. He rushed to the grocery store to pick up ground beef, hamburger buns, frozen fries and sloppy joe sauce for his son DJ's favorite meal. DJ's birthday was that weekend. Deandre had to work, but he'd set a personal objective to try and make every other day of the week special for his kid.

They'd moved to Sunshine Beach right after DJ's mom, Jamila, passed away suddenly. The aneurysm took her from them quickly when no one was at home to deliver first aid or call the hospital in enough time to possibly save her. As much as it had pained him to find his wife like that, he was thankful that he'd gotten home before DJ. She'd passed away a few days before his son's birthday, which was why Deandre tried his best to make DJ's birthday special.

He made it home in enough time to get the sloppy joes created and was just taking the first batch of fries out of the fryer when the back door opened. He turned off the deep fryer and spun toward his son.

"Hey! You're just in time. I've got dinner ready," Deandre said cheerfully.

DJ gave him a look that said the cheerfulness wasn't needed or very much appreciated. Not surprising. DJ was a good kid, but he was filled with teenage attitude. Deandre spent a lot of time trying to figure out when he'd gone from being his son's best friend to the person he wanted to spend the least amount of time with. They'd been close before his wife passed and had grown closer in the years after they'd lost her. But, sometime in the past year and a half, his relationship with DJ had shifted. His son's answers were short, his eye contact brief to nonexistent, and the time they'd spend hanging out together only happened when Deandre forced it.

"Yeah, I'm here," DJ said in a flat tone.

DJ reminded him a lot of his mother, with the same wide-set brown eyes, flat nose and dimpled chin. His height, broad shoulders and growing muscles all came from Deandre. His son wore a pair of dark blue joggers and a white hoodie. He'd let his hair grow out. The curls at the top were thick and wild enough to make Deandre want to cut them, but he was trying to let his son express himself. That's what Jamila would have wanted.

"I made dinner." Deandre pointed toward the plate of hot fries and the pan with the sloppy joe mixture on the stove.

DJ glanced at the food and shrugged. "I'm not hungry." He turned to leave the kitchen.

"Hold up," Deandre called.

DJ didn't sigh out loud. He wasn't outright disrespectful, just mildly disdainful with receiving attention from his dad. Still, Deandre *felt* the sigh and eye roll as he watched his son's shoulders lift and lower.

DJ turned around. "Yeah?"

Deandre raised a brow. "Yeah?"

"Yes, sir?" DJ replied in the same flat tone of voice he'd used before.

Deandre wrestled back his growing annoyance with considerable effort. "You've been in school all day and then you had wrestling practice afterward. I don't believe you're not hungry."

"I already ate."

"Ate? When and where?"

"My boy Jay wanted to get some pizza so we stopped by the place down on the strip and got something to eat."

Deandre looked at his watch. DJ wouldn't have had time to eat if he was coming home straight from wrestling practice. "When did you have time to do that?"

"After school."

"What about wrestling practice?"

DJ shifted his stance. He glanced away quickly before meeting Deandre's eyes and lifting his chin. "Oh, I quit."

"You quit?" Deandre asked, narrowing his eyes. He braced his hands on his hips and stared at his son. DJ had loved wrestling. He'd won a medal the year before. "Why would you quit?"

DJ shrugged. "The coach started changing stuff up. I didn't like it, so I quit."

"Change things up how? And, why didn't you tell me?"

"Just new rules and stuff. This is why I didn't tell you. I knew you'd have a bunch of questions."

"I'm going to ask questions because you liked wrestling. If the coach was acting weird, then you tell me and I can talk to him."

DJ waved a hand. "See, that's why I didn't tell you. I knew you'd go all *cop* on me and want to make it a big deal. I was just tired of wrestling. It took up too much time and I want to hang with my boys. So, I quit when he started changing the rules. That's all."

Deandre's argument deflated. He didn't want to *go all cop* on his son. Deandre set rules and insisted on order in his house, but he never wanted his son to feel like he was being treated as a suspect. It was one of the things he'd promised Jamila when they'd gotten married. She'd said if they were going to build a family they had to treat each other like family. Meaning Deandre couldn't come in setting law and order as if they were the people he arrested every day.

Deandre dialed back the steel in his voice and tried to sound more like a father and less like a cop. "I still think you should have talked to me about it."

"I'm talking to you about it now."

Deandre took a deep breath. He would not get frustrated with his son and let this spiral into an argument. "Before you make big decisions like that I need to know."

"Okay," DJ said in a flat tone.

"Okay what?"

"I'll tell you before I make big decisions."

The quick agreement wasn't a win. It was a deflection tactic. Something DJ had also started in the last year. Instead of talking about anything Deandre tried to discuss, he said "okay" or agreed to whatever Deandre said. It had taken Deandre a few weeks to catch on that his son was using the quick agreement to end the conversation faster.

"And you need to call me if you're going somewhere after school. Anything could happen and I wouldn't know where you were."

"Okay."

Deandre waited for more, but the wait was a waste of time. DJ wanted the conversation to end and, honestly, he wanted to move on and try to salvage the rest of the night. "Let's eat and we can talk some more."

DJ rubbed his stomach. "I'm full from pizza and I've got homework."

He tried a different approach. "Did you want to do anything for your birthday?"

"You're working, so no. I'll just hang with my boys."

There wasn't any accusation in his son's voice, but the reminder still sent a knife through Deandre's heart. He'd tried to find a way out of working, but the police chief was scheduled to speak at a community event with several politicians on Saturday, and she wanted him, as the new head of the Community Outreach Division, to also be there.

"But we could still do something. I'll be done by three or four."

DJ lifted a shoulder. "Okay. You just tell me where you want me to be."

"I want you to tell me what you'd like to do. We could go to dinner with your grandparents. Or check out a movie."

"Grandma and Grandpa said they'd take me to breakfast. I'm going to a movie with my friends. I'm good."

The guilt wrapped around Deandre's heart tightened its grip. DJ already had plans for his birthday. Plans that didn't include or require him. "Squeeze in some time for me. Let's grab something to eat before you go to dinner with your friends. That work?"

"Okay. Now, can I go do my homework?" DJ asked.

Deandre bit back suggesting DJ to do his homework downstairs so they could talk while he ate. He already knew what the answer would be. Instead, he nodded. "That's fine."

DJ turned and walked out without another word. Deandre watched his son go, then looked at the sloppy joes and French fries he'd made. He didn't know how they'd gotten to this point, and what scared him even more was that he didn't know how to change things, either.

Chapter Five

Sheri went inside the Kings store, now the home of the south end's neighborhood watch, for her meeting with Deandre. She'd spent most of the day making sure everything was settled at the restaurant so she could leave in enough time to meet him that afternoon. She didn't like to leave the rest of the workers by themselves at closing time. Not because she didn't think they could close up without her, but because she didn't want to give the impression that she wasn't just as willing to work late and hard with them. After the attempted break-in, they were all more than willing for her to leave early and meet with Deandre. They'd practically pushed her out of the door.

Inside was dark compared with the bright sunshine outside the building. Only half of the overhead fluorescent lights were on. Deandre sat at a desk in the back corner of the open space. He'd been looking at his phone when she'd walked in but gave her his full attention when the doors opened. He put his phone down and stood.

"Come on in." He pointed to a seat in front of his desk, one of the folding chairs they'd set up in rows for the neighborhood watch meeting. "Have a seat."

"Is this your office?" she asked, raising a brow. She looked around the wide, empty space as she crossed over to him. During the neighborhood meeting, she'd been so caught up in what was happening that she hadn't paid attention to what the inside of the building looked like.

Without all the people inside, it was dark and dreary. There wasn't anything in the space except for the desk in the corner. She supposed the tables and chairs put out for the meeting were stored away behind one of the doors along the back wall.

Deandre shook his head. "No, I have an office down at headquarters. But since I started working in the Community Outreach Division, I try to meet people in their neighborhoods. When I'm in the south end, this is where I meet people. Coming down to the police station isn't always comfortable for everyone."

Sheri hung her purse on the back of the folding chair before sitting down. "Can you blame them for not being comfortable?"

He shrugged and his broad shoulders stretched the material of the dark blue polo shirt he wore. "Not really. I understand why they would feel leery about being down there. Our conference rooms look a lot like interrogation rooms. I'm trying to build bridges, not intimidate."

"That's good to hear."

"Why is that?"

"Some cops like to intimidate people."

She waited for him to deny it. Or get defensive. Instead, he nodded. "Some do. I don't."

She watched him, impressed and surprised by his answer. She lifted a brow and studied his shoulders. "Come on, a big strong man like you. You've never intimidated anyone?"

The corner of his mouth quirked. "I learned long before I became a cop that my size and voice intimidates some people. Just my presence can heighten the tension in a situation. Instead of leaning into that, I chose to figure out the best way to diffuse the situation versus making it worse."

Dang, she was even more impressed. He was self-aware. She thought back to when he had arrested her. She could tell he'd been irritated with the situation, but he hadn't tried to tower over her, talk over her or try to make her feel afraid. She'd been pissed off, angry and afraid of what would happen that night, but she hadn't been afraid when he was around.

"I think I'm going to be okay working with you." She stretched her legs out in front of her.

Deandre leaned forward and rested his forearms on the desk. They were muscled and toned, just like the rest of him. "You didn't think you'd be able to work with me before?"

Sheri jerked her eyes away from his arms and back to meet his direct gaze. "I wasn't sure. You're the cop who arrested me. But the more I talk to you, the more I think you're okay."

This time the lip twitch turned into a half smile. "I appreciate that."

He continued to hold her gaze as he smiled. The air electrified. Sheri's pulse increased and sparks shot across her skin. The man was handsome but when he smiled, he was devastating.

His cell phone chimed. He looked away, breaking the spell and allowing Sheri to breathe. She rubbed the back of her neck. She had to get a hold of herself. Yeah, it had been a while since she'd had sex, but she wasn't so hard up that she would risk embarrassment by trying to hook up with the cop that arrested her. Besides, he was cool with her and everything, but he did not seem like the type of cop who also tried to slide his phone number on the traffic ticket he wrote you. She'd bet money he was not interested in her in any kind of way outside of helping him reach out to the south end community.

"Dammit, DJ," he muttered. His fingers tapped against the screen as he frowned down.

"Anything wrong?" she asked.

He looked up and then looked embarrassed. "I'm sorry. I didn't mean to curse."

Sheri chuckled. "*Dammit* is far from being one of the worst words I've ever heard. Any trouble?"

He shook his head. "No, it's my son. He was supposed to be going back to wrestling practice but instead he's gone home."

"You have a son?" Which meant there was a mother. Which meant he might be married or in a relationship. Further proof why she did not need to be salivating over the man in this meeting.

He nodded. "Yeah, he's sixteen. A sophomore in high school. He suddenly decided to quit wrestling but won't give me a good reason."

"Oh. Well, I'm sure he has a good one."

"I wish he'd tell me." He gave her a curious look. "Do you have kids?"

She shook her head. "No. Wanted one or two one day, but just haven't met the right person to impregnate me."

He blinked. "Oh."

Sheri laughed at his stunned expression. "You don't have to look so… I don't know, surprised. Having a kid is a big deal. I can't be having one with just anybody."

His shoulders relaxed and he held up a hand. "I'm sorry. I just never heard it phrased that way. But I understand what you mean."

"What about your son's mom? Is she your wife?"

He nodded. "She was. She died, six years ago."

Sheri put a hand to her chest. "I'm so sorry. I didn't mean…"

"I know. It's a little easier to say it now. That's why we moved to Sunshine Beach. Her family lives here. I wanted my son to grow up with family around. My family is…not as reliable."

"In what way?" she asked, then flinched. "Sorry, I'm being nosy."

He shrugged. "And I'm dumping personal stuff on you. My bad."

She kind of liked that he was talking to her. It made him seem a little less off-limits. Not that she was going to cross those limits. But seeing a personal side of him took away some of the space she'd expected to be between them.

"It's okay. I've been told I'm easy to talk to. You'd be surprised the personal things my customers say to me when I bring them their food. I guess I've got that kind of face."

"It is a nice face," he said.

Heat flooded Sheri's cheeks. She pressed a hand to one. "Oh, well, thank you."

He glanced away and then shifted in his chair. "I mean, you seem trustworthy. I get a sense about people. You're a good person."

"I try to be." She got a vision of the disappointment in his face when he'd taken the baseball bat from her the night of her arrest. Her cheeks burned even more. "At least, I've been trying harder to be a better person."

He cleared his throat. "So, about the community outreach."

She snapped her finger. "Yes, about that. I was thinking a fair or something. We invite people over to talk about what's happening in the area and what we'd like to see."

"People like who?"

"I don't know. Like folks who work for Sunshine Beach. We haven't heard from council members. Or the ones making plans for the area. Then there are the people in law enforcement."

"People don't just come out for a panel discussion from politicians and bureaucrats." His words held a hint of humor that surprised Sheri. He could also tease. She liked that.

Sheri slid forward in the chair. "Then let's make it more than that. Let's make it fun. Draw them in and then teach them something while they're here."

"That could work."

"I know it can. We can bring it up at the next neighborhood watch meeting. Get some ideas and form a committee to help plan."

"You came with all the ideas already, huh?"

She grinned. "I mean, it is why you asked me to help. You could tell I'm a good person and that I can get things done."

"That is true. Okay, Sheri, let's plan a fair."

Chapter Six

Deandre sat at his desk in headquarters working on paperwork when there was a knock on the door. Looking up, he spotted LaTisha Fuller. They'd worked together when he was on patrol, and he'd become friends with her and her husband, Omar. Their son was about the same age as his and he'd quickly latched on to other people he could connect with and give his son a community when he'd moved to Sunshine Beach.

"What's up, Tisha?"

LaTisha pointed over her shoulder. "Chief wants to see you. What did you do now?"

Deandre thought about everything he'd worked on this past week and couldn't think of anything. Not that he made a habit of messing up and being called to meet with the chief. He played by the book and followed the rules. "Nothing that I know of."

LaTisha laughed. She was a little under six feet tall, with golden brown skin and a halo of curly hair she wore slicked back in a tight ponytail. When he'd left patrol and accepted the offer to head up the Community Outreach Division, he'd hoped she would've accepted the role of heading up the section with him. But she hadn't wanted to be strapped to a desk. He couldn't blame her, and, thankfully, their friendship remained intact.

"Well, she's itching to see you, so you've probably done something."

Deandre scooped up a notepad and pen and headed out the door. "If I did something, then I'll deal with it."

Latisha shook her head. "You're always acting like stuff doesn't bother you."

"It bothers me, but I put things in perspective. I realize what's worth the effort and what isn't. Chief wanting to see me, that's not worth any anxiety until I get there and find out why. No need to borrow trouble. She may have something good to say."

Latisha shrugged. "I hope so. Lunch later?"

He checked his watch. "Nah, I'll be taking a late lunch. Maybe tomorrow."

"Sounds good." She held out her fist.

He bumped his fist with hers before turning the corner to head to the chief's office. The police chief was still considered new, since the previous chief had worked for the department for twenty years. She'd been hired to take over the Sunshine Beach Police Department six months after he'd moved to the town and taken a job with the force. Higher-ups had brought her in because the previous chief had been caught up in one too many scandals with his subordinates. The final affair was with a married woman in Dispatch. Her husband had blown the whistle, sending text messages, pictures and emails to the local news. Once his bad deeds could no longer be hidden, the department went under scrutiny and everything wrong about the way he ran things came to light. The previous chief had created a lack of trust in the community, a high turnover rate of officers and a toxic environment that didn't offer any benefit for doing the right thing. Chief Montgomery had been hired and given the task of fixing all of that. And she'd taken her job seriously.

Suddenly, people were held accountable for their actions. Transparency and integrity were valued over sweeping things under the rug and an unwritten policy of talking through smoke and mirrors. She'd slowly made changes and they were finally starting to see the benefit of her efforts.

He knocked on the door and entered after hearing a terse "come in." Chief Montgomery gave him a quick glance before looking back at her computer. Her fingers flew furiously over the keyboard as she typed.

"Lieutenant King, come on in and have a seat."

Deandre entered and sat down in the chair across from her desk. "I heard you wanted to see me."

"I do. Let me finish my thoughts on this." She was short but had enough confidence and attitude to make up for her stature. She wore her brown hair in a short style. Her cheeks were slightly flushed beneath her pale skin and her eyes narrowed as she typed. Whoever was on the other side of her email had obviously pissed her off.

"Go right ahead."

Her chin lifted and lowered before her brows knitted and she went back to typing. Chief Montgomery had spent the past fifteen years in law enforcement after an eight-year stint in the army. She was straightforward, no nonsense and one of the few people he knew who truly believed in always doing the right thing. She was a stickler for following the rules but was also empathetic enough to try and understand why decisions were made. He liked that about her and believed that was the reason why she'd been able to make the department better.

She finished with a few hard taps on the keyboard before her lips moved as she read over the email. Then she hit the enter key hard. "There, that's done."

"Who's getting eviscerated now?" Deandre teased.

She looked at him and raised a brow. "The town manager. I swear that guy likes to push my buttons."

"What's the problem now?" On the one hand, the town manager respected the way Chief Montgomery had improved the police department. On the other hand, the popularity she received for doing so and the love of the community meant her power with the elected officials and the public was higher than his. The battle of egos commenced whenever the two were together.

"That's why I want to see you," she said. "What's happening in the south end?"

"I met the with community liaison. We're looking at dates to have an outreach event in the neighborhood. Why?"

Chief Montgomery pointed at her computer and frowned. "He's once again griping about crime in the area. Mostly because business owners are griping to him. He doesn't want to hear about the community outreach team. Instead, he wants to hear about the number of arrests we've had."

Deandre scoffed. "Why, so he can turn around and blame us for ruining the town's reputation with the residents?"

"The Community Outreach Division wasn't his idea, and he doesn't like it. The man hired me to make things better, but he fights me on everything I'm trying to do."

"Your work proves him wrong all the time. That's what matters." Deandre had seen that for himself several times over the past six years. The chief and town manager would argue about one of her ideas, but things would turn out great and her approval ratings in the community went up several more points.

"Yeah, well this time he's got at least two council members on his side. They want to see arrests for the break-ins, and they want more patrols to handle the hoodlums in the area." She held up a hand. "Their words, not mine."

Deandre nodded but his shoulders tensed. "There aren't any hoodlums. Just teenagers with nothing to do."

"Well, I need to give them something. Maybe your outreach event will work out. I can ask them to come and speak. Elected officials love a chance to speak."

"If they're willing to come, we'll have them. We were even thinking about asking the public defender and solicitor's office to show up. We'll take a few council members."

She nodded. "Good. Let me know when you finalize a date and I'll get it on their calendar. This has to work out. I don't need him to give me any more crap about the community outreach division. If we can show that having a presence in the neighborhoods that's positive and not just to scare people but still get results, then I can shut him up."

"I'll get on it. I'm meeting with Sheri later today to go over possible dates and locations."

Chief Montgomery stopped in the middle of turning back to her computer to give him a sharp glance. "Who's Sheri?"

"She's the community liaison. She agreed to help after the last neighborhood watch meeting. She wants the area to get better, but not at the expense of kicking out the kids who rely on the area as a place to hang out."

The line between Chief Montgomery's eyes lifted before she nodded. "Good. Let me know what you'll need. I'll see if I can get it for you."

"I will." He stood and turned toward the door.

"And Lieutenant,"

Deandre faced her. "Yes, ma'am."

She clasped her hands on her desk and met his eyes with

an intense stare. "We've got to make this good. I don't know if he means it, but he threw out dissolving the Community Outreach Division to focus more on a tactical team that focuses on crime. I can't let that happen."

Deandre understood exactly what that would mean. An increased police presence and a heavier hand from law enforcement. A stronger push to not only remove the teenagers from the area, but revitalization efforts that also pushed out the current businesses for ones that were higher-end like the north side of the beach. Gentrification in the name of community improvements.

The Community Outreach Division had been Chief Montgomery's idea—an idea Deandre had supported and been more than willing to support after seeing how well the similar division had worked back in his hometown. He'd accepted the offer to head the division because he'd wanted to be part of the solution to rebuild trust in the police force. He'd become a cop because he wanted to make a difference, not because he wanted to be in control or scare people. The Community Outreach Division could make a difference not just by reducing crime in the area, but also by building a much-needed bridge between the force and citizens that hadn't trusted in the town's willingness to meet their needs.

He gave her a thumbs-up. "We won't let that happen."

Sheri held her breath and leaned forward as she watched and waited for Deandre to take a bite of the fried chicken she'd brought him. They'd agreed to meet up at the neighborhood center to talk about plans for the "Connecting the Community" outreach event—a name she'd come up with that morning while making biscuits. Her kitchen was good at making sure they didn't have too much leftover food by the time they closed, but today she'd asked them to try and have a few extra pieces of chicken available. She'd also packed some of the biscuits he'd liked and a side of her special collard greens. He'd already mentioned not eating breakfast, and when she'd visited him the other day to discuss plans, she'd seen the protein bar and sandwich that looked like it had come from a gas station on his desk.

She didn't need to feed the man. He wasn't her responsibility, but there she was. Arriving with a basket packed and insisting that he eat.

"Mmm." Deandre's eyes closed. He licked his full lips and nodded. "This is good."

Sheri's lips parted as she sucked in a shallow breath. She wasn't sure if it was the compliment or the way her eyes followed the movement of his tongue on his lips, but either way she clapped her hands. "I'm glad you like it."

His eyes opened and he raised a brow. "You *knew* I would like it."

She shrugged and tried not to look too smug. From the way he'd enjoyed the biscuit the other morning, she'd been confident he would love her fried chicken. Her chicken and waffles was the most popular item on the menu. "I assumed you would, but it's always good to get confirmation."

"You didn't have to bring food."

Sheri reached down in the bag she brought and pulled out a bottle of water. "I had some left over. We're meeting and I figured we needed to eat. It should be enough for you to take home." She twisted off the top and set the bottle on his desk.

"How much do I owe you for this?" He took a sip of water from the bottle.

"You don't owe me anything. Consider it a bonus for working with me to put together the community event."

"You don't have to feed me because of that. I'd help regardless."

"Yeah, but hopefully the food will really put your heart into it." She winked.

He chuckled and quickly looked down at the food. "Believe me, my heart is already into this. I want to make this event just as successful as you do."

"Oh really? Why?" She sat back and crossed her legs.

She was still in her jeans and The Breakfast Nook T-shirt, which was stained after a busy day. Whereas he looked neat and put together in his wrinkle-free police station collared shirt and khakis. She wished she'd thought to bring a change of clothes before they'd met.

"The Community Outreach Division is still new. Although our chief wants it to be successful, some of the higher-ups aren't convinced that this is the fastest way to clean up the South End."

Sheri sat up straight and pointed a finger at the sky. "The south end doesn't need to be cleaned up. We're not dirty."

Deandre held up a hand as if to surrender. "I didn't mean it like that."

"I know what you're trying to say, but words matter. Saying the area needs to be cleaned up makes it sound like something is wrong with the south end. We just need more help for the businesses, investment from the town and meaningful things for the kids in the area to do. That's not cleaning up, that's just providing support."

"I hear what you're saying. I won't use those words anymore."

Sheri studied his features and didn't see any signs that he was just agreeing to make her be quiet or move along. His gaze remained steady and his voice was sincere.

She nodded and returned to leaning back in the chair.

"Thank you. You're the officer most of the people in the area will deal with. Think about what you're saying so that you don't push them away."

"Point taken." His voice remained even. He didn't seem upset or irritated by her correction.

"What kind of support do the higher-ups think the area needs?"

"Not the community outreach kind. The town manager wants to create a tactical team to focus on crime. There are concerns about gangs and the access to opioids in the community."

"That doesn't sound like support." In fact, it sounded like a scare tactic.

"For the people that are complaining about the break-ins and drug trafficking, it sounds like the perfect answer."

Sheri let out an annoyed breath and shook her head. "I remember what it was like dealing with the police in Sunshine Beach when I was a teenager."

His head tilted to the side. "What was it like?"

She considered trying to find a nice way to say what was on her mind. But the interest in his eyes made her want to speak the truth. If they were going to work together on bringing the community together, then he would need to know how some people still felt about the police department.

"Don't trust them. Don't call them. Don't say anything because they're always looking for trouble. I was terrified when I found out one of Tyrone's neighbors called the cops on me."

"You didn't think someone would call the cops when you went over with a baseball bat?" A spark of amusement lit his eye.

Sheri shrugged and looked to the ceiling. "I was listening to my cousin and blasting angry, love-gone-wrong songs. I wasn't thinking clearly." She focused back on him and patted her chest. "But when the blue lights pulled up, it hit me just how bad things could go."

"I didn't want to terrify you."

"I'm glad it was you and not someone else. I was surprised by how…calm you were." She thought back to that night and the way he'd quickly diffused the situation. He'd been direct and to the point and taken charge without throwing his ego around. "I could tell you were disappointed maybe, but you weren't belittling, and you didn't treat me like I was nobody. I don't ever want to get arrested again, but if I have to, then I'd prefer it be like that."

"Going in guns blazing only makes a situation worse. I'm not that kind of person or cop. Our chief is the same. She spent her first year or two weeding out the bad apples in the bunch. We're not perfect, but we're on the right path."

"That's good to hear. Honestly, my family warned me about working with you."

"Because of our past connection?"

She shook her head. "Nooo! I did not tell them you were the cop who arrested me. I try not to bring up that part of my life with my family."

"Then why didn't they want you to work with me?"

"Just because you're a cop. They remember the old days even more than I do. They're worried you'll take the hammer approach to helping out the neighborhood."

"The hammer isn't my first approach."

She narrowed her eyes and grinned "But you will use it?"

The corner of his mouth quirked before he lifted one broad shoulder. "Only when necessary. My late wife talked about how she used to love hanging out on the beaches when she grew up here. She loved this place and always talked about us moving back here one day."

"She was from here? I know you said you moved after she passed because your in-laws were close, but we have a lot of people who move to Sunshine Beach later in life."

"She was. Grew up here and then moved to Greensboro after graduating from North Carolina A&T."

"Hold up? Was your wife Jamila Davis?"

Deandre blinked and froze for a second before nodding. "You knew her?"

"I mean, I knew who she was. She was what…two years behind me in high school. Her family goes to my aunt's church, so I'd see her around. I heard she went to A&T and that she passed away a few years back."

Sadness filled his eyes and a bittersweet smile hovered around his lips. "Yeah, that was her."

The sorrow in his eyes made her want to get up and give him a hug. Which was completely inappropriate, so she asked a question that would hopefully remove some of the pain. "How did you two hook up?"

The sadness left his eyes and he let out a soft laugh. "We met at a protest."

"Wait, what? Don't tell me you arrested her?"

He grinned and shook his head. "I didn't arrest her. It was a peaceful protest. I was there to protest, too. Against a new ordinance the city was passing. We caught each other's eye in the crowd. She came up and said hi and… That was it."

The way he spoke the words, as if some magic spell had come over him that granted him everything he ever wanted, made her want to believe fairy tales existed. She leaned forward and rested her elbow on his desk. "How long were you married?"

"Eleven years," he said slowly. His eyes still focused on the past.

She nodded but didn't know what to say. That was a long time to be with one person only to lose them so permanently. She didn't have the right words and instead of saying something wrong she decided to stay quiet.

"It was a good eleven. I wouldn't trade them. Even if I knew how they'd end."

"Sounds like you really loved her."

"I did. Maybe one day…" He looked at her and their gazes connected.

He didn't have to finish his words; the wistful look in his gaze told her the rest. Maybe one day he'd fall in love again. What would it be like to be loved by this man? To be loved so much that even knowing the ending would be tragic, he still wouldn't walk away?

Sheri's breath caught in her throat. She was fantasizing about falling in love with him while he talked about his late wife. To make matters worse, she'd leaned on his desk and was right in his face. He looked away quickly and she pushed back to sit fully in her chair.

"I hope that one day, if you're ready, that you can find someone who makes you happy."

He glanced back at her. She couldn't read his expression or what he was thinking. That didn't stop her heart from racing faster or for the air to feel thin and hot around her.

The door opened. And a voice called out. "Hey, Dad, you here?"

Deandre blinked and stood. "Yeah, I'm here. Meeting with Ms. Thomas to talk about the community event. Come and say hi." His words were rushed, almost guilty.

Or maybe Sheri was projecting. Thank goodness for the interruption. His heart had been given away a long time ago and wasn't going to be given away anytime soon, much less to her. Plus, he had a teenage son. She was far from ready to be anyone's stepmom. Her attraction to Deandre wasn't going to go away, but she would have the decency to be professional while they worked together and keep all fantasies to herself.

She stood as well and turned to meet his son. When she spotted the kid, she had to blink twice. His son froze in place, his eyes wide.

"It's you," Sheri said.

Deandre frowned. He looked from Sheri to his son. "You've met."

"The other day," Sheri said. "He offered to help me with my sign." Right before trying to hit on her and calling her an "old ass."

Deandre's frown cleared up and he smiled. "Oh, good. I'm glad to see that DJ was being helpful."

"Yeah, real helpful," Sheri said dryly.

"You know me, Dad. I'm always trying to help my elders." DJ looked at Sheri and gave an innocent smile.

Sheri's eyes narrowed. Was he was calling her old? Again! Sheri pulled back the attraction she felt for Deandre and shoved it to the darkest corner of her mind, slammed the imaginary door with a kick and locked it. Being interested in a man who had no interest in her was one thing. Being interested in a man with a sly teenager who liked to play games was 100 percent out of the question.

Chapter Seven

Sheri was flipping through the rack of shirts in TJ Maxx with her cousin Cora by her side talking endlessly about the last date she'd gone on, when the sound of a familiar voice caught her attention. She stopped searching and lifted her head. Sure enough, walking across the store to the men's section was Deandre, a cell phone pressed to his ear.

"Deandre!" she called before she could think.

He stopped walking and glanced around. Her cousin stopped flipping through the clothes and followed Sheri's gaze toward him. Deandre caught her eye, lifted a hand and smiled.

Cora leaned over and whispered. "Lil Bit, who is that?"

"The cop I'm planning the community event with."

"Oh? Then why are you calling him like he's your man?" Cora cocked her head to the side and narrowed her eyes.

Sheri elbowed her cousin. "Shut up. I'm not calling him like he's my man."

"Mmm-hmm," was Cora's unconvinced reply.

Deandre spoke into the phone before pulling it away and sliding it in his back pocket. He walked over to talk to her from the other side of the aisle. He was dressed in regular clothes, a basic black T-shirt that fitted his muscled arms and broad shoulders perfectly and a pair of blue basketball shorts that stopped right above the knee.

"Everything good?" His gaze scanned the area before gliding across her face as if checking to make sure everything was okay around her. Or, maybe she was projecting. The guy probably always scanned the perimeter.

"Yeah, everything is good. I recognized your voice when you were walking by. You didn't have to get off the phone. I just wanted to say hey."

He nodded. "I was looking for a reason to end that call. My friend LaTisha can sometimes get on a roll."

Sheri's heart dimmed. Based on the name, she assumed his friend was a woman. Did he mean friend as in, they were cool, or friend as in *girlfriend*? Why did she care? She'd already decided she was not going to do anything about the attraction she felt for Deandre.

"This is my cousin." She pointed to Cora watching intently next to her.

Cora shoved her hand over the rack. "Nice to meet you." She leaned forward, nearly spilling her cleavage out of the tank top she wore, and poked her tongue out of the corner of her mouth. Sheri rolled her eyes at her cousin's familiar flirty move.

Deandre shook her hand. "Deandre. Nice to meet you, as well." When he tried to pull back, she didn't let go.

Cora tilted her head to the side and eyed him. "You look familiar. Have we met before?"

Deandre shrugged. "I'm not sure. I'm around town a lot. You might have seen me. I'm in the Community Outreach Division of the Sunshine Beach Police Department."

Cora finally let go of his hand. "Maybe that's it."

Sheri was glad Cora didn't immediately recognize him. She'd been with Sheri the night Deandre arrested them for acting like some broken-hearted vigilantes. No telling what Cora would say when she put two and two together.

"Well, it was good seeing you," Sheri said quickly. "I'll see you Wednesday at the neighborhood watch meeting, right?"

"You will. I hope the rest of the neighborhood is as excited about your idea for the event as I am."

"I hope so, too."

Cora tapped her chin. "I swear we've met before."

Time for them to go. She looked at Cora. "We better check out if we want to get to the grocery store and pick up the stuff your mom needs for the potato salad."

Cora's attention immediately snapped back to that. "Girl, you're right. We've been in here way too long. Nice meeting you." She waved and headed to the register.

"Same here." Deandre looked back to Sheri. "See you on Wednesday."

"If you need anything before then just give me a call." She should be following her cousin instead of prolonging the conversation, but she didn't always make the best choices when she talked with a guy she was feeling.

"I think we're good. Even though I have been thinking about the chicken you dropped off the other day."

Pride ballooned in her chest. He'd been thinking about her. Well, her chicken, but she'd take that. Maybe he'd told someone about her food who would check out the restaurant. "If you've been thinking about it, then I'll have to bring some over."

"No need to do that."

"I don't mind feeding you." Honestly, she'd like to do a lot more than feed him, but she kept that thought to herself.

Her thoughts must have shown on her face because his smile faltered and he glanced away. Her mom always said everything she thought came through on her face.

Deandre pointed to the men's section. "I'd better go. I was looking for some shirts for my son."

Yes, the son who called her old. A good reminder of why she needed to keep her thoughts in her head instead of showing up in her expressions or words. "I'll let you go. See you around."

Sheri turned away and followed her cousin to the checkout. They'd put their purchases in the back of the car and were driving to the grocery store when Cora slapped the steering wheel.

She pointed at Sheri. "He's the cop that arrested us!"

Sheri closed her eyes and groaned. "Damn. I'd hoped you wouldn't remember."

"I remember everything. Why didn't you tell me?"

"Because I didn't want to make a big deal out of it."

"Does he know who you are?"

"He does. He remembered me almost immediately."

"And he doesn't mind working with you?"

"No, and I don't mind working with him. We talked about it, and for the sake of supporting the businesses in the south end, we agreed to work together."

Cora glanced at Sheri from the corner of her eye. "But you like him."

Heat spread across Sheri's face. She focused extra hard on keeping her expression neutral. Cora could always read her like a book. "Yeah, he's nice."

Cora pursed her lip. "Don't play with me. I mean you want to sleep with him."

Sheri scoffed and looked out the window. "No I don't."

"Girl, if you don't quit lying to me. I've known you all my life and I can tell when you like a guy. You get that horny look in your eye."

Sheri spun back toward Cora. "I don't have a horny look."

"Yes you do, it's like this." Her cousin batted her eyes, pursed her lips and lifted her shoulders with exaggerated breathing.

Sheri crossed her arms. "You ought to stop! I am not that bad."

Cora laughed and fixed her face. "You're bad enough. So, are you going to sleep with him?"

"Hell no! We're working together."

Cora sucked her teeth. "You're working together on a community event. That's not the same. And my man is sexy." Cora's voice dipped with the last sentence, and she licked her lips.

"He's a widower with a teenage son who called me an old ass the other day."

"Wait, what?"

Sheri recounted the story and running into him later. "I didn't want to tell Deandre what happened."

"Why not? He should know if his kid is acting up."

"It's not my place." Sheri didn't have kids and therefore tried not to get into the business of parents. She didn't know his parenting style or how he'd handle her saying anything negative about his son.

"We knew that everything we did as a kid in Sunshine Beach would get back to our moms. That's why we didn't act the fool too much. These kids don't think we will say anything. Besides, if he's hanging with the kids who the other business owners are saying are the problem, it'll get back to him sooner or later. You might as well give him a heads-up."

Cora had a point. Deandre's eyes lit up when he talked about his son. He'd be embarrassed if he found out his son was causing problems. "You really think I should tell him?"

"Yep. And then, you can sleep with him."

Sheri laughed. "I'm not sleeping with anyone. I'm not signing up to be a stepmom."

"Who said anything about being a stepmom to his kid? I said sleep with him." Cora shook her head. "There you go being all romantic and delusional again. Girl, just get yours and move on."

The words put Sheri on the defensive. Cora loved pointing out that Sheri was too quick to get caught up in a fairy tale when dealing with guys. Cora was only about getting what she could and moving on when the guy no longer served a purpose. Sheri had tried to be detached with her hookups and that had gotten her arrested. Proof that she could not separate feelings from sex.

"I'm not set up to just sleep with someone. Call me old-fashioned if you want to, but I'm ready to settle down. I don't want to get caught up in a guy who is only looking to have a good time."

"I told you not to get attached just because the sex is banging," Cora said in a lecturing tone.

"You did and I thought I could be okay. Well, I wasn't. Every time I try, I catch feelings. Let's face it. I'm not built for the hookup lifestyle."

Something Sheri had finally accepted about herself. Since high school she'd tried to be like Cora. When Cora said she needed to date multiple people, Sheri had done that. When Cora said never like a guy more than he liked you, she'd pretended as if she wasn't waiting by the phone for a guy to call. She'd spent so much time trying to be the independent, *I don't need a man*, love-and-leave-'em type that her friends and the single women in her family said she should be because she'd been too afraid to admit that she wanted what her mom and aunt hadn't had—a long-term committed relationship with a man. Marriage, a house and kids. All that jazz. But she was almost forty with no prospects in front of her and a police record because she spent too much time lying about what she really wanted in a relationship. No more.

Her cousin sighed and patted her shoulder. "You know what. You're right. I've accepted that."

Sheri brushed off Cora's hand. "I'm not about to sleep with Deandre only to find out I don't like his kid and he's not looking to settle with a woman he once put in handcuffs. Not in the good way. We'll just be friends."

"What if I sleep with him?"

Sheri cut her eyes at her cousin. "Don't even go there."

Cora sighed as if Sheri was asking for her right ovary. "Fine. Gotta ask. I won't go there."

"Thank you."

After the Tyrone situation, she and Cora had a "Come to Jesus" talk. Her cousin had been interested in Tyrone and admitted she was jealous when Sheri started seeing him. That's why she encouraged her to damage his car and started rumors online about his dating habits to try and sabotage his career. Sheri didn't agree with what her cousin had done, but she was family, and Sheri's mom always instilled in her that she couldn't turn her back on family. They'd made a truce with a strict rule. If one liked a guy, even a little bit, the other didn't mess with him. They didn't need any more messy situations.

She glanced at Sheri again as she started singing along to the song on the radio. She just hoped her cousin would stick to her side of the bargain.

"I don't see how this is going to help us," Belinda spoke up in the middle of Sheri's presentation.

Sheri stopped talking midsentence and raised a brow.

Oh, we're interrupting people now? Sheri thought to herself. She'd barely started talking about why they wanted to have the Connecting the Community event and how it would benefit the area when Belinda started shifting in her seat. Sheri could feel the heat of her hard stare. Now she wasn't even going to let Sheri finish making her case?

"I see you're eager to jump in," Sheri said. "Since you won't let me finish my presentation, why don't you give us your thoughts."

Belinda had the decency to look halfway chastised. "I'm just saying, I don't see how a community event is going to stop the crime or the kids hanging out in the area."

"First of all, the goal isn't to stop the kids from hanging out. This is their town, too, and they deserve to have access to the beach just as much as your yoga clients. So, let's get that clear. The goal of the community event is to give residents and business owners information about what's happening in the area, give them a chance to hear from more than just the police department, and bring people together."

Belinda crossed her arms and raised her nose in the air. "Well, it sounds like more of a warm-and-fuzzy approach to our problem."

"Are you saying you want a cold-and-hard approach? For the police to come through and treat the teens and residents like criminals and not form any type of connection with the community?"

Belinda glanced at Deandre before looking back at Sheri. "That's not what I'm saying."

Sheri put a hand on her hip. "Then what are you saying?"

Belinda sputtered, "You're trying to make me sound horrible."

"You're doing a good job yourself."

Mumbles went through the group. Belinda's eyes narrowed. Sheri raised a brow and dared her to clap back.

Deandre stepped forward. "No one is trying to make anyone look bad." He spoke in an even, "everybody calm down" tone of voice. "We know that there are a lot of challenges in the south end. We hope this event will allow us to reach the people in the area who may not be coming to the neighborhood watch meeting. Not all business owners are here or all residents, but they have concerns. We don't want to leave them out of this conversation. We also don't want to increase the police presence just to scare the people who live and work in the south end. If we increase patrols, we want people to know we're here as a community partner as well as to keep them safe. Not to hurt anyone or make them feel unwelcome." He smiled at the end, the dimple in his cheek peeking out.

The fight in Belinda's eyes melted and she grinned back, her head tilted to the side. "I think that's a great idea."

Sheri blinked. "Seriously?" Belinda wouldn't let Sheri get through her presentation, but Deandre flashes a dimple and she's cheesing and agreeing with the event?

"Thank you, Belinda," Deandre said. "I hope this means you'll help us plan for the event."

Belinda nodded so fast she looked like a bobblehead doll. "I'd love to help."

"That's great." He looked at Sheri and nodded.

Sheri rolled her eyes. "I guess so."

Deandre gave her a look. Sheri shrugged. She could read the "play nice" in his eyes. She didn't want to play nice. She wanted to call out Belinda for being a hypocrite, but now wasn't the time. They were trying to convince people to be excited about this event. If Deandre's dimples made

Belinda shut up and go along with her idea, then that would have to work.

The rest of the meeting was spent going over ideas for the community event. They even agreed on keeping Connecting the Community as a name after Belinda said it wasn't "the most clever" name she'd ever heard. Sheri stuck around after the meeting to talk with some of the other business owners and residents. Despite Belinda's original negativity, most of the others were excited about trying to do something that wasn't going to scare people away from the area.

"I mean, I moved over here because I want to see the area revitalized," Kelly, the owner of the comic book shop, said after the meeting. She wore a superhero T-shirt and jeans. "I'm glad that the city is willing to invest in this area and not just write us off as a bad part of town."

Sheri was vindicated hearing other people didn't feel the same way as Belinda. "It's on us to remind them that we're just as relevant as the north end of the beach."

Kelly's eyes lit up and she snapped her fingers. "Exactly. Hey, I'm having a drop-in at my comic book store this weekend. If you're not busy, you should come on through."

Sheri lifted a brow. "Really?"

"Yeah. I invited some other business owners, too. It's another way for us to get to know each other. And, with me being fairly new in town, it's a good way to meet up with new people."

She wasn't a big comic book fan, but she liked Kelly. She only hung out with family members, and if she was going to be staying in Sunshine Beach and wanted to make new friends, she'd need to make an effort to get out of her comfort zone. "Sounds like fun. I'll come through."

Kelley grinned and gave her a thumbs-up. "Great!" She looked over Sheri's shoulder.

"What about you, Lieutenant King? Will you be able to come by?"

Sheri turned as Deandre walked up beside her. "If I'm invited. Is it okay if my son comes with me?"

"Sure, the more the merrier," Kelley said with enthusiasm.

"Then I'll try to come through," Deandre said.

"Awesome! I'll see you both later." Kelly smiled and waved before leaving.

Sheri turned to look up at Deandre. He didn't try to tower over her, but when he stood close she was reminded of how tall he was. Tall, strong and tempting. Heat flooded her midsection and spread through her body. Sheri took a step back before her thoughts started playing out on her face again. "The meeting went okay."

He nodded. "It did. I'm hoping that means we'll have a good turnout."

"I think we will. If every business promotes it and the residents tell their neighbors, then we'll have a lot of people show up."

"I'll borrow some of your enthusiasm," he said with a half smile.

Sheri's stomach flipped. She understood why Belinda had changed her mind so quickly just because he smiled. The man was good-looking and seemed to be a decent human being. Basically, he was perfect.

"Belinda seems to like you," she blurted out.

He frowned. "I knew you were going to say that."

Sheri grinned and pointed. "So you know she likes you."

He waved a hand and shook his head. "I don't know that. I said I knew you were going to say that."

"Why, because she looked like she wanted to throw her panties when you popped that dimple on her?"

Deandre laughed. "Like she wanted to do what?"

Sheri waved her finger toward his face. "That dimple. You have to know the effect it has on women."

He rubbed his cheek. "It has an effect, huh? Well, then, I'll make sure I use my power for good instead of evil."

Sheri rolled her eyes and grinned. Good-looking, decent and has a sense of humor. He was everything she wanted. *If* there was a chance they could be anything more than temporary lovers.

"Be sure you do that." She looked around the now empty space. "Where are all the helpers who stayed behind last time to help you lock up?"

"I only have one or two, and they had to leave early. I'm good. It doesn't take much to clean up. I'll leave the tables and chairs out until tomorrow and get my son to help."

"Why doesn't he come to these meetings?"

Deandre walked toward the front of the room and she followed. "Even though I enjoy working in the community, these meetings are technically work. I don't bring him to work with me." He stopped at the front door.

"You seem to be out in the community a lot. He isn't interested in getting involved?"

"I'd love for him to take an interest, but he's at the age where dad being a cop isn't as cool as it was. When he was younger, I could show up in my car and turn on the lights and he'd think I was the best dad in the world."

Sheri smiled, imagining a younger version of his son being excited to see the lights on his dad's car. Then she thought about the way he'd called her "old ass" and couldn't imagine him being thrilled about blue lights. "Teens are like that."

He crossed his arms and leaned against the wall. Sheri was glad to see that he didn't seem to be in a hurry to leave, but instead appeared to be enjoying talking to her. "I know, but it's still taking me some getting used to. We were close before his mom passed and got closer after. It's hard watching him pull away. I wish I knew what was going on with him, but I don't."

She opened her mouth, ready to tell him about running into his son that day, but then closed it back. Now wasn't the best time. Not when he was already feeling bad about his kid growing further away from him.

Deandre's brows drew together. "What?"

She shook her head. "Nothing."

He straightened and gave her a no-nonsense stare. "No, it's something. What did you want to say?"

"It's not that big of a deal."

"Obviously it is, or you wouldn't hesitate to tell me. Is something wrong?"

"Not exactly." When he continued to watch her with concern, she decided to take Cora's advice and be honest with him. "I just... Well, I ran into your son. Before you introduced me to him."

"When?"

"Outside of my restaurant when I was closing up. He was with a group of teens. Some of the same kids that the other business owners have complained about. He was kind of rude."

Deandre's stance shifted and his gaze sharpened. "Rude how?"

Sheri held up a hand and shook her head. "Damn, see, I wasn't trying to get him in trouble."

He reached over and wrapped his hand around hers. He gently lowered her arm before letting her go. The touch was firm, but surprisingly gentle, and way too brief. "If he's acting out in the community, I need to know. What happened?"

Sheri forced herself not to rub her wrist. Not because he'd hurt her, but because she still felt the heat of his quick touch and she wanted to savor the feeling. To rub it in so she could melt in it later.

She told him the entire story. "It was just kids being kids," she said. "I wasn't hurt or anything, but I just thought you should know since you're trying to connect with the people in this area."

He frowned and ran a hand over his face. "I'm sorry, Sheri."

"For what? You didn't do anything. Please, if you talk to him, don't be too hard on him. It really wasn't that bad."

He raised a brow. "I'll talk with him and get him to apologize."

Sheri closed her eyes and groaned. "Now he really is going to think I'm a mean old woman."

"He'll know that if he acts up in this area that it'll get back to me and that actions have consequences."

She opened her eyes and met his gaze. He seemed concerned, but not upset with her for telling him about what happened. She'd been right in her assumption that he wouldn't go off on her for pointing out flaws in his kid.

"Fair enough," she said. "But I still feel like a snitch. And you know snitches get stitches."

His lips quirked and he laughed again. "No one in my family will be giving you stitches. Seriously, thank you for being honest with me. It's good to know. I want my son to grow up into a responsible person. If he's being rude to adults in the area, then I need to know."

"Hopefully, this won't come up again. And we can only talk about fun stuff when we're together."

"Fun stuff?"

He pushed away from the door. He didn't come closer,

but with him standing straight and giving her his complete attention, it made her mind think of all the fun but inappropriate stuff they could do. Like the two of them wrapped in each other's arms. His body between her legs.

She blinked and pushed that thought out of her head. "You know, like the community event, the chicken I bring you, stuff like that."

"In between the fun stuff, can you let me know a little bit more about you?"

She pressed a hand to her chest. Her heart beat frantically beneath her rib cage. "Me?" Thank goodness her voice didn't tremble like her insides.

He nodded. "Yes. I'd like to know more about my partner."

"Your partner?" Her cheeks heated. Damn, she liked the sound of that.

"Yeah, my partner on planning. Plus, I'll be in the area a lot. We can be friends."

Friends. He wanted to be…friends.

Sheri's stomach plummeted. Even if she were able to be a hit-it-and-quit-it girl, she still didn't have a chance with him. She was holding back from salivating over him, while he'd, very easily, put her in the friend zone.

She grinned but the movement felt stiff. Embarrassment churned her stomach, but thankfully, he didn't seem to have any idea about the fantasies going through her mind. She would be a professional and work with him on this project without making a fool of herself.

She took a step forward and opened the door. "We sure can. Friends it is."

Chapter Eight

Deandre drove home with the weight of what Sheri told him pressing down on him, urging him to speed the few miles to their house, but the reminder from his late wife that he should always get the full story before going into "cop mode" with the family held him to the speed limit. He would get to the bottom of things and find out if what Sheri said was the truth. And if it were, why would DJ do that?

Deandre knew his son wasn't perfect, but he'd always believed he was a good kid. Good kids didn't go around trying to hit on women old enough to be their mother or call them names when they were rejected. As much as he didn't want to believe what Sheri said, he'd also dealt with enough delusional parents in his career to hesitate before saying "my kid would never do that."

His in-laws' car was in the driveway when he pulled up. He'd forgotten they'd mentioned coming over to check on DJ while Deandre worked late at the neighborhood watch meeting. They often stepped in to spend time with DJ when Deandre had to work. Their support for him and DJ after Jamila's death was invaluable. His parents currently lived in a rental house in Denver. Since retirement, his parents embraced the "live it up" lifestyle and spent most of their time traveling to places they'd always wanted to visit. He didn't blame them; they'd raised him and his three brothers and wanted to enjoy their life. A part of him wished they'd spend more time with DJ, but he was forever thankful for Jamila's parents for providing a level of consistency even Deandre couldn't handle on his own.

He went inside and found Cliff and Rose sitting on the couch with DJ. The three of them watched a sitcom on television. His in-laws laughed at something on screen while DJ looked unamused. Which was his typical look lately. At least he didn't have his phone in his hand. Rose and Cliff had a strict rule that DJ couldn't scroll when he was with them. A rule DJ followed with minimal complaint.

Rose spotted him first. "Hey, Deandre, how was work?" He'd liked Rose from the start.

She'd treated him like family from the moment Jamila had introduced him to her. They got along well, and, with his own mother so far away, he'd easily accepted and absorbed the love she'd given him when he'd married her daughter.

"It was pretty good. The area seems excited about the event. So that's a good thing. I didn't think you would still be here."

Cliff pointed to the television. "We were going to go, but then I remembered my show was coming on. DJ was okay with watching it with us."

He glanced at DJ. "Well, that was nice of him."

DJ shrugged. "I'm a nice kid."

"When you want to be," Deandre countered.

Rose reached over and patted DJ's shoulder. "He always is."

Deandre sat in the chair next to the couch. "I want to believe the same thing, but I've been hearing some things."

"Things like what?" DJ asked.

"Things like you're going around saying inappropriate things to some of the shop owners on the south end."

Deandre didn't mind having the conversation in front of Cliff and Rose. If anything, DJ would be more likely to tell the truth in front of them. The glacier-cold wall DJ had built in the past year didn't extend to the relationship with his grandparents. He was more patient and accepting of their questions and prodding into his life. Deandre wished he'd get the same treatment, but, thankfully, Cliff and Rose and Deandre were a team in parenting DJ. If he came to them with any problems, they wouldn't hesitate to bring the situation to Deandre for them to work together on a solution.

DJ rolled his eyes. "She's lying. I didn't say anything to her."

Rose turned to DJ. "Her who?"

Deandre leaned forward. Disappointment tightened into a knot in his stomach. "Yes, DJ, her who, because I didn't say anything about where I heard it."

"I don't have to guess," DJ said with an irritated sigh. "I already know. I was just joking with her. That's all."

Deandre cocked his head to the side. "Joking? Do you joke with me or your grandparents like that?"

DJ huffed but shook his head. "No, sir."

"Then what makes you think it's okay to joke around with any other adults that way? Come on, DJ, what's going on with you? You quit wrestling and now you're hanging around, insulting adults you don't know."

Cliff sat up straighter. "You quit wrestling?" He sounded just as shocked at Deandre had.

DJ shrugged. "It's no big deal. Nothing is going on. I just didn't want to wrestle anymore, and I really was just joking. I'm not going through something."

Deandre pointed at his son. "You're going with me on Saturday to apologize."

DJ threw up his hands. "Come on, Dad."

"You're coming. You understand me? I'm working hard to build trust with the people in that area and I can't have you going behind my back undermining the trust and proving to them that the kids in the area are part of the problem. There are some business owners who think you and your friends are the reason for the break-ins and increased crime. They want us to come through arresting you all and scaring you away. If you're running round with a group of kids who think it's funny to hit on older women and call them *old ass* when they tell you no, then you're not helping. You understand?"

Rose pressed a hand to her chest. "Old what? DJ, did you say that?"

DJ closed his eyes and let out a heavy breath. He hesitated a beat before opening them back and nodding. "Okay. I get it. Don't embarrass you."

"It's not about embarrassing me. It's about also protecting you. Look at me, DJ."

His son slowly turned and met his eye.

"There are people who want to take my job and weaponize it against you and your friends. Don't give them a reason to do that. That's what this is about. Do you understand that?"

Some of the defiance left DJ's eyes. "I get it."

"Good."

"Can I go to my room now?"

Rose reached over and patted his leg. "You want to leave us now that we know what you did? Don't do something if you'll be embarrassed for us to find out about it later."

"Yes, ma'am. I've got homework," DJ said in that same, unconvincing voice that irritated Deandre.

Rose sighed but nodded. "We'll see you another day."

"Okay, Love you." DJ hugged her and then Cliff before disappearing down the hall to his room.

"Teenagers," Cliff said shaking his head.

"Tell me about it," Deandre replied. "He's still a good kid, but he's pushing boundaries."

"They'll do that. I remember when Jamila would fight us on everything," Rose said.

"Hold up," Cliff cut in. "She fought you on everything? She never argued with me."

Rose rolled her eyes and grinned. "That's because she was a daddy's girl through and through."

Deandre lifted his lips in a wistful smile. "DJ's personality is so much like hers. I wonder if he'd still be doing this if she were around."

"He would," Cliff said matter-of-factly. "Teenagers like to spread their wings and see how far they can go."

"Maybe, but boys are different with their mommas," Rose said. "He'd still be butting heads with you, Deandre, but he'd have a softer side in the house to calm him down."

Deandre leaned back in his chair. "I'll work on developing my softer side."

"Or, you can find a nice woman to settle down with," she said with wide, hopeful eyes.

Deandre closed his eyes and smiled. In the past year, Rose had gotten it into her head that Deandre needed a wife. At first, he'd been surprised. Not because he expected his in-laws to want him to remain alone for the rest of his life after losing Jamila, but he just hadn't expected them to actively try and push him into the arms of another woman, either. But they both were strongly on the side of him getting back in the dating pool.

"If I find the right person I'll consider that. But not because DJ needs a new mom. We're doing okay."

"Have you been looking for the right person?" Cliff asked curiously.

A vision of Sheri drifted into his mind. Her bright eyes, wide smile and sexy figure. She wasn't as dramatic as he'd assumed she would be, but she did have a fiery spark to her personality. One she'd wanted to let out on Belinda today.

He sat up straight and his eyes popped back open. What was that? Yeah, he found her attractive, and yes, she'd awakened his sex drive, but why would he think of her when he thought of a potential future wife? She wasn't even in the running.

"Hmm." Rose narrowed her eyes on him. "I think there may be someone."

Deandre shook his head. "Nah, there isn't. It's not like that."

Rose and Cliff shared a look and grinned. "What's not like that? Who is she?"

Deandre held up a hand. "There is no she and there is no situation to update you on. Right now, I'm focused on keeping DJ out of trouble and making sure the town sticks behind their promise to support the revitalization of the south side of the beach."

"There's always time for a little romance," Cliff said with a wink.

"He's right," Rose agreed. "We want to see you happy, too, Deandre. And, you know Jamila would have wanted you to be happy, as well."

Deandre nodded. "I know. I'm not trying to rush into

anything. But I hear you and I appreciate that you want good things for me."

They exchanged another look, communicating silently in a way that Deandre had once hoped he and Jamila would get to. But they never would get to that point, and while the pain of her loss would never go away, he was no longer too gutted to poke at the scar.

He did have a quick moment with Sheri earlier. When their eyes met, and she'd wanted to keep arguing with Belinda but he'd pleaded with her to be nice. She'd understood him. He'd imagined her voice saying *"Fine, this time for you,"* before she'd let the conversation drop. Maybe that's why he was imagining her as more than just a partner in this project. But deep down, he knew it could be more if he let it. The instant attraction, the connection, the way he just *liked* her. He hadn't felt that since…

"Anyone want something to drink? I'm going to get some tea." He cut off his own thoughts before they could take hold.

"I'll take some. We'll leave after the show is over," Cliff said.

Deandre nodded and looked at Rose, who shook her head and said she was good. He went to the kitchen and prepared the drinks. He'd deal with getting through today, helping his son and the community event. That's it. He wasn't quite ready to deal with the weird message his libido, or maybe his heart, was trying to deliver to his brain.

Chapter Nine

DJ sighed for what had to be the hundredth time since Deandre told him to get in the car so they could go to the gathering at Kelly's comic book store. Deandre hadn't expected DJ to jump up and down with excitement to apologize to Sheri, but he had hoped his son wouldn't act as if he were being dragged to the guillotine. Comic books were one of the few things DJ still enjoyed reading.

"Come on, DJ, what's the sigh for?"

DJ looked at him as if he should know exactly what the sigh was about. "I didn't have to come here tonight."

"You're here to apologize."

"I can do that anytime. Why tonight in front of everyone?"

"I won't make you apologize in front of the group. You like comic books. I thought you'd enjoy coming to the store."

"Manga."

Deandre frowned. "Say what?"

DJ rubbed a hand over his face and gave Deandre a "you're clueless" expression. "I read mangas. Not comics."

"Aren't they the same thing?"

DJ closed his eyes and shook his head. "Bruh…" he sighed. "They are completely different things."

"Well, *bruh*, maybe there are mangas in here."

"There aren't."

"How do you know?"

"I've been in that shop before. It's all comics, maybe a few mangas, but not what I'm reading."

"Well, check out the comic books anyway. Maybe you'll find something you like."

"Yeah, maybe," he said just a tad shy of sarcastically.

Deandre accepted that he wasn't going to get anything more positive out of his son, and parallel parked the car in a spot a few storefronts down from the comic book store. They got out of the car and went inside. Several other business owners and some residents mingled inside the store. Deandre's eyes searched the crowd until they landed on Sheri standing in the back talking with Kelly. Sheri threw her head back and laughed at something Kelly said and Deandre's breath hitched in his throat. Damn, she was fine.

"Can I go after I apologize?" DJ's voice cut into Deandre's thoughts.

He blinked and looked over at his son. "I may not be ready to leave."

"My boy Julian is at the pizza place. He said he'll pick me up."

Deandre shook his head. "You came with me, and you'll leave with me. End of discussion."

"Oh, man," DJ muttered.

"Come on. Let's go say hello."

"And get this over with," DJ mumbled.

They were stopped by several people who recognized him as they made their way across the room. Even though DJ didn't want to be there and was more than happy to show his irritation to Deandre, the kid had enough home training to not act out or say anything rude while they spoke with the people in the store. DJ was all yes ma'am and no sir with eye contact and a pleasant expression when he spoke. Pride swelled in his chest. DJ was "pushing boundaries" as Cliff said, but he was still a good kid.

They got to Kelly and Sheri just as soon as it looked like Sheri was about to walk away. She caught his eye and smiled. It was so bright, he wondered if she'd been waiting for him to arrive. No, he was reading too much into that. She always smiled like that.

"Lieutenant, how are you?" Kelly asked.

"I'm good, Kelly. How are you?"

"I'm great. Is this your son?" Kelly asked, grinning at DJ.

"It is. This is Deande Jr., or DJ for short."

DJ nodded to them both. "It's nice meeting you."

"Likewise. Do you read comics?" Kelly asked.

DJ shook his head. "Not really. Mostly mangas."

Kelly pointed to a section across the room. "Ah, I've got a few but not many. I hope to expand the section one day. Maybe you can tell me some of the series you're reading, and I can get them in stock."

DJ's brows lifted. "You'd do that?"

"Of course. I like mangas, but comics are my true love. But I would like to bring in all types of customers. Just let me know." She nodded at someone who called her name from across the room. "Let me check on this. Thanks for coming, Lieutenant. Nice to meet you, DJ." She left the three of them.

"I'm going to check out the mangas," DJ said, turning away.

Deandre cleared his throat and placed a hand on his son's shoulder. DJ sighed and turned back. "Yes, sir."

"Aren't you forgetting something?" Deandre tilted his head toward Sheri.

DJ looked like he wanted to roll his eyes, but his son was also a smart kid and knew better. He turned to Sheri. "I'm sorry for what I said the other day. It was rude and it won't happen again."

Sheri's eyes widened. She looked at Deandre, then back at DJ. "Oh, well, thank you for apologizing. It's accepted."

DJ nodded then looked at Deandre. "Now can I check out the mangas?"

"Fine, go ahead." DJ quickly ran off.

Sheri chuckled. "How much did it hurt him to have to apologize to me?"

"Enough to warrant about fifty million sighs on the car ride over and a request to leave immediately afterward."

Sheri crinkled her nose. "That much, huh? You didn't have to get him to do that, but I do appreciate it."

She wasn't dressed in her usual The Breakfast Nook T-shirt and jeans. Instead, she wore a sleeveless tan-colored shirt that fitted her breasts perfectly and a pair of distressed jeans that hugged her curves. A gold chain with her nickname, Lil Bit, hung just above the swell of her breast. He forced himself to keep eye contact and not let his gaze wander over the smooth brown skin of her neck, chest and shoulders.

"I did have to get him apologize. I let him know that kind of behavior is what's making some people want him and his friends banned from the south end of the beach. I think he understood."

"Well, for what it's worth, that was the only thing I've seen happen with him and his group of friends. They don't really cause any trouble as far as I know. I don't think he's running around with a really bad crowd."

"That's good to know. He doesn't know how much I worry about him. I get it, he's sixteen and able to be out in the world on his own to an extent, but it's still hard for me to not want to protect him like he's still six years old."

Sheri placed a hand on his arm. "I think I get what you're saying, but don't let him hear that. I don't know any sixteen-year-old who wants to still be viewed like they're six." Her eyes sparkled with humor.

She gently squeezed his bicep before her hand fell away. He didn't know if the movement was meant to be reassuring, or a way for her to feel the muscle, but either way, his arm seemed to sizzle from where she'd touched it.

"I'll try and remember that," he said.

She glanced away and nodded as she caught someone else's eye. Was she about to walk away? He wasn't ready for their conversation to end. "How long have you been here?" he asked quickly.

She looked back at him. "Not too long. It's a nice thing to get to mingle with the other shop owners and learn more about Kelly's store. I think I may host something at the restaurant later for everyone."

"That would be a good idea."

"Yeah, keep the vibe going and help us all get to know each other as we build up the area." Her eyes darted to the side again. Whoever she'd noticed before must have gotten her attention.

Deandre shifted his stance a little to the left. Sheri's dark brown eyes lifted back up to meet his. "I hope I get an invite."

Sheri's tongue darted out and touched the edge of her mouth. "You'd come?"

He would, but the hope in her voice and the way her lips lifted in the sexiest of smiles triggered something in his brain. He'd rearrange his entire schedule to make it to anything she ever put on. "For you? Of course I'd come."

Her hand lifted to toy with the chain around her neck. His eyes followed the movement of her slim fingers above her breasts and there was a stirring in his groin. He quickly lifted his eyes back to hers.

Sheri sucked in a breath, then pointed to his left. "I'm going to go say hello to Ivy and see if she wants to host something at her tattoo parlor. I'll talk with you later."

Deandre wanted to find another reason to keep her talking to him, but he was also blurring the line between their working together and flirting. Sheri solved his problem by dashing across the room before he could think of something else to say. Which was probably for the best. What was wrong with him? A few weeks ago he wasn't even entertaining the idea of doing anything about his attraction to her. Now he was searching for ways to keep her nearby? He'd better get this under control because she was obviously not interested in him that way. He wanted this project to succeed and hitting on his project partner was a surefire way of ruining everything.

Sheri spent most of the night trying to avoid being alone with Lieutenant King again. Not because she didn't enjoy his company. That was the problem. She enjoyed his company *too* much. The man was handsome, thoughtful, kind and funny. He was all the checkboxes she made for herself after realizing that one-night stands and friends-with-benefits type situations weren't going to work for her anymore. Which meant her attraction for him was about to have her make a dumb decision. A potentially embarrassing decision when he rejected her if she hit on him.

Sure, there had been that one time when he'd checked out her cleavage. She had to admit, her cleavage was amazing in her shirt. She'd worn it partially because she'd wanted him to see her. But, like a gentleman, he'd lifted his eyes quickly and looked apologetic. The man was a man, but he obviously was not a man coming to her for anything other than the community event.

Despite her growing attraction for Deandre and her efforts to avoid him, Sheri had a good time at the comic book shop. It was the first time she'd had a chance to mingle with some of the other business owners and not focus on crime in the area or ways to get support from the city. Outside of her cousin Cora, Sheri didn't have a lot of friends. When she'd moved home, family was her support system. They were whom she spent time with when she wasn't working. The friends she'd had while she'd grown up had either moved away or were married with their own kids and things to deal with. So hanging out with Kelly and Ivy from the tattoo parlor made her want to branch out and expand her social circle.

"Let's do this again," Sheri said when she was saying goodbye to Kelly later that evening.

"Have a get-together at the comic book store? Sure."

Sheri shook her head. "No, I mean let's hang out sometime. I'm just going to be straight up. I mostly hang out with my cousin, and even though I love her, I wouldn't mind expanding my social circle. If you're cool with it, let's hang out sometime."

Kelly grinned and nodded. "I'm cool with it. I need to get out more." She looked to Ivy. "What about you?"

"I work late hours at the shop, but if you give me enough heads-up, then I can make it work. I'm down."

"Cool. I'll send out some dates and we'll see what works." Sheri kept her voice calm and collected even though she wanted to bounce with excitement.

She was finally making some new friends. She wanted

new friends. Not because she didn't like hanging out with Cora, but she also needed different viewpoints. Cora was cool and all, but she didn't always encourage Sheri to make the best decisions.

Speaking of her cousin. Sheri pulled out her cell phone and texted her. She'd let Cora borrow her car while her car was in the shop, and she'd dropped Sheri off and promised to be here by nine to pick her up. Sheri had texted her to make sure she was still coming, but the return texts had stopped.

R U on the way?

Can u catch a ride?

Sheri cursed and looked up at Ivy and Kelly. "My bad. I need to make a call. We'll catch up soon."

They waved as she walked outside. She was going to have to curse out her cousin and she didn't want to do that in front of everyone in the room.

Once outside, she dialed her cousin's number. Cora answered on the fourth ring. "What do you mean *catch a ride*?" Sheri said immediately.

"Look, I thought I'd be done, but Tim needed a ride." Cora didn't sound the least bit apologetic for leaving Sheri stranded while she gave someone else a ride.

"Who the hell is Tim?" Sheri put a hand on her hip.

"You know, the guy I've been trying to hook up with?"

"You said you needed my car to run an errand while yours was in the shop. Not because you were taking some guy for a ride."

"He's not just some guy. Do you ever listen?" Cora had the nerve to sound exasperated with Sheri.

"I'm listening now while you tell me you're giving some-one a ride in my car."

"I said it was an errand. I didn't say what kind."

Sheri pinched the bridge of her nose. She took a deep breath before asking. "When will you come and get me?"

"See, what had happened was—"

"Cora!" Nothing good ever started with those words.

Cora plowed ahead. "I told Tim I would take him to pick up some money from his boy's house."

"I don't give a damn about his boy."

"But he owes me the money," her cousin said as if that were explanation enough. "So, I said I'd take him to get the money."

Sheri tapped her foot. She wanted to shake Cora. "Still not my problem."

"Well, his boy lives in Myrtle Beach."

"Myrtle Beach! You're an hour away."

"And his friend is having this party, so, can you catch a ride? I promise I'll be back as soon as I can."

"You're gone with my damn car! How am I supposed to get home?"

"Uber? Lyft? Call your momma?" Again, Cora didn't sound apologetic. She had the nerve to sound as if Sheri should already have the answer for how to get home.

"I'm not calling my mom. You said you'd be here to get me by nine."

"My bad. Look, I'll pay for the Uber."

"You know what. Forget you and Tim. You owe me and when I see you, I'm going to cuss your—"

"I know you will. Send me the cost for the Uber and I'll send you the money. Bye!" She ended the call.

Sheri stomped her feet and cursed again. "I don't want to call a damn Uber!"

"I'll give you a ride home." Deandre's voice came from behind her.

Sheri spun around. Deandre watched her with a concerned expression. His son watched her as if she were as pitiful as she felt. Stranded at the beach while her cousin ran off with her car.

Sheri shook her head. Her cheeks burned with embarrassment. "You don't have to do that."

"I couldn't help but hear some of your conversation. I wouldn't want you waiting out here for some stranger to take you home. Let me give you a ride."

"But…" She glanced at his son. "I live kind of far out."

"I'll drop off DJ and then take you. I live about five minutes from here."

She could order an Uber and go back inside to wait. She was sure she'd have fun talking to Ivy and Kelly some more. But it was embarrassing enough to be stranded. And he was there, and he was offering to give her a ride. And, even though she'd tried to stay away from him most of the night, the reckless side of her brain couldn't resist a man who was willing to step in and help when the opportunity presented itself.

"If you don't mind, then sure," she said before she could second-guess or remind herself how this was not going to help her get over her attraction to him.

Deandre looked as if he'd been hoping that would be her answer. "Good, let's go."

Deandre was parked a few cars down from the store. DJ got in the back seat and Sheri took the passenger side. When they were in the car, Sheri tried to think of something cool or interesting to say but her mind drew a blank. Not that it mattered. Other than showing mild irritation when his dad offered to give her a ride home, DJ had shown more interest in his phone than he had in Sheri, or his dad, for that matter.

"Thanks for this," she finally said once they'd dropped DJ off and were heading to her place. She'd given him the address and he'd known the area.

"You don't have to keep thanking me. It really is no problem."

"I know, but you could be doing anything other than dragging me out to my house. I swear I'm never letting my cousin borrow my car again."

"Does she usually leave you hanging like this?"

"It depends. I don't usually have to go so far as to let her use my car. Hers is in the shop, and she swore this would just be a quick trip. But when it comes to Cora and a man, then, yes, she will drop me like a balled-up receipt."

Deandre shook his head, then chuckled. "Damn, not like that."

"Exactly like that. She's my cousin, and I love her, but she doesn't always make the best choices. Or support me making the best choices."

"Is she the friend that encourages bad behavior?" His voice was light, not judging.

She nodded. "Most definitely. To be honest, she's part of the reason you got called out to arrest me that night."

He turned to look at her quickly before glancing back at the road. They were farther away from the town now. The streetlights were now nonexistent, and the sliver of a moon barely lit up the road. "How?"

"I don't throw all the blame on her. I mean, it was me holding the bat. But she did encourage me to use it." Sheri shook her head and groaned. "I still can't believe I did that. It took me way too long to live that down."

He was silent for a second before asking hesitantly, "Were you and he...very serious?"

"We weren't. I knew it, but when you get caught up in something, reason doesn't always make sense. So, when my feelings got hurt, and Cora and I were watching *Waiting to Exhale,* that's how we ended up there. It wasn't until later that I realized Cora also liked Tyrone. That may have played into her encouragement."

"For real?"

"For real."

He was quiet again. Sheri looked out the window, wondering what he was thinking but also hesitant to ask. She didn't like to play the mind-reading game, but she couldn't help but worry that he was thinking she was immature and overly dramatic.

"The event tonight was cool," she blurted out. Anything to keep him from thinking about her bashing the car of a guy she was no longer interested in.

"It was," he said evenly.

"We're thinking of having more. It'll be a good way to bring the community together."

"I like that idea. I don't get out much, so it'll give me a reason to socialize."

"Why don't you go out much?"

Did that mean he wasn't dating? They'd been planning the event for a few weeks, and he hadn't mentioned a girlfriend. Not that she'd asked. There also hadn't been phone calls, texts or anything that gave the appearance of him having someone in his life.

"Between the job and raising DJ, I didn't worry about a social life. Now that he's getting older, it's time for me to try to figure out how to interact with people again."

"I think you interact pretty well."

He nodded. "Most of my interactions aren't in a social setting. My former partner and friend LaTisha, along with my in-laws, keep asking me to get out there and start living my life again. In fact, if they don't drag me out of the house, I don't do much of anything."

"I love going out and doing stuff. I had a side job as event staff at the convention center in Myrtle Beach. It was a great way to get out, meet people and see interesting events. But once I opened the restaurant, I gave it up. Now, I'm kind of like you. Looking for excuses to get out and do stuff."

"Do you hang with your cousin a lot?"

"We hang a little, but we haven't as much since I opened the restaurant. She's got her thing and I've got mine. We catch up when we can, but lately it's been a lot of her dropping me for other interests."

"Hmm."

She raised her brow and looked at him. "Hmm, what?"

"Nothing, just looks like we're in the same boat. Need a reason to go out and socialize."

"Well, if you ever see something you're interested in and want a partner, let me know. I'll go with you."

Damn, why had she said that? Did it sound like she was asking him on a date? Because she wasn't. Not really. She said the words before she could think about them and talk herself out of making the suggestion.

"We're friends, you know," she said quickly. "Friends hang out."

He nodded slowly. "They do."

That wasn't much of a reply. Her cheeks burned and she wanted to get out of the car and walk the rest of the way home. What in the world was wrong with her? She was Sheri "Lil Bit" Thomas. She wasn't afraid to talk to anyone or try something new. She knew her own mind and was confident in herself and her abilities. So why did conversations with this man make her wonder if she was somehow lacking? Sure, he'd seen her at her worst, but that wasn't all of her. She had to get herself together. They were friends and working together on this project. That was it. She was not going to act like a schoolgirl with a crush on the popular boy that was so hard she couldn't even speak to him.

"So it's settled, then, friend," she said. "We'll hang out if we see something interesting." She infused her voice with confidence, and an "I will not be hurt if you say no" string of steel. The string was micrometers thick and could be bent, but it was still steel.

He glanced at her again. "Settled."

They were silent for the next few minutes. The radio played soul music thanks to the local station's *Saturday Night Juke Joint* playlist. She sang along to some of the songs and was pleasantly surprised when Deandre did the same. She glanced his way and their eyes caught. They both grinned and continued to sing along with the lyrics. The rest of the trip went by fast but was the most fun she'd had all night.

She wished it would last longer, this impromptu sing-along with Deandre that didn't make her feel immature or overly flustered.

"Thanks for dropping me off."

He put the car in Park. "I'll walk you to the door."

"You don't—"

"I know I don't have to," he cut in. "But blame it on my upbringing and being a cop. Your house is dark, you live away from town and I'd feel better walking you to the door."

She pointed to the house next door. Her family owned most of the property on the road. Two years ago, before her grandmother passed, she'd split two acres so her daughter could build a home and given the quarter acre where she'd built her home to Sheri.

"My mom's light is on, so I'm sure she's watching from behind her curtains."

"Even more reason for me to walk you to the door. I don't want her to think I don't have any manners."

Sheri couldn't help but laugh as she opened the door. "You're worried about what my mom thinks?"

"You never know when I'll need to make a good impression."

Her heart rate tripled. She shook her head as she got out of the car. He was just being nice. He walked her the short distance from the gravel drive to her front door. She hadn't left the porch light on, and with the limited moonlight, the only illumination came from the tall light on a pole along the border of her property and her mom's they'd installed to light up the side yard where they had cookouts long into the night with family.

She unlocked her door, then turned back toward Deandre. "Thanks again, for the ride and bringing me home."

"You're welcome." He shifted his weight.

Sheri got the impression he had something to say. "Anything wrong?"

"That guy… Tyrone. Do you still have feelings for him?"

The question was so out of the blue that she took a step back. "What? No. Why would you ask?"

"If we're going to hang out, I just wanted to know if there was someone you had feelings for."

"Definitely not him. You know he's getting married, right? We made our peace with each other, and I wish him well."

He slowly lifted and lowered his head as if letting her words settle in. "No other guys in the picture?"

"Not right now." She cocked her head to the side. Her pulse pounded as a wild thought entered her mind. "Are you asking for a reason?"

"Just curious."

"No, you don't ask that kind of stuff just because you're curious. Is there a reason?" She had to know. Otherwise she'd be up all night wondering why he asked and what he meant. She wasn't about to put herself through that kind of torture.

He straightened his shoulders, and even in the darkness of the porch she could feel the intensity of his gaze. "Because I want to know for personal reasons. If you're available."

Her breathing hitched. Okay, so maybe he was interested. "I'm available," she said quickly.

He nodded, a short, succinct movement of his head. "That's good to know."

"Why?" She shifted closer.

"I'd like to get to know you. Not just for the community event and not just as a friend."

Sheri's knees felt like Jell-O. She wanted to jump up and down and twerk, but instead, she held in her excitement and nodded. "Oh…well… I like that idea."

God how she wished there was more light for her to see. She could swear his body stilled, but she couldn't see his face. The humid night air felt electric and ten times hotter, thicker. Was that just her? Did he feel it, too?

"Good. Then it's official."

She blinked. "What's official?"

"You and me. We're…officially getting to know each other."

She smiled, loving his direct manner. "We are."

"I'll call you tomorrow, then."

"I like that."

He nodded and took a step backward. Sheri was excited, but she wasn't ready to let him go. Not just yet. "But you can kiss me tonight."

There was just enough light for her to see the way heat flared in his gaze. He glanced at her mom's house. Then back at her. Time seemed to slow down before he stepped forward and pulled her into his embrace. The kiss was soft, and sweet. He explored her mouth with the same direct confidence he'd used to confirm that they would officially get to know each other. She wanted him to kiss her deeper, harder. If she were honest, she wanted him to back her against the wall, and kiss every part of her body. She pressed forward, but he pulled back.

"I'll call you tomorrow," he said in a deep, rumbling voice.

"But…"

He silenced her with another kiss. When he pulled away, he smiled. "Tomorrow."

Chapter Ten

Sundays were the busiest day in the restaurant, and Sheri typically didn't have time to have any thoughts in her head other than prepping food, serving customers and making sure everything was happening on schedule. But this Sunday, she had an extra bounce in her step and nothing but personal thoughts filled her head.

He'd said they were officially "getting to know each other," so did that mean she was officially dating Lieutenant Deandre King? Did that mean she could refer to him as her man, or was "getting to know each other" not an automatic step into official relationship status? Was she being silly for overthinking this? Shouldn't she just go with the flow and let whatever happened happen? No. Going with the flow meant not knowing where she stood and misunderstandings. Clarity was important.

"Lil Bit, if you don't quit daydreaming and get your food off the counter, then I'm going to throw an egg at you." JD's gruff voice broke into her thoughts.

Sheri blinked and shook her head. "I'm not daydreaming." She was preoccupied. There was a difference.

Cora came up to her side. Her cousin sometimes helped on the weekends. She hadn't agreed to come in today, but Sheri assumed she'd shown up in an attempt to make up for ditching Sheri the night before.

"Yes, you are," Cora said. "This got anything to do with whatever man dropped you off last night?"

Sheri's head whipped to the side so she could eye her cousin. "Who said a man dropped me off?"

Her mom sidled up next to JD in the kitchen and peered at Sheri with a hand propped on her hip. "I said it because I saw it. It was dark last night, but I recognize a man's shoulders."

JD slapped his spatula on the griddle. "I don't care who dropped her off. I made those waffles and eggs and they're gonna get cold if y'all keep clucking like chickens. Take the food and worry about the man later."

Sighing, Sheri grabbed the plates off the serving station and hurried from the kitchen before she could be further questioned. She wasn't ashamed to tell her family about her and Deandre, but she wasn't ready to get their input, either. A part of her was dying to talk to someone, but she could guess her mom's and Cora's opinions. Her mom would warn her not to trust or date a cop and Cora would find something negative about Deandre to put a damper on Sheri's excitement. She wanted to enjoy this moment, before she let family come in and cast their shadows of doubt.

She took the food to the table for her customers. "Here you go. Can I get you anything else?"

The two women glanced over their food, eyes brightening the way she liked to see. "No, I think we're good for now."

"Extra napkins, please," the other lady said at the same time.

"I've got you." Sheri got the napkins and then went to serve the next table that had just been seated.

They were busy, as usual. They even had a waitlist started. She glanced at the people lined up outside through the window and nearly stumbled. Was that? She squinted and leaned forward. Her heart jumped. Yes, that was Deandre standing outside. He was with a woman she didn't recognize, another man and had DJ with him. He'd said he'd call her today, but she hadn't expected him to show up.

"What are you smiling at?" Cora scooted up next to Sheri. She looked out the window, too. "Isn't that the cop you saw at TJ Maxx the other day?"

Sheri turned and hurried away to fill the drink order for the table she'd just visited. She hoped Cora would move on to her own tables, but no, her cousin just followed her to the back where they prepared the drinks.

"Is he the one who dropped you off?" Cora's voice dripped with judgment. For what reason, Sheri didn't know. Cora tended to go straight to judging Sheri's relationship decisions from the start.

"Why are you worrying about who dropped me off?" Sheri grabbed the sparkling wine out of the cooler to make mimosas. "No one would have had to drop me off if you hadn't left me hanging."

Cora held up a hand. "Didn't I say I'm sorry? Besides, I'm here now helping out."

"You're not helping. You're over here bothering me. You know we're busy. We can talk about it later."

"He did drop you off, didn't he?" Cora's eyes lit up with the excitement of new gossip. "Girl, wait till I tell your mom."

Sheri reached out and grabbed Cora's shirt before she could head in the direction of where her mom worked with JD making the food.

"What, are you a snitch now? Why are you going to tell her?"

"Because she was worried about you. I'm just looking out." Cora tried, and failed, to look and sound innocent.

Sheri didn't believe that for a second. Cora was eager to

tell Sheri's mom to start drama in the middle of the busiest shift. "No, you're being messy. I don't want messy right now. Not with him, okay."

Cora raised her brow. "What's that supposed to mean?"

"It means what I just said. He's a nice guy. He wants us to get to know each other. So that's what we're doing."

Cora scrunched up her nose. "Get to know each other? Sounds like a simple way to say he just wants to sleep with you."

"He's not trying to sleep with me. He's taking it slow."

"For what? You're both grown. Girl, something is probably wrong with him."

Sheri rolled her eyes and groaned. Why had she even bothered to give an explanation? Cora didn't believe in taking things slow. She got hers and moved on and dealt with guys who wanted the same. "Nothing is wrong with him. He's just a nice guy. Can I be with a nice guy for once?"

Cora threw up her arms. "If you say so. Let me go help at the front." She turned and walked out of the kitchen.

Sheri closed her eyes and groaned. Damn, Cora, and her negative attitude. She would immediately jump to saying something was wrong with Deandre instead of seeing what he'd done as something decent.

Sheri left the kitchen to deliver the mimosas. Cora was at the front talking to the hostess, their younger cousin D'asa. D'asa looked outside, grinned, then nodded. Sheri had to take her customer's order, so she couldn't run up and find out what Cora had said. The next few minutes were harried as she put in the order, delivered more food and greeted another set of customers. When she was able to check on Deandre's progress again, he and his party were seated, but they were across the room. Not in her section but in Cora's.

Double damn! So that's what Cora was up to. And her

cousin wasted no time rushing up to Deandre's table to take their order. Sheri took a step in that direction to intervene. She did not need Cora's messiness this early in whatever kind of relationship she was starting with Deandre.

"Excuse me, Sheri, can I get a refill?" the customer at the table next to her asked.

As much as she wanted to curse for being interrupted, she remembered customer service was something she prided herself in and overcame her need to snatch Cora by her ponytail and pull her away from the table with her man. She turned and smiled.

"Sure, I've got you." She took the cup and went back to refill it and prayed Cora wasn't going to do something to sabotage this relationship before it started.

Deandre hoped he would be seated in Sheri's section but felt he did a decent job hiding his disappointment when the hostess put them across the room from where she worked. He hadn't intended to come here for breakfast, but when LaTisha and her husband, Rob, called to see if he was up so they could drop off the chain saw they'd borrowed before going to breakfast, and then mentioned they were checking out Sheri's place, he'd found himself inviting him and DJ along before the thought could finish forming in his mind.

"Now I know why you wanted to come eat here," DJ said with a smirk.

LaTisha raised a brow and gave DJ a curious look. "Why?"

His son looked across the room at Sheri talking to a couple at another table. "For her."

LaTisha and Rob both turned in that direction. "The waitress?"

"She owns the place," Deandre said quickly.

DJ sat forward in his chair, a frown on his face. "Is this why you made me apologize? Because you like her?"

"Wait? You like her?" LaTisha asked with a big smile as she pointed over her shoulder.

Rob chuckled and shook his head. He was shorter than Deandre, with a bald head, golden brown skin and well-defined muscles gained from hours in the gym. He was a paramedic who'd met LaTisha when they'd both responded to an emergency. Twelve years later, they were still together. "I knew you had a reason for coming," Rob said.

Deandre focused on DJ instead of the teasing looks in his friends' eyes. "I had you apologize because it was the right thing to do. Not just because I like her."

DJ shook his head and glared down at the menu. Deandre didn't get a chance to respond to his son's mumbled "whatever" because LaTisha was tapping his arm.

"Hold on. You like her for real?" LaTisha's voice rose in pitch with her excitement.

"Can you not announce it to the entire restaurant?" Deandre said, looking around at the other tables. Who, thankfully, seemed to be preoccupied with their own conversations.

LaTisha lowered her voice, but her enthusiasm was still visible in her eyes. "When did this happen? How did you meet her?"

"She's helping me with the community event."

The waitress walked up to their table, immediately blocking Deandre's view of Sheri across the room. He looked up and recognized her as Sheri's cousin Cora. Cora studied him through squinted eyes. She was sizing him up. For what he didn't know. Had Sheri already told her about what happened the night before?

"Well, hello, Officer." Cora's voice was syrupy sweet. "It's good to see you again."

"Good seeing you, too."

She looked at LaTisha. "This your girlfriend?"

Deandre coughed. "What? Nah?"

LaTisha returned Cora's smile with a fake one of her own before slipping her arm through Rob's. "I'm with him. And I'd like coffee and orange juice, please."

"Water and coffee for me," Rob replied.

"I'll take an apple juice," DJ ordered.

"Coffee and water," Deandre finished with a nod.

Cora looked at the four of them. He could see the irritation in her eyes. He'd bet she wanted to linger and get more information out of him, but thankfully LaTisha peeped her game as well and cut it short.

"I'll be right back with those drinks." She turned and walked away.

"What's up with her?" LaTisha asked as soon as Cora was out of earshot.

Rob shrugged and picked up his menu. "It's not the first time someone asked if you were with Deandre."

"Yeah, but she said that with intention." LaTisha cut her eyes in the direction Cora had gone.

LaTisha had been his partner and they hung out after work, so people had assumed they were together before. Nothing ever happened between them, and Rob was just as much his friend as hers. Most of the time the assumption wasn't made was when the three of them were together.

"That's Sheri's cousin Cora," Deandre said. "I think she's a bit of a troublemaker."

DJ lowered his menu. "Didn't you warn me to stay away from girls with drama?" he said. "I'd think you'd do the same."

"Cora is not Sheri, and we're just…getting to know each other."

DJ rolled his eyes. "Sure."

"Leave your dad alone." LaTisha waved her hand at DJ. "It's good that you're testing the waters."

"And Sheri is not her cousin."

Cora returned with their drinks. "Have you been here before?"

LaTisha answered, "It's our first time."

"I can tell you the specials."

"No need," LaTisha said with an unwavering smile. "I want the chicken and waffles."

Rob ordered, then DJ and finally Deandre. Which didn't leave Cora much time to chat. She hurried away. Sheri came out of the back as Cora was heading into the kitchen. Sheri stopped her cousin, who said something that made Sheri cringe and glance their way. Cora continued to the kitchen and Sheri made a beeline their way.

"Is everything good over here?" she asked.

Deandre shifted forward and smiled. A sheen of sweat beaded her brow, her ponytail was tousled and what looked like syrup stained her yellow The Breakfast Nook T-shirt, but she still managed to look sexy as all get-out. She was obviously busy, with many more things to focus on besides him and his friends. He shouldn't have come to distract her, but when he'd been faced with the chance to see her, he hadn't been able to stop himself from coming.

"We're great. Busy morning?"

She nodded. "Yes, Sunday is our busiest day." She looked to LaTisha and Rob and held out her hand. "Hey, I'm Sheri Thomas."

Latisha took Sheri's hand. "LaTisha and Rob Fuller. I've been wanting to try this place for a long time."

"Well, I'm glad you decided to give us a try." She looked at DJ. "Good to see you again, DJ."

DJ barely glanced up from his phone. "Yeah, same."

Sheri's smile stiffened at the edges. Deandre nudged his son's foot under the table. DJ gave him a "What's the matter?" look before sitting up and giving Sheri a plastic smile. "Good seeing you, too, ma'am."

Deandre placed a hand on her forearm. "We dragged him out early."

"It's no problem. I'm just glad to see you." Her eyes met his and he knew that despite the rush of people, her nosy cousin and his rude kid, she meant the words.

"Likewise."

"You all enjoy your meal. Give me a call later, okay?" She squeezed his shoulder before going back to her tables across the room.

LaTisha and Rob both beamed at him. "She likes you, too."

"I'd hope so," he said, trying not to let it show how much those words made his morning.

DJ sucked his teeth but kept looking at his phone. Deandre decided to let it go for now. No need to make a scene in the restaurant and ruin breakfast. DJ was more than likely still upset about having to apologize. He'd eventually come around.

The conversation drifted to the neighborhood and the latest renovations to LaTisha and Rob's house. The food came and Cora realized they didn't want to chat with her and went on about her business. At the end of the meal, she came back and gave him a smug look with her hand on her hip.

"Looks like your food was comped today," she said.

"What?" Deandre looked around the room. Sheri met his eyes and winked. "No, I can't let her do that."

"She's the owner and can do what she wants. You better not hurt her, that's all I've got to say."

Deandre frowned. "I don't plan to hurt anyone."

Cora snorted. "That's what they all say. Have a good rest of your day." She turned and sauntered off.

"Ignore her," LaTisha said. "Your girl really likes you."

"Free food is cool," DJ agreed.

"I really shouldn't," Deandre said.

"Dad, why you arguing? She's *your girl* now, right? Just take the W and move on. I'll meet y'all at the car." He got up and walked out.

He looked at Rob and LaTisha. "It's too much."

"It's her restaurant, don't make a scene. Just make it up to her later in a nice way," LaTisha said.

"How?"

Rob winked at him. "You'll think of a way." They got up and headed to the door.

Deandre stood as well, but instead of going to the door he crossed the room to where Sheri was turning away from a table. She grinned at him, and he had a funny sensation in his chest that he hadn't felt in years. Something that told him that if he wasn't careful, he could fall hard for Sheri. It was part of the reason why he wanted to take things slow. He'd tried quick hookups and casual flings after his wife passed, but that life wasn't for him. He was open to a long-term relationship, maybe even getting married again one day. He wasn't sure if Sheri was the person he'd do that with, but he didn't want to rush into sex with her and create an awkward situation.

"Did you enjoy the food?"

She had the same hopeful look in her eye that she always had when she brought him food. She looked so cute he couldn't help himself. He placed his hand on her hip, pulled her forward and kissed her quickly.

"I enjoyed seeing you more. I owe you."

She leaned into him. The light press of her breasts against his chest caused a stirring in his midsection that made him want to pull her closer and kiss her deeper. He definitely needed to take things slow with Sheri or else he'd lose himself.

"You don't owe me anything."

"I do." He'd figure out something nice to do for her. "Call me when you're done. Okay?"

She bit the corner of her lip and nodded. "Okay."

He needed to pull away but couldn't help himself. He kissed her again before letting her go and walking out. He could feel the eyes of the entire restaurant on him as he left. He didn't care. Sheri had agreed to be with him, and with the way he was feeling, he didn't care if the entire world knew.

Chapter Eleven

Sheri jumped in the shower and changed clothes as soon as she got home from work. As promised, she'd called Deandre when she was leaving work. He'd asked her to go out on their first official date. Bonus point, he'd already planned what they were doing that evening. They were going to the movie at the park downtown, and he was bringing a picnic basket of treats. She'd nearly swooned when he'd told her the plans. He'd put some thought into their first date. She couldn't remember the last guy who'd taken the time to plan a date. Most of the guys she'd dated asked her out and then put all the effort of planning on her shoulders. Deandre was a take-charge kind of person and she liked that.

The thoughts that bothered her at the start of the day no longer took up as much room in her brain. When he'd kissed her, no matter how quick and sweet the kiss was, it had been a definite show of them being together. At least, that's how she was taking it. She would still tell him what she wanted out of a relationship. She was too old to play games or be dishonest with herself. If they were dating, she wanted it to be exclusive and she'd tell him she was looking for something that could be serious. If that scared him away, then she'd be better off in the long run. Having her feelings bruised now was better than being heartbroken later.

She'd agreed to meet him at the park, even though he'd offered to pick her up. She did not want her family to see him coming by. If they knew she had a date with him, they'd immediately find a reason to come to her house just so they could see and talk to him. She'd barely been able to get out of the restaurant on time after he'd kissed her. Her mom hadn't seen, but Cora had, and she'd made a point to make sure everyone in the kitchen knew what happened.

She'd seen the look her mom had given her, but they'd been too busy for her to pull Sheri to the side and talk. That, and JD had already said he wasn't in the mood to have his kitchen slowed down by gossip. So, her mom had lct things slide. She'd had to leave before closing to run an errand with her aunt Gwen, and Sheri had thanked her lucky stars when she didn't see her mom's car in the yard when she'd pulled up.

She wasn't meeting Deandre for another hour, but she was going to get out of the house before her mom had time to come and question her. She was showered, dressed and heading to her front door in no time. She'd opted for a light blue jumpsuit with spaghetti straps. The soft material was thin enough to keep her cool and her shoulders and décolletage looked amazing when she wore it. She'd taken her hair out of its usual ponytail so it hung thick and loose around her shoulders. She slid her "Lil Bit" necklace around her neck and paired it with large, silver hoop earrings. She hoped she looked casual but sexy at the same time.

She opened the front door and froze immediately. Her mom and Aunt Gwen both stood on the front porch. Her mom's finger hovered just above the doorbell.

"Where you going?" her mom asked.

Sheri barely stopped herself from stomping her foot with frustration. She tried not to show her irritation on her face, but something must have crept through because her mom crossed her arms and gave her *the look*.

Sheri fixed her face and smiled. "Just got to run some errands. I may hang with Cora later."

Her aunt Gwen shook her head. "I know you're not going out with Cora because she's running behind that man in Myrtle Beach tonight. So what man are you running behind?"

Sheri sighed and walked out onto the porch. If she let them in the house, she was trapped for at least an hour. "I'm not running behind anyone. Just going out real quick."

"It's that cop, ain't it?" her mom asked. "Cora told me he kissed you today."

No need lying to her mom about what happened with Deandre. "He did."

"Why's he kissing you all in the middle of your job?" Aunt Gwen asked, sounding affronted.

"Because we're dating."

That was met with silence as the sisters exchanged looks. Sheri couldn't decipher the look, but she could imagine the things in their head. *There Sheri goes again. What's going to happen with this guy? Is she going to embarrass the family one more time?*

Ever since the Tyrone fiasco, her mom had questioned Sheri's dating decisions. She was afraid Sheri would get caught up with another guy who would have her acting out and doing foolish things like damaging a car. Her mom was a firm believer in not playing the fool for any man. Something she'd preached to Sheri, which meant when Sheri had done just that over Tyrone Livingston, a known playboy at that time, she'd been so disappointed to have her daughter acting "desperate and dumb" over a man. Sheri swore her mom viewed her actions as a personal failure on her mothering abilities.

"Dating, huh?" her mom said.

"Yes. Dating. He asked me and I said yes. Anything wrong with that?" She would not feel bad about wanting to be with a guy instead of pretending as if she were good with keeping things casual or claim she didn't need or want a man. Sheri didn't need one to provide for her, but she did enjoy having a guy in her life.

Her mom threw up a hand. "Nah, nothing wrong. I'm just saying…"

"That you're happy for me and hope things work out," Sheri insisted.

Her mom's eyes narrowed. "You know he's got a kid. You ready to play step momma?"

Sheri wasn't sure if she was ready to play stepmom. She wasn't even sure what was going to happen with this. She doubted DJ liked her, but she wanted to at least see what it was like to date a nice guy. She'd only focus on her relationship with Deandre and worry about how things would play out with her and his son if things progressed that far.

"I'm ready to see what happens. No one is playing step momma."

"You be careful," Aunt Gwen said. "I'm not hating or anything. I just don't want you to get hurt."

Her mom grunted and studied her nails. "Or act out like you did last time."

Sheri was used to them bringing up her past dating mistakes, but her defenses rose. She'd messed up, but she'd learned from her mess-ups. No matter how much she tried to prove that, she was getting tired of her family's inability to focus on anything else.

"I'm not going to act out. That was a one-time thing. Can we not bring it up again?"

Her mom stared longer but nodded. "I guess you're not letting us in so you can run and meet him?"

"I just have stuff to do before I catch up with him later."

"Bring him to the house so we can meet him," her mom said.

"Why? You don't need to meet him yet."

Gwen nodded. "Dorothy Jean is right. We need to make sure he's good people. I think I know his in-laws."

"He's not married."

"Well, his late wife was from around here and I know Cliff and Rose. They go to your cousin's church, and they are really involved with their son-in-law. So, he may not be married but he has in-laws."

"And a kid," her mom chimed in. "Think about that while you out having fun with him tonight."

Sheri hadn't considered the rest of his family despite his mentioning he'd moved to Sunshine Beach because his late wife's family was from here. Sheri had known who his late wife was, but she didn't know her parents like that. If her aunt knew them, then she could get all the information she wanted on Deandre, DJ and his family. Which also meant his family could get any information they wanted on her, too. So many people in town knew she'd been arrested after damaging Tyrone's car. The gossip had died down until the brothers got the television deal and then it came back up thanks to internet trolls. Trolls stirred up thanks to her cousin Cora's digging into his past. Would his in-laws be okay with him dating her? Did he listen to them?

She shook the thought out of her head. She wanted to learn about him from him. Not from what people thought of him. Deandre seemed like the type of guy who would feel the same. The good thing was, he already knew her shady relationship past better than anyone and they'd talked it out. She wouldn't worry about his in-laws unless they became serious.

"I've really got to go."

"Go on, have a good time. But be careful, Lil Bit." Her mom's voice was serious in the end.

She and her mom had different views when it came to relationships, but she knew her mom cared about her. She'd been hurt by Sheri's dad when he'd left her and she shielded her heart. She didn't want Sheri to have the same heartbreak.

She gave her mom a hug. "Ma, don't worry. I know what I'm doing this time."

The date was even better than Sheri hoped it would be. Deandre had ordered sandwiches along with a meat, fruit and cheese tray from a local restaurant that he already had spread out on a blanket. He'd paired it with a blackberry lemonade that was delicious. When she'd asked about wine, he let her know that he didn't drink due to the job. When he was a patrol deputy, he'd stopped drinking alcohol and the habit stuck even when he was no longer on patrol.

The movie was *Grease*, and he hadn't believed her when she said she'd never seen the entire movie before.

"I'm not really a musical person, plus, I didn't even know what it was about."

"I was in chorus in high school, and they made us watch it because we sang all the songs from the movie for our end-of-year performance," he'd told her as they sipped lemonade and waited for the movie to start.

Sheri's eyes widened. "You were in chorus?" That explained the impromptu sing-along in his car when he'd driven her home. He liked singing.

"I was."

"Did you play any sports?"

"I played football and ran track. I sang in the choir at my grandmother's church growing up, so I liked music. I wasn't really interested in the band, but chorus was fun. Plus, they had the best field trips. What about you? What activities did you do in high school?"

"I was a cheerleader, but that was about it. I wasn't in any other clubs or anything else. I couldn't wait to graduate and get out of Sunshine Beach."

"What brought you back?"

"My mom got sick. I thought I'd stay in Charlotte working at that steak house until I got a job at another high-end restaurant. But I moved back to help take care of my mom after her stroke. My aunts and cousins were around, but I didn't want to leave her in their care."

"She seems to be doing a lot better now."

"She is. Sometimes I can't believe she recovered. Thankfully, my aunt had just watched something on the news about recognizing the signs of a stroke. She saw my mom was dizzy and numb so she called 911. She got to the hospital in time, but she still had to go through rehabilitation. When she started physical therapy, she asked if I planned to move back to Charlotte, but by then I knew I couldn't leave her. I started working at Waffle House for the flexible hours and decent pay and then got the wild idea to open my own restaurant."

"Are you happy here in Sunshine Beach?"

She thought about it, then nodded. "I am. Growing up I just wanted to experience a new place. But when I came back I realized how much I love this town. I might have been able to open a restaurant in Charlotte, but opening my restaurant here was so much better. I had people I could call on and help me like Aunt Gwen, my cousin D'asa and even Cora. Then there's JD. He left Waffle House to come and work with me. My family is here and can help me fill in while I work to build up my staffing levels. Then there are the people who knew me growing up and want me to succeed. It's just a different sense of community that I didn't have in Charlotte."

"Did you have friends up there?"

"Yeah, some work friends and a few from college. We keep in touch. When I get a chance, I go up and visit every once in a while. What about you? Do you still keep up with friends and family back in Florida?"

He shook his head. "Not so much. DJ was ten when my wife died. We moved to Sunshine Beach a year after. At first it was too hard to keep in touch with the people and the life I left behind. It was easier to start over here."

"I'm surprised you moved closer to your in-laws instead of your own parents."

"Her parents are the ones who stepped in and helped me with DJ when I needed them. I love my parents, but they're off living their own life. They felt bad for me when I lost Jamila, but they'd already moved to Destin. Just last year they moved to Denver. They're enjoying their retirement, and I can't blame them. They come down and visit us, but they weren't ready to move closer and help me raise DJ. When Rose asked me to move to Sunshine Beach so they could help with DJ, I didn't hesitate. I turned in my resignation, packed our stuff and moved."

"It's good that you're close with your in-laws. Even after…"

"I love them just as much as I love my parents. I'm forever grateful for them and the way they helped out."

"My aunt Gwen says they go to my cousin's church."

"Mount Olive AME?" he asked.

She nodded. "That's the one. My cousin Faith and her husband, Gary, go there."

"I'll ask them if they know them."

She shook her head. "No need. My cousin Faith is cool, but she's messy. They probably know all my business and the trouble I've gotten into. They may tell you to stay away from me if they know who she is."

She tried to keep her voice light, but a part of her worried that was the case. Even before Tyrone, back when she was a teenager, she would sometimes get into trouble. She wasn't ashamed of her past or the mistakes she'd made, but she was tired of defending herself. She liked Deandre, but she didn't want to have to defend herself to him or his family.

Deandre leaned forward and met her eyes. "They can tell me, but it doesn't mean I'll listen."

A flutter when through her chest. "Why not?"

"Because what they think about you, or your cousin, doesn't matter to me. All I care about is how *I* feel about you."

The words settled over her and wrapped her in a comforting embrace. She eased closer to him and warmth spread through her chest. "How do you feel about me?"

"I'm still figuring it out, but so far, I'm feeling pretty good about you."

"Pretty good, huh? What does *pretty good* mean?"

He reached for her hand and threaded his fingers with hers. "It means that I want to get to know you. I don't want to see anyone else while I do that. That I'd like for us to take our time to see where this goes. Is that cool with you?"

More than cool. In fact, it was perfect. Sheri squeezed his hand. "Cool with me."

They didn't talk as much during the show. She watched

as many people sang along to the songs in the movie. Deandre didn't sing along with as much enthusiasm, but he did hum and nod his head a few times like a true chorus kid. After the movie, they packed up their items and he'd walked her to her car before suggesting they walk to the ice cream place downtown.

"I've got ice cream at home," she said.

He frowned. "Oh, are you ready to get back?"

She lifted a brow. "That's my not-so-subtle way of inviting you back to my place."

His eyes darkened. She'd parked on a side street about a block away from the park. The streetlights kept the roadway well lit, and there were several other people who'd watched the movie who'd also parked in the area, but the look in his eye made her feel as if they were the only two people on the street.

"I don't know if that's a good idea."

She poked out her lip. Not the least bit embarrassed to show her disappointment. "Why not? It's just ice cream."

Deandre raised a brow. "It's more than ice cream. Or, at least, I'm going to be thinking about more than ice cream."

"No rush or no other expectations. I just don't want the date to end just yet." Which was true, but she wouldn't pretend as if she didn't want to kiss him again. The brief kisses he'd given her before only made her crave more.

"Neither do I."

She stepped forward until their bodies almost touched and lowered her voice. "Then come by. Just for ice cream. Nothing else. We'll both be good." Though the way he looked at her, with so much heat and longing she felt like her skin would catch fire, made her want to be anything but good. She wanted to be naughty.

The question flashed in his eyes for another second before he nodded. "Just for a few minutes. I need to get home and check on DJ."

She grinned. "A few minutes works for me."

Chapter Twelve

Deandre watched Sheri get into her car before walking around the corner. His stomach churned as if he were about to go on the most important job interview of his life while his heart pounded as if he'd just won an Olympic gold medal. He was just going to her place for ice cream. He wasn't trying to push for anything more. This was their first date, and he'd never been the type of guy who expected something on the first date. But that didn't stop his imagination from going to all kinds of places. Places where he had Sheri in his arms again. Felt her lips on his and got to spend endless amounts of time kissing and caressing her skin.

"Deandre? I thought that was you."

The sound of Chief Montgomery's voice stopped him in his tracks. He turned, caught her eye and smiled. "Chief, how are you doing?"

Deandre kept his voice pleasant, even though he wanted to just wave and hurry to his car. Most days he wouldn't mind stopping to talk to the chief, but the memory of how Sheri looked at him before she'd gotten in the car, as if she was thinking the same thoughts as him, had Deandre ready to be rude and on his way.

"I was here for the movie in the park. The family just went to the car." She pointed over her shoulder where her husband and two daughters were chatting next to her large SUV.

Deandre waved at her husband before focusing back on her. "Tell everyone I said hello. I was just about to leave."

"I know, I saw you here earlier." She took a few steps forward. "With Lil Bit Thomas."

Deandre blinked, surprised to hear the chief use Sheri's nickname. "You know Sheri?"

She crossed her arms and watched Deandre with an assessing gaze. "Not very well. I know who she is. She's the one you arrested back when you were on patrol." The words weren't a question.

Deandre's defenses went up. "She was."

"And now you're dating her?" That was a question, and the chief's tone said she hoped the answer was no.

"She's also working with me on the community event for the south end of the beach."

"Are you telling me that you're just working together?"

Deandre respected Chief Montgomery, but he didn't like the questioning or the judgment in her eye. "Can I know why you're asking?"

Chief Montgomery stepped closer. "Look, I don't like to step in and make comments on my employees' personal lives. But I want you to also know that the work we're doing in the south end is important. They already think I'm going too soft on the crime in the area. If the higher-ups find out that the officer I put in charge of the area is also, I'll just be frank, sleeping around with one of the business owners down there, it won't look good."

"I'm not sleeping around with anyone. And even if I were, it doesn't matter."

"Look, I'm not telling you this to be mean. I'm telling you this because I need you to understand the situation we're in. Everything we do is going to be scrutinized."

"Look, I understand what you're trying to say, but I don't

plan to stop seeing her because the higher-ups are going to scrutinize my motives. She cares about the neighborhood as much as the rest of the community and she's the one who stepped up to help. If they have a problem with me seeing her, then they can come tell me to my face."

"I'm just trying to look out for you."

Deandre held up a hand. "I appreciate the thought, but I don't need you to look out for me when it comes to my personal life."

She looked like she wanted to say something else, but instead she pressed her lips together and nodded. "Fine. I'll stay out of it."

"Thank you." He turned to walk toward his car.

"But…"

Sighing, Deandre faced her again and raised a brow.

"If this becomes a problem, then you deal with the fallout. Understand?"

"I understand, but there won't be any fallout."

His irritation at the intrusion grew with each step he took toward his car. He wished he could ignore her worries and warning as foolishness, but he'd worked in the department long enough to know that if Montgomery thought it was necessary to say something to him, then her concerns had some validity. People may look at any relationship he formed with Sheri and their past together and try to use that to undermine any work he did in the area. It was messed up and unfair but knowing Chief Montgomery had pressure on her to use a stick approach versus a carrot to reduce crime in the area meant that those in favor of the stick weren't afraid to pull out their own.

The thoughts bothered him on the ride to Sheri's place. He arrived at her home several minutes later and tried to push them to the back of his mind. He didn't want to ruin the night with talks about what Chief Montgomery had said.

Sheri greeted him at the door with a smile and a bowl of ice cream. "What took you so long?"

He took the bowl of ice cream and grinned. "Ran into the chief on the way to my car."

"Oh really?" She took his free hand and pulled him farther into the house. "Is everything okay?"

"Yeah, she was there with her family. She stopped me to talk about something."

Sheri's house was cute and decorated with comfortable-looking furniture. Pictures of her family lined the walls. They stopped in her living area that was separated from the kitchen by a small island.

"Nothing too bad, I hope." She grabbed another bowl of ice cream off the counter.

"Nothing bad, but she was…concerned." When Sheri raised a brow, he decided to be honest. Otherwise, she'd notice he was distracted and that would ruin the night. "About us."

He recounted what she said and his response for her to stay out of his personal business. By the time he finished, Sheri had put down her bowl of ice cream and paced in front of her couch.

"Are you serious? No one will ever let me live down one mistake."

He put his ice cream on the coffee table and placed his hands on her shoulders. "This isn't about your past mistake. This is squarely on me."

"Yeah, but if I was Belinda or some other Goody Two-shoes in the town they wouldn't care so much. They'd probably applaud you."

"Did you hear what I said? I told her to stay out of my

personal business. I don't care what they think. I mean it, Sheri. I haven't been this interested in someone in a very long time. I'm not going to stop getting to know you because of something like this."

The corner of her mouth lifted. "You're so straightforward and honest."

"Is that a bad thing?"

"No." She raised her arms and wrapped them around his neck. "It's actually very, very sexy."

Fire flooded his veins and stirred in his groin. If she kept looking at him like that, he was going to be hard as a rock. "You know I only came for ice cream?"

"I know, but that doesn't mean you can't have a little sugar." She lifted on her toes and kissed him.

Thoughts of ice cream fled as her tongue glided across his lower lip. Deandre opened his mouth and let her deepen the kiss. She was just as straightforward with her kiss as she'd said he was with his words, and he loved it. She tasted like strawberry ice cream and he loved strawberries.

His cell phone rang. He wanted to ignore it, but not many people called his cell. "Sorry." He pulled back and reached to get his phone out. To his surprise, his son was calling. "It's DJ."

She stepped back and pushed her hair behind her ear. "Handle that. It could be important."

She licked her full lips and he bit back a groan. He had to clear his throat before he answered. "DJ, what's up?"

"You still at the movie?"

Sheri played with the Lil Bit necklace around her neck, drawing his eyes to the swell of her breasts just below the neckline of her jumpsuit. "Huh…ah, nah, it just ended."

"I've got a problem."

Deandre's focus immediately went to his son. "Problem, what's wrong?"

"I'm kind of embarrassed to say, but I locked myself out of the house. Can you come home and let me in? I didn't want to call because I thought you were still on your date."

Guilt twisted his insides. He never wanted his son to feel as if he couldn't call him. If he'd gone straight home like he'd planned, DJ wouldn't be locked out. "Nah, don't ever feel like you can't call. I'll be home in a few minutes."

"Cool, thanks, Dad." The relief in DJ's voice made Deandre feel like his son's superhero. He hadn't felt like his son's hero in a long time.

"I'm on my way." He ended the call and looked at Sheri. "DJ's got a problem. I need to check on him."

"I get it. Please, go check on him." Even though he could see the disappointment in her eyes, her voice was understanding. He could relate to the disappointment. Now that he knew DJ wasn't in any immediate danger, the passion he'd felt in her arms came rushing back.

He took her hand and pulled her closer to him. "Rain check on dessert?"

She grinned before lifting up to kiss him again. "Rain check." Her lips pressed his once more before she lightly bit his lower lip.

He thought his erection would burst out of his pants. He wanted to linger over the kiss. To trail his lips across her chin to her chest just in the spot where her necklace sat. But the sound of DJ's voice pulled him back. His son was locked out of the house. Sure, he could call Rose and Cliff, but DJ had called and asked him for help. He wouldn't pawn him off on someone else. He'd have time to kiss Sheri later. "I'll call you tomorrow," he said before leaving.

Chapter Thirteen

Sheri entered the storefront that was starting to feel like a second home to her. They were a few days away from the Connecting the Community event. Which meant this was the last planning meeting before the big day. Most of the business owners and residents were excited. Everyone had come together to think of ways to encourage people from outside the South End to attend. Ivy had created a social media campaign to drum up interest. Deandre and the police chief had encouraged the city to promote the event on its social media pages. The city of Sunshine Beach even sent out a press release to local media, which Sheri had also forwarded to her childhood friend Vanessa Steele-Livingston. Vanessa lived in Charlotte, but she was a news anchor and had roots in Sunshine Beach. She'd reached out to her connections at the local affiliate to get them interested in following the story.

The event started as a forum for community members to learn about what the city was doing to address crime in the town and ways the community could participate. As interest grew, they'd expanded the day to include several vendors from the area who didn't have a storefront but lived nearby selling their goods along the sidewalk. All the shops would be open during the event and Sheri had extended her hours so that the restaurant wouldn't close until two hours after the event ended.

The team of people they'd pulled together to help were all at the last planning session. Sheri's eyes narrowed when she spotted Belinda giggling next to Deandre. She and Deandre hadn't hidden their relationship from the group, but they also hadn't made a big deal about it. Most had guessed there was something going on, because he offered to take her home or they talked openly about getting together later in the week. But Belinda still flirted as if Deandre were single.

Sheri was mostly amused by Belinda's attempts. Deandre was clearly not interested and hadn't followed up on of her blatant hints about them getting together to discuss "the neighborhood." But, when Belinda put her hand on Deandre's shoulder, Sheri's eyes narrowed. She barely got to touch him the way she wanted. She wasn't about to stand by and watch Belinda grope him.

"Hey, everyone, sorry I'm late," Sheri announced herself a little too loudly.

Deandre looked her way and the light in his eyes when he saw her that hadn't been there when he looked at Belinda cleared away the storm clouds of jealousy swirling over Sheri's head. "We were just getting started."

He left Belinda behind and met Sheri halfway across the room. Sheri rose up on her toes and pressed her lips against his. The kiss wasn't long enough. Not for her, but it was good enough for her to make her point. Deandre was spoken for.

Deandre's eyes widened. "What was that for?"

"Just because," she said loud enough for anyone listening to hear. She lowered her voice. "And because we didn't get to finish what we started last night."

The light in his eyes quickly flared into a fire. They'd made a point to try and see each other whenever they had time. But every time they went on a date, DJ seemed to have some type of crisis. Locking himself out of the door was just the first of many times. Since that night three weeks prior he'd run out of gas, lost something he needed help finding, or needed his dad to help him get something last minute for school. All of the calls were legitimate, but Sheri was starting to suspect DJ was interrupting them on purpose. She just didn't know how to say that to Deandre without sounding paranoid.

"I do plan to finish what I started," he said in just as low a tone.

"When? I'm growing anxious." She tried to keep her voice light, but some of her frustration crept in. She appreciated that he liked taking things slow, but she was tired of having to handle her own needs when she was dating a deliciously sexy man.

Some of the heat left his gaze and was replaced with an apology. "Soon."

His eyes were filled with the same frustration, making her want to jump him in a crowded room. He wasn't just teasing her or playing hard to get. Deandre felt some, if not all, of what she felt, which made her not want to make him feel guilty for having to cut things short because he was being a good parent.

She patted his chest. "It's no problem. I was just teasing."

"You sure?"

She nodded. "I'm sure."

"Good, because DJ is hanging with his grandparents tonight, and I was thinking that maybe…"

"You can come over for ice cream?" She grinned so hard her cheeks hurt.

"Most definitely."

She did a hip shimmy to celebrate, then looked back to Belinda. She didn't bother to hide her smug "he's mine" smirk. She'd been patient enough with Belinda. Now it was time to clearly put up her boundaries.

Deandre lightly tapped her hip. "Let's get started." He called the meeting to order. Sheri grabbed a seat next to Kelly.

Kelly leaned over and lightly elbowed Sheri. "Finally giving Belinda the hint to back off, huh?"

Sheri smirked and winked. "She's lucky I didn't snatch her hand off him."

Kelly held out her hand palm up and Sheri rubbed her palm over hers. They both giggled; the modified high five was something they'd started when they'd hung out after the first neighborhood get-together. Sheri didn't want to jinx anything, but she was pretty sure she and Kelly were on the way to becoming good friends.

The door to the center opened. DJ walked in followed by two older adults who looked familiar. A second later, everything clicked. They were Jamila's parents. Deandre's in-laws.

Deandre gave them a puzzled look. "What are you doing here?"

Rose led the three of them farther into the room. "Well, DJ was telling us about all the work you put into planning the community event, and we decided to come and see if we can help in any way."

Deandre seemed surprised, but pleased. "Sure, I'd love for you to help out. Everyone, this is Rose and Cliff, DJ's grandparents."

Several excited exclamations came around the room as everyone welcomed them. Sheri joined in the welcomes and watched as Belinda quickly ushered them over to the empty seats next to her. Sheri tried, and failed, not to feel some type of way about that. Instead of acting jealous, she focused on what she was there for. Rallying the community to support revitalizing the south end.

The meeting went by quickly. Everyone knew their assigned tasks and was ready to see everything come together that weekend. After things wrapped up, Sheri chatted with Kelly and some of the others before approaching Deandre. He was talking with his in-laws, DJ and Belinda. She wasn't sure if Cliff and Rose knew about her, and she didn't want to make a bad impression. She took a reassuring breath. All that mattered was how Deandre felt.

"Deandre, we were taking DJ to get some tacos. You should come eat with us," Rose was saying as Sheri walked up.

Deandre glanced Sheri's way. "Uh… I already—"

"We're going to the place you like," DJ cut in. "Come on, let's all have dinner together."

Deandre caught Sheri's eye. "I was going out with Sheri."

Sheri stepped next to Deandre. "Hi, nice to meet you all."

Rose's brows rose and she looked at Sheri with interest. "Oh, so you're Sheri."

Cliff snapped his fingers. "You're Dorothy Jean's daughter." He spoke as if he'd just figured out the answer to a riddle.

"I am. I think one of my cousins goes to your church."

"They sure do," he said. "How's your aunt Gwen doing? Me and her were close back in high school."

"She's doing good."

Rose's eyes narrowed on her husband. "You still asking about her? All these years later." Rose sounded more exasperated than upset.

Cliff shrugged. "It was just a question."

Sheri looked from them to Deandre. Deandre raised his brows and looked just as confused as she felt.

Rose looked back at Sheri. "Your aunt Gwen was his high school sweetheart."

"Oh... Well, I didn't know that." She wasn't sure what she was supposed to do with that information.

"Dad," DJ cut in. "Come with us to get tacos. I'm thinking of joining wrestling again."

"I thought it was too late?" Deandre asked.

DJ shook his head. "Coach said I could still join. But I'm not sure. I wanted to talk to you about that."

Deandre glanced from DJ to Sheri and back. She wasn't a detective, but she could deduce what was going on. He wanted to be with her, but also wanted to find out about DJ rejoining the wrestling team. He'd mentioned his frustration with DJ quitting suddenly. As much as she wanted them to finish what they'd started numerous times, she wouldn't pull him away from his kid.

She shrugged. "Go on with them. We'll catch up later."

"Sheri you can come with us," Cliff offered.

Sheri quickly shook her head. Rose didn't seem seriously upset about him asking after her Aunt Gwen, but Sheri was not about to potentially put herself in a situation where she'd have to answer questions about his high school sweetheart all night. "Nah, you all got it. I've got stuff to do. I just wanted to say hi and meet you."

"Maybe next time. A friend of Deandre is a friend of ours," Rose said, sounding friendly enough.

"She's more than—"

"Good, let's go," DJ cut Deandre off. "I'm hungry."

"Me, too," Rose agreed. "Nice to meet you, Sheri. Let's go."

Sheri walked out with them. She caught DJ's gaze as Deandre locked the door. The smug satisfaction as he looked at her proved she wasn't being paranoid. Deandre's son was purposely trying to keep them apart.

"You ready to tell me what you're doing?" Deandre asked DJ when they walked into the house after dinner. DJ had decided that he no longer wanted to spend the night with his grandparents and was going home since Deandre was done with work and was also going home.

DJ looked up from his phone. "Checking my phone."

Deandre shook his head. "That's not what I'm talking about. You wanted me to come to dinner so we could talk about you joining wrestling again, but you never brought it up."

DJ shrugged. "We talked about other stuff."

"And you came to the meeting tonight."

"*You* said I need to be more involved so that people won't treat me like I'm some thug. I thought you'd be happy I showed up."

Deandre took a long breath and gathered his thoughts. "You know what I mean."

"I don't know what you're talking about." DJ turned to go toward his room.

"You're always calling when I'm with Sheri."

DJ faced him again with a raised brow. "I can't call you when you're with her?"

"That's not what I'm saying. But I've noticed the pattern. You went from barely wanting to spend time with me to suddenly needing my help whenever I'm with her."

"I can't help it that things mess up when you're around her. If you don't want me to bother you when you're with her I won't." DJ tried to sound pitiful, but Deandre didn't miss the dare in his son's eye. He hadn't wanted to believe that DJ was intentionally trying to keep him away from Sheri, but tonight proved something he'd tried to pretend wasn't happening.

"Don't twist my words."

"I'm not twisting your words. I'm just saying what you're telling me."

"What's your problem with her? Is it because I made you apologize?"

"I don't have a problem with her. I don't see why you're interested in her in the first place, but I don't have a problem."

"You don't have to see why I'm interested in her. You just have to understand that she and I are together right now."

DJ looked away and shook his head as if he couldn't believe what he was hearing. "Did you arrest her?"

Deandre's head snapped back. How in the world did DJ know about that? He didn't come home and talk about the stuff he'd see when on patrol. He also hadn't talked about Sheri's past with him.

"Who told you that?"

He shrugged. "I overheard it somewhere. That she was acting all ghetto and you had to arrest her. You always told me to avoid girls with drama, but you're with someone like that."

The judgment in DJ's voice made Deandre's neck tighten. He took a second to take a breath and count to five before responding. If he reacted negatively, DJ would lash back and they'd get nowhere. "First of all, what you heard and what happened are not the same. Second, Sheri isn't dramatic or ghetto. So, mind what you say."

DJ threw up a hand. "Fine. Are we done now?"

"No, we aren't done."

"You want me to like her, fine, I can like her. But she better not come in here trying to act like she's my momma, 'cause she ain't."

Deandre shook his head, confused by how the conversation had just gone left. He and Sheri had just started dating. DJ had known he'd gone on dates before. He'd even joined in with Rose and Cliff when they'd started pushing him to date again. So, why was DJ suddenly against it? Or was it just he was against Sheri?

"She wouldn't do that." DJ snorted and Deandre narrowed his eyes. "Listen, you're going to be nice to her and you're going to stop playing these games when I'm with her. I'm always here to help you. Don't doubt that, but I know what you're doing. I don't know why, but I don't like it. So, if you've got something to say, now's the time to say it."

"I don't have anything to say." DJ closed his mouth and stared at the ceiling as if suddenly bored with the entire conversation.

Deandre wanted to shake him. DJ was shutting down again. He didn't know what to do or how to make his son open up to him. He wanted to make DJ sit down and not move until he told Deandre what was going on in his brain. Deandre couldn't ever remember struggling with his own dad like this, but then again, he also hadn't spent a lot of time having heart-to-heart conversations with his dad. To this day, other than the weekly call to check in on his parents, he didn't talk to his dad much. He wanted more than that for him and DJ. In a few years he'd be going to college and become even more distant. But he didn't know how to bridge this gap.

"Fine, DJ, but when you're ready to talk, I'm ready to listen."

DJ nodded and turned. "Uh-huh," he said before going down the hall to his room.

Chapter Fourteen

Sheri took a deep breath and then glanced at the crowd. The committee agreed that holding the question-and-answer session with town leaders at the Connecting the Community event outside instead of crowding everyone inside the store used for the neighborhood watch meetings was the best way to get more participation. The town agreed to set up a stage in the vacant lot between the old record store and the pizza parlor. They'd also supplied the chairs for people to sit, and a microphone.

The amount of people who were picking their seat for the question-and-answer session surprised Sheri. The entire turnout for the event had surprised her. Sure, she'd hoped they would have a lot of people come through, but Sheri was a realist. She hadn't had much hope that a huge crowd would show up for what was essentially a public meeting. But they had. The amount of participation in the event had blown everyone away. The shops along the strip had several new visitors. The vendors stayed busy, and the weather was perfect enough for the beachgoers who'd come just to enjoy the water to also wander up to see what was happening.

Someone stepped to Sheri's right. Sheri turned and met the eyes of the police chief. She liked Chief Montgomery well enough. The woman seemed to be interested in turning around the police department and doing what was right for the town and the residents. But, after what Deandre said about the chief's concerns with their relationship, she wasn't sure if the woman liked her.

"You ready?" Chief Montgomery asked, nodding toward the crowd.

Sheri shrugged. "Ready as I'm going to be."

"How did you get picked to moderate the panel discussion?"

"Since I'm the de facto chair of the planning committee, I was *encouraged* to do it."

She kept her voice light, but her stomach was a jumble of nerves. Sheri could talk to almost anyone, but public speaking wasn't her thing. She'd wanted to help from the background, but when the rest of the group had urged her to serve as moderator for this panel, she'd agreed. The discussion had been her idea. She'd been up half the night practicing what she was going to say so she wouldn't screw anything up.

Montgomery stared at her quietly for a second before nodding as if the answer were acceptable. Sheri just stopped herself from rolling her eyes. She didn't like being assessed by the police chief.

"I'm not here because Lieutenant King wants to show off his new girlfriend," Sheri said. "You don't have to worry about that."

Montgomery's shoulders stiffened before her eyes narrowed. "I wasn't worried about that. Lieutenant King knows how important this event is. For all of us."

"I do, too. I care about this area because I'm from Sunshine Beach and I hung out here as a kid. I don't want to see the town turn it into a carbon copy of the bougie, touristy north end, and I don't want them to ignore us and treat it like a crime-riddled problem. We're on the same side."

Again, Chief Montgomery stared at Sheri for a long moment before lifting and lowering her head. "He said you cared."

Sheri lifted a brow. "Believe him now?"

"I do."

She wouldn't dare show it, but relief rushed through her. Instead, she gave Chief Montgomery the same stiff nod that she'd given Sheri. She believed Deandre when he said he didn't care what people thought about their relationship. That didn't mean she wanted his boss to think she was somehow going to ruin his career or reputation.

"The rest of the group is here. Let's get started."

Chief Montgomery took her seat. They'd pulled together an impressive panel—the town manager, solicitor, county sheriff, mayor and district attorney. Sheri hoped everyone's participation was a good thing and meant they took reinvestment in the south end seriously.

Sheri looked back at the crowd. Deandre stood at the back with several other officers. He gave her a smile and thumbs-up. She lifted her hand in a quick wave, before bringing the microphone to her face.

"We'll get started now. Thank you all for coming out to the south end neighborhood's Connecting the Community event. The growth and success of the south end equals growth and success for all of Sunshine Beach. Which is why we have many of the leaders from the town and the county here today to talk about their plans to continue to reinvest and keep the south end safe for everyone."

There was a round of applause and cheers from Kelly and Ivy. Sheri grinned and relaxed. Having the rest of the business owners here helped calm some of her nerves. She wanted this event to go off perfectly, so everyone would see the great things the south end had to offer.

"Administrator, I'll start with you. The town has invested heavily in retrofitting the vacant buildings here and partnering with small businesses like mine as part of their revitalization efforts. Can you tell us what led to that decision?"

The panel discussion went smoothly. As a business owner, Sheri was glad to hear from everyone on the panel about the ways they wanted to see the community continue to thrive—from more investment by the town to help businesses grow, to the connection of law enforcement to connect people to mental health and substance abuse assistance as a way to help address crime. By the time they opened the discussion to questions from the audience, Sheri was leaning back in the chair relaxed and happy about how great things had turned out.

Kelly gave the sign that there were five minutes left. Sheri sat forward and spoke in the mic. "We've got time for one last question." She looked at the woman standing at the microphone they'd set up in the crowd for questions. "Go ahead."

"This question is for you," she said with a raised brow and pursed lips.

Sheri sat up straight and returned the woman's direct stare. She looked kinda familiar, but Sheri couldn't immediately place her. "Okay, what's your question?"

"I think it's great that you pulled this together, considering you also have a criminal record. Was that part of the reason why you chose to have this event?"

Sheri sucked in a breath. Had she misheard? She must have misheard, because that question had nothing to do with the event and was a shot aimed right for Sheri.

She focused on her again and realized she was someone from her aunt's church. One of the people who always had something negative to say. Sheri didn't want to sit here and accept being disrespected. She also couldn't curse the woman out like she wanted to with so many law enforcement officers on the stage. No, Sheri had to be the bigger person. She had to prove she wasn't the same hotheaded person this woman was trying to prove her to be.

"Ma'am, I have no criminal record." Mostly true. She was never convicted for the damage to Tyrone's car. "I'm a business owner who cares about the community. I also know the importance of second chances. I don't shy away from any mistake I may have made. I got the chance to be a part of the city's program to bring life back to a part of town I care about. I want to do my part. I don't participate in idle gossip or spend energy trying to tear other people down. I suggest that anyone who wants to see things get better do the same."

There was applause from the crowd. Kelly was already next to the woman and took the microphone before she could answer. The lady glared at Sheri. Sheri stared back with a fake smile on her face. She was not going to give this woman the benefit of getting a rise out of her.

Sheri stood, and the rest of the panel thanked her for doing a great job. She smiled and nodded patiently, but she wanted to get off that stage, find the woman and ask just what the hell did she think she was doing. But that would only embarrass Sheri and make a scene.

Despite the negative last question, several people came up to Sheri when she left the stage and thanked her for doing a great job pulling everything together. By the time she escaped them, the crowd had dispersed, she didn't see her hater anywhere and the only ones around were family and friends.

Her mom and Cora came over. "You did a great job!" her mom said, pride in her eyes.

"Don't worry about that woman," Cora said. "We'll deal with her later."

A hand rested on Sheri's shoulder. Deandre. "No need to deal with anyone. Sheri already dealt with her."

Sheri grinned at him. "Did I?"

"She ran out of here with her tail tucked between her legs." He squeezed her shoulder. "Great job."

That was true. Sheri had long moved on from the mistakes of her past. The life and relationships she had now was more important than having it out with someone whose opinion didn't really matter.

"Everything did turn out pretty good, didn't it?" she said. "Hopefully it'll help. And we'll get more people to join the neighborhood watch." She looked at her mom. "How's the restaurant?"

Her mom had managed things for Sheri earlier in the day, but said she would leave to see the panel. "Good. Don't worry. We know how to close things out. I told the family to come to my house later this evening to celebrate you showing the town who's boss."

"I didn't do all that," Sheri said, grinning.

"Girl, you know your mom don't need much of a reason to have a cookout," Cora said.

"True." She looked at Deandre. "Want to come eat with us tonight?"

"You won't be tired after all this?" Concern filled his dark eyes and he squeezed her shoulder again.

The last of Sheri's irritation melted away. She was tired, but she'd drink ten cups of coffee if she needed to stay up and spend more time with him. "I'll be good. Besides, it's just a small family thing. Bring DJ with you."

SYNITHIA WILLIAMS 147

Maybe if his son was with him, he wouldn't have a good reason to pull Deandre away.

"You sure?"

She nodded. "I am." She had a feeling DJ didn't like her, but she was going to at least try.

"Cool. We'll swing through."

Chapter Fifteen

Deandre had a different definition of "a small thing" compared with Sheri. That's what he thought as Sheri introduced him and DJ to her aunts, uncles and several cousins. He was pretty good at remembering names, but he doubted every name would stick. There were at least three Willies and four Ericas.

DJ had not been excited about coming. Not that he'd said anything, but his lack of words and excess sighs expressed his lack of interest more than if he'd complained. Thankfully, some of Sheri's younger cousins knew DJ from school and pulled him in with the group of other teenagers.

Sheri took him over to a table with her uncles and a few male cousins. "Sit tight while I fix you a plate."

Deandre shook his head. "I can fix my own plate."

She grinned and patted his shoulder. "I know. It's my rule. First time you're here, I'll fix your plate. After that, you're on your own."

Her uncle, the first Willie if he remembered correctly, chimed in. "You better let her go on and fix you a plate." The other guys at the table agreed.

"You all be nice to Deandre until I get back." Sheri pointed at each of the men at the table.

Willie waved her away. "We got him. And make sure you bring him the big piece of chicken."

Sheri rolled her eyes before walking away. Deandre sat in one of the black plastic chairs set around the fold out table.

"Lil Bit must really like you," Willie said, grinning. "I ain't never seen her fix any man a plate."

The guy next to him, her cousin Kenny, he thought, nodded. "She sure doesn't. Not even before that mess with Tyrone."

Willie elbowed Kenny. "Don't be telling all of Lil Bit's business."

Kenny pointed to Deandre. "Hell, he knows. He's the one who arrested her."

Willie's eyes widened before narrowing. "You a cop?"

Deandre nodded. "I am. Hope you don't hold it against me."

"Depends. You a good one or a bad one?"

"I try real hard to be a good one. And I don't put up with the bad ones."

That seemed to satisfy her uncle because he nodded. "Well, if Lil Bit likes you, then you might be alright. But, for real, you arrested her?"

He wasn't about to dig up that situation today. "So, Willie, I heard that red sixty-seven Chevy out front is yours," Deandre said. "You remodeled that yourself?"

Willie laughed and wagged a finger at Deandre. "I see what you're doing. Cool, cool. You must like Lil Bit, too. Good. She's a good woman. Treat her right."

"That's my plan."

"That is my Chevy out front. Man, I had to drive all the way to New Jersey to get that engine."

Willie spent the next thirty minutes talking about the work he'd done to remodel the truck. He followed that up by taking Deandre to look under the hood and then for a test drive to see how well it ran. Deandre took it all in stride. He had a feeling Willie was partially checking him out. He found out through their conversation that he was Sheri's mother's brother. He'd been the father figure in her house after, per Willie, Sheri's dad hadn't bothered to live up to his responsibilities.

Sheri rushed up to him as soon as he and her uncle pulled back onto the side of the road. The driveway and front yard were filled with cars.

"Uncle Willie, where did you take him?"

"Just for a ride. What? Your man can't spend some time with your uncle?"

"He's here to spend some time with me," she said with a sly grin.

Deandre walked over and wrapped his arm around her shoulder. "I had fun with your uncle. The truck runs like a dream."

"Told you it would," Willie said as if Deandre shouldn't have expected anything less. "You two go on and get your time in. I'm going to get me a piece of pound cake."

"You better hurry," Sheri said. "They cut it ten minutes ago. I made it, so you know it's going to go fast."

"Damn, let me hurry up. Come around again, Deandre." Willie threw up a hand before power walking toward the backyard where the food was set up.

Sheri laughed and turned to him. Deandre kept his hands on her hips. "Sorry about that. Uncle Willie loves that truck, and if you show a hint of interest, he'll take up all your time."

She'd changed into a loose, dark blue sundress that skimmed over her curves and constantly drew his eyes to the sway of her hips. The Lil Bit necklace sparkled in the late afternoon sunlight just above her cleavage.

Deandre tried to pull his mind away from how good her hips felt beneath his hands. And how much he wanted to pull her closer kiss the spot above her necklace. "I really didn't mind. He's a cool guy. Loves you, a lot."

"I know. He's like a dad. He helped mom a lot when I was growing up. I think he still tries to look out for me. He likes you if he told you to come around again."

"That's a good thing. I'd like to come around some more." He glanced toward the backyard. "How's DJ?"

"Good, actually. He's still hanging out with my cousins. They were playing Uno a little while ago."

Deandre pulled out his phone with one hand and texted. You okay? To DJ. He quickly texted back. I'm good.

Deandre smiled and slid his phone back into his pocket. "I'm glad he's having fun."

"I was going to my place to grab the other pound cake I made. I didn't lie when I said the first one was going to go fast. I always keep an extra hidden so that I can have a slice. Want a piece before everyone else gets it?"

"You had the energy to make a pound cake after the event today?"

She gave a sly wink. "Me and my momma made them yesterday. She planned this cookout weeks ago to celebrate me becoming a community activist."

She walked toward her house, and he followed from behind. He put his hands on her bared shoulders and gently massaged. He couldn't help but touch her. "You know you're amazing, right?"

She grinned over her shoulder. "I know."

The quiet inside her house was welcome after the noise of the music and conversation from everyone outside. Even though Uncle Willie was cool, he'd talked nonstop for the past hour. The few minutes inside her place were the first moments they'd had the chance to be alone for a long time.

Deandre took Sheri's hand to stop her from picking up the cake. She faced him and raised her brow. "What's up?"

"Nothing. I'm finally alone with you. I can't help but want to do this." He pulled her into his arms. She came willingly. Her arms wrapped around his neck, and she lifted on her toes to kiss him.

He felt like he hadn't kissed her in years. Had it only been a few days since he held her in his arms? Why did a few days without her feel like he'd gone nearly a lifetime? Why did every moment he spent with her still not feel like enough time? He knew why, but he wasn't ready to say it out loud. But damn, if holding her like this didn't make his feelings impossible to ignore.

She pulled back and smiled at him. Emotion tightened around his heart. He was so close to losing himself when it came to this woman.

"If you keep kissing me like this I'm going to forget about that cake and take advantage of us having a few minutes alone." The devilish spark in her eye combined with the huskiness of her tone made him instantly hard.

He knew exactly how he wanted her to take advantage of their time alone. "Will anyone come looking for you?"

The teasing light left her eye and desire flashed instead. "No. What about…"

"He's good and distracted."

They stared at each other, contemplating how long they had before they'd be missed or people would start wondering what was taking so long. He wanted their first time together to be special. Drawn out. Where he had the chance to savor every part of her body. But the look in her eye and the way her hips pressed forward against him said there would be enough time for drawn out and savor later. He hadn't been spontaneous or felt this rush of excitement in years. The responsible cop and parent in him knew they should get the cake and go back to the cookout. The man who'd had the time with her in his arms interrupted too much said take everything he could get now.

Sheri saw the moment he made the decision and she wanted to jump for joy. There was no time for jumping. Not when they only had a few minutes together. She lifted on her toes, wrapped her arms around his neck and kissed him with all the restrained desire pulsing through her body. The second he'd gotten out of his car wearing a beige T-shirt that clung to his chest and shoulders and those shorts that showed off his strong legs she'd wanted to climb him like a tree.

Deandre's kiss was just as hot and urgent as hers. Did he feel the same way she did? As if she would explode into a thousand pieces if she didn't get the chance to touch him? To feel his body against hers? The way his hands gripped her breasts and behind said he had to. She wished they had more time, but that would wait until another day. The weeks of interruptions and broken dates were the longest foreplay she'd ever had.

They moved frantically, knowing each second could be interrupted like so many precious seconds before. She slid her fingers beneath his shirt, marveled at the warm softness of his skin over the hard muscles beneath. Deandre moaned, low and deep, before his large hand palmed her breast through the thin material of her dress. His fingers rubbed over, then toyed with the hardened tip until she whimpered and pushed forward for more.

He wrapped an arm around her waist and lifted her up.

Sheri grinned and wrapped her legs around his waist. Yes, he most definitely felt the way she felt.

Deandre moved and set her on the kitchen table. The table wobbled, nearly toppling Sheri to the floor.

"In the chair," she said laughing. "If this ends because you drop me I'm going to strangle you."

Deandre grinned as he kicked out the chair and sat with her straddling his waist. "I'll strangle my damn self."

She rolled her hips to push his erection against the juncture of her thighs. Pleasure exploded through her body. She reached down and pulled at the button of his shorts. Deandre stopped her movement by tugging on the straps of her sundress and bra. Pinning her arms against her side, she wiggled and he tugged until her arms were free and she reached around to unhook the bra until her breasts spilled out.

Deandre moaned. "You don't know how much I think about your breasts."

The raw desire in his voice nearly pushed her over the edge. "How much?"

"Every damn time you wear this necklace." He leaned forward and kissed her chest right above her Lil Bit necklace. "You play with it and usually when you're wearing a low-cut shirt. Then all I can think about is your chest, your breasts and what I want to do to them."

Sheri's breathing hitched and she arched her back. "Show me what you want to do."

"Yes, ma'am." His warm hands cupped her breasts, lifting them before he sucked the hard tips between his lips. Sheri twisted her hips. Her hands grasped the sides of his head. Wanting more and never wanting this moment to end.

She reached for his waistband again. Deandre dropped one hand to quickly unfasten the button while his other hand and mouth remained on her breast. They shifted and shoved until his pants and underwear were out of the way and he sprang free.

"Do you have a condom?" she asked.

"My wallet." He reached down into the back pocket of his shorts and pulled out the wallet and then the condom.

"You're always this ready?"

"Since we started dating? Hell yes."

Sheri grinned, loving the need and urgency in his voice. He quickly opened the foil package and covered himself. Then he placed his hand on her back and pulled her forward. "Come back here."

"Yes, sir," she said, her voice thick with need.

She took his solid length in her hand. He was thick and hard and felt so damn wonderful as she slid down on him. They both groaned with pleasure before their lips came together in a hard kiss. She rocked back and forth. Taking him deeper. Moaning with each movement because every touch and slide was better than the one before.

Deandre's hands gripped her waist. His strong arms guided her up and down first in slow, deep strokes that grew fast, more frantic and urgent. She gripped his shoulders, her head thrown back as her world constricted to nothing else but the feel of him inside her, his strong hand on her hip, his lips on her breasts and the pleasure rushing through her body. He pulled the tip of her breast deep into his mouth and she was lost. She shattered into a million stars as her body squeezed around him. He cried out with his own release, his fingers digging hard into her hip as his body jerked.

Sheri collapsed against his chest. Their breathing was choppy as they both came down. She lifted her head. He watched her through slitted lids, contentment and another emotion she couldn't quite name on his face. Because she believed in fairy tales and perfect endings, she wanted to believe that was love on his face. But it was too soon for that, right?

Deandre cupped the back of her head and pulled her forward to kiss her slowly. As if they had all the time in the world and didn't need to rush back before people came looking for them. Her heart fluttered. Maybe it was too soon, but it was too late for Sheri. She was falling hard and fast in love again.

Chapter Sixteen

"Another good day," Sheri said to her mom and Cora as she put the bank deposit for the next morning in the safe.

"Sure was," her mom said. She leaned against the doorframe of the office. "I think more people came out after seeing you at the event on Saturday."

"Well, I'll take it." Sheri closed the safe and double-checked the lock. "We were doing good already, but I'll never turn down more business."

Cora pointed at Sheri and grinned. "Ain't that right."

Sheri and her mom both laughed. Sheri's phone chimed. She picked it up and checked the text message.

I've got an hour alone.

Sheri grinned as she quickly replied. Where?

My place? DJ just left to see his grandparents.

OMW!

"Sheri!" Cora's voice snapped. "Girl, why are you grinning at your phone like that?"

Sheri shrugged and stood. "I've got to go."

Her mom shook her head. "It's Deandre. That man has her acting brand-new."

Sheri let out an incredulous laugh. "No he doesn't."

"Yes he does. Normally, I'd tell you to be careful, but I like Deandre. Even if he is a cop. Willie said he's a nice guy."

And that's all it had taken for her mom to warm up to Deandre. She didn't trust most men, but if her brother gave a guy the stamp of approval, then she was willing to give him a chance. Sheri didn't care if her uncle's cosign was what it took for her mom to be okay with her dating Deandre. She was just glad that their relationship wouldn't be a problem.

"That's because he *is* a nice guy," Sheri said. "I guess it's true that there are a few of them left out there."

Cora smirked. "Are you sure he's nice or are you just blinded by the sex?"

"What?"

"You heard me. We all know it don't take that long to get a cake from your house."

Sheri's cheeks burned. Really? Cora had to call her out right now in front of her mom. Her mom knew she wasn't a virgin, but that didn't mean she wanted to be called out for getting a quickie at a family cookout.

"Mind your business, Cora," Sheri warned. "Let's get out of here." She left the office and went toward the back door.

"I'm just saying," Cora said, following her.

"No, you're just doing too much."

Her mom spoke from behind them. "It's okay, Lil Bit. He is a nice guy. Don't be embarrassed for enjoying each other."

"Thanks, Ma." Sheri wanted the entire conversation to end.

Cora, unfortunately, wasn't ready to let it end. "You don't have to be embarrassed, but you do need to be careful."

"Careful for what? Deandre is cool. He's respectful and isn't about playing games. It's all good."

They went out the back door and Sheri pulled out the key to lock it behind them.

"Yeah, well, you better watch that son of his."

Sheri frowned. "DJ? Why?"

"Emory said that he was bragging about being in a gang," Cora said, referring to one of their younger, teenage cousins.

Sheri nearly dropped her keys. "What? He's not in a gang."

"Well, that's what he said," Cora spoke as if she were repeating the God's honest truth. "He said him and his boys control this end of the beach and that everyone knows not to go messing with their group."

"Emory must have misheard. DJ wouldn't be in a gang. His dad is a cop."

"Yeah," her mom agreed. "Let's be honest. I love Emory, but the girl likes to exaggerate. Besides, there aren't any gangs in Sunshine Beach."

Not exactly true, but DJ and his friends hardly qualified as a gang. "I've seen DJ with his friends, and they don't look like a gang. They look like regular teenagers who hang around the area."

Cora waved off Sheri's words. She gave Sheri a look that was both pitying and disbelieving. "You're just being delusional because you're all into Deandre."

Sheri stopped walking and faced her cousin. "I'm not being delusional. I'm also not going to start spreading rumors about gangs in the south end. Especially rumors that Deandre's son is part of one."

Cora put a hand on her hip. "It's not a rumor when the boy said it himself."

"Did you hear him say that?"

Cora glanced away before lifting her chin defiantly. "I'm telling you what Emory said."

"We all love Emory, but Mom is right. She can exaggerate. I think you just want to try and find something wrong with Deandre."

Cora's jaw dropped. "Ain't nobody trying to find something wrong with Deandre."

"Really, Cora? Don't even play like that. It's what you do. You always hate on whatever guy I'm dating. I'm not following you down the yellow brick road this time." Sheri turned to stalk away from her cousin.

"I don't know what you're talking about. I don't lead you down any roads."

Sheri spun back. "Yes you do. You always try to find something wrong and push me into doing something dumb."

"You make your own decisions. Don't blame me because you pick the wrong guys."

"No, Cora, you pick the wrong guys. And then you want to find something wrong with every guy that I try to spend time with. It's not going to work this time. I'm not going to let you bad-mouth Deandre or his son."

Her mom stepped between them. "Both of ya'll stop right now. You are not about to fall out in this parking lot over a man. You're family. You understand me?"

Her mom's intervention did nothing to calm Sheri's irritation. "I understand, Ma, but it has to be said. Cora is going too far."

Cora rolled her eyes. "You know what, I don't know why I'm even talking to you. When you figure out that his son is some wanna-be thug, then I'll be the first to tell you I told you so." Cora turned and stomped off.

"You won't be telling me anything," Sheri called after her.

Her mom put her hand on Sheri's arm. "Lil Bit, stop. Why are you being like that with your cousin?"

"Because, Ma, you know how she is. She makes everything worse and always looks for the negative."

"But she doesn't mean you any harm."

"Yes she does. She did it before and she'll do it again."

Her mom pointed. "Don't go blaming Cora for the decisions you made. Did she egg you on? Yes, but at the end of the day you took the bat to that man's car."

"Ma." Sheri wanted to argue. Her mom was supposed to take her side. Dorothy Jean didn't give her a chance to continue.

"Don't 'Ma' me. It's the truth. Cora isn't perfect, and she was wrong for encouraging you, but you can't go putting all your activities on account of her."

"But she made things worse." Not just that night, but by spreading rumors when she was jealous. Not to mention the way she constantly ditched Sheri whenever some new guy came around. Cora was family, but she didn't always act like a good friend.

"Then be mad at her for the things *she* did. Not for the things you did. And I don't know if Emory is right or not, but where there's smoke there's usually fire."

"You think DJ is in a gang? Seriously?"

"I don't know enough about the boy to say anything about him. But if Deandre really is your man, then how about you tell him what was said at the party. Let him figure it out before you get lost in love. Because if he is in a gang, then honey, you're signing up for a lot more than what you bargained for."

Deandre bit the corner of his lip as he watched Sheri stretch as she sat on the edge of his bed. She raised her arms high over her head with her back arched and her breasts pushed forward. Even though they'd just made love, he wanted to pull her back into the bed and get lost in her body all over again.

"I needed that." Sheri grinned at him over her shoulder.

"Did you?" He shifted on the bed until his legs straddled her and his feet rested next to hers on the floor. He wrapped his arms around her waist and brought her back to his chest.

She nodded and leaned into him. "I did. It was a busy day at the restaurant."

Deandre kissed her shoulder and breathed in the sweet scent of her skin. "There are a lot more people on the south end of the beach since the event. Which is a good thing."

"Do you think things will get better?"

"I think it showed the town leaders that the people in the area are serious about making things even better. Montgomery also told me they heard loud and clear that the business owners and residents don't want us coming through with a heavy hand. I think they finally understand and are good with us becoming a part of the community."

Her eyes widened and she squeezed his arms still around her waist. "That's great. I'm telling you things aren't that bad."

"I know they aren't."

She moved to get up, but he held on to her. "You sure you don't want to stick around for dinner? DJ will be home soon and can join us."

Her body stiffened. Deandre let her go. She didn't pull away but she shifted so that she could look at him. "I don't know. I'm trying not to come on too strong around him. I think we need to ease into the time together."

"I know what he's been doing."

She glanced away. "What do you mean?"

"You know what I mean. We both know he's been trying to keep us separated. I talked to him about it."

Her body relaxed and relief filled her gaze. "What did he say?"

"He said he wasn't trying to do that. Then made me feel guilty for saying that he was calling just to interrupt us."

She cringed. "Dang."

"Yeah. I don't want him to think I don't want him around or calling when we're together. That's why I asked you to stay. I'm thinking you and I are going to be together for a while. I want him to get used to you being a part of our life."

"You want me to be a part of your life?"

The hopeful smile on her face made his lips turn up. "Yeah. I told you I'm not about sleeping around. I like you. We're good together. I'd like to see where this goes."

The seconds she took to study him while chewing on the corner of her lip were the longest, sexiest seconds in his life. "So would I."

"I'm not asking you to step in and be DJ's mom or anything. But I would like for the two of you to start getting along."

"I would like to get along with him."

"So will you stay?" She glanced away again. Deandre frowned. "What's wrong?"

She shifted until she could face him better, her hand resting on his thigh. "I need to tell you something. It's part of the reason I was so wound up when I got here."

Dread tightened his shoulders. Things were going so well, he hoped she wasn't having any concerns about their relationship. "What is it?"

"Something my cousin Cora said. Which, I don't believe because she's always stirring up trouble."

"What did she say?"

She sighed and looked like she didn't want to say it. He gently squeezed her hand. She met his eyes. "She says that at the cookout the other day, DJ was bragging about being in a gang."

Deandre jerked back. "A what?"

"I know. It's the dumbest thing. There's no way he would be in a gang when his dad is a cop. Then she started talking about how I shouldn't get involved with you because of DJ and that you weren't as great as I thought. That's why I don't believe her. I think she's just trying to start problems."

Deandre swung his leg from around her and sat on the edge of the bed. He shook his head. "He couldn't."

"I don't believe it."

Deandre thought about the last few months. The withdrawal from the things DJ usually liked. The new set of friends that he didn't want to bring around. The way he was cagey with his answers about whom he'd been with and what they were doing. "He wouldn't."

Sheri placed a hand on his knee. "I know. Cora is just being messy."

"But if he's saying things like that, then I need to talk to him about it."

"I'm not trying to get him into trouble."

"I know you're not, but I'm glad you told me." All kinds of thoughts and concerns spiraled through his brain. Had he missed something so big with DJ?

"Look, I can't prove he really said that. It's what I got from Cora, who said our younger cousin Emory heard him say this. This is literally hearsay."

"Even if it's hearsay, I still need to let him know. If he said it, then I need to know why. If he didn't say it, then I need to find out what he said that could have made them think that."

Maybe it was just a mix-up. Confusion over a turn of phrase. He could make sure DJ was aware that words held power and could cause big problems if he wasn't clear.

"Wait, do you think there's something to this?"

The concern in her eyes mirrored his own. He was glad that she cared. Glad that she'd told him and was still willing to stick with him in this relationship after hearing something so negative about his kid. Something he prayed was not true.

"I don't know. But he has changed in the last few months. I don't know what's going on with him. I'd rather rule this out than pretend as if he never would get involved with the wrong crowd and be wrong."

Chapter Seventeen

Deandre sat up on the couch when the sound of the key in the front door's lock echoed through the quiet. Sheri had left two hours ago when it was obvious that DJ wasn't coming home anytime soon. When he'd called his in-laws to see if they were still with DJ, he'd been shocked to learn that DJ had never made it to their place.

Deandre had been disappointed and confused. DJ's lie wasn't one that he would be able to get away with. Which meant he didn't care about being caught. Deandre wasn't sure what was going on with his son, but he was going to get to the bottom of everything tonight. He'd tried to respect DJ's space and give him the room he needed to go through whatever teenage transition he was having. But lying to him was something he was not going to accept.

The front door opened, and Deandre waited. There was no need to rush forward. DJ would see him as soon as he crossed the threshold. His son walked in slowly, his brow furled and shoulders slumped. He quietly closed the door and locked it behind him. When he turned and entered the living area, his gaze collided with Deandre's. He paused for a second, eyes wide as if for a split second he was surprised to find his dad there. Maybe a part of him had hoped he wouldn't get caught. But the second of surprise quickly faded, and DJ straightened his shoulders and lifted his chin.

Deandre clenched his hands into fists. This was what they were doing? His son was really going to flex on him? After he'd done wrong? The level of audacity made Deandre's stomach churn and his blood boil. He took a long breath and calmed himself. They were going to have a showdown, but he was the adult. This wasn't going to go anywhere if he let anger rule him.

"Where have you been?" Deandre asked.

DJ glanced away and rubbed his chin before looking back. "With some friends."

"You were supposed to be going to your grandparents' house."

DJ lifted a shoulder. "My plans changed."

"You didn't think to tell me about your change of plans?"

"I didn't think you'd care."

Deandre frowned so hard his forehead hurt. He slowly stood and crossed his arms. "Why wouldn't I care? When I called your grandparents, and they said you never came by, they were worried. They thought something happened to you."

Guilt flashed in DJ's dark eyes before he blinked it away and lifted his chin again. "I didn't tell them I was coming. There wasn't any reason for them to worry."

"But you told me that. I expected you to be with them. They weren't the only ones worrying. I worried."

"Well, I'm fine now." DJ patted the front of his hoodie and joggers as if to support the statement.

"Fine now?" Deandre paused, breathed, then continued. "Boy, have you lost your damn mind? You don't change your plans and tell me you're going one place and then go somewhere else. That's not how this works. You're supposed to call me."

"You told me not to call when you're with *Sheri*." DJ

rolled his eyes and said Sheri's name as if it were some kind of disease.

Deandre uncrossed his arms and planted his hands on his hips. "You know good and damn well that isn't what I said or what I meant. Now, if you have a problem with Sheri, then you tell me that straight up. What you won't do is try to use that as a reason to lie to me. Now give me your phone."

DJ scowled. "For what?"

"You know what for. You're on punishment. You aren't allowed to leave this house except to go to school, to be with me or with your grandparents. You can't use your phone, laptop or any other electronic device in this house for anything other than homework. I'm disabling the internet on everything in here."

DJ scoffed. "Whatever." He pulled out his cell phone.

Deandre crossed the room and snatched it from his son. Then he froze. He sniffed the air and leaned in closer. His eyes narrowed as he realized what he smelled. "Were you smoking weed?"

DJ's eyes widened. "What? Nah! I swear!"

"You've already lied to me once. Don't lie to me again. I know what weed smells like and I smell it on you. Is it true? Are you in a gang?"

"Dad, I wasn't smoking weed. Some guy I knew had it—"

"Some guy you knew? Are these the so-called friends you're hanging with? No, we're not doing that. I didn't want to believe Sheri but—"

"Sheri? So, she's snitching on me again?" Disbelief filled DJ's voice.

"She's not snitching. If there's something going on with my son, then I need to know. Gangs and drugs? DJ, how could you?"

"I'm not—"

"You're getting tested."

"What?" DJ's eyes bugged with disbelief. He threw up his hands.

"Right now." He grabbed his son's arm and pulled him down the hall to Deandre's room. Deandre went into the bathroom and pulled out the at-home drug test he kept. Something he never thought he'd have to use.

"Do this. Right now."

"Dad, you're really going to drug-test me?"

Deandre tossed the box and DJ caught it. He crossed his arms and glared. "Yes. I really am."

Sheri didn't see Deandre again until later in the week. He'd given her an update via text and phone calls of what DJ had been up to. She was glad that he'd made his way home safely, while also hating the fact that Deandre had worried about him. She'd even called her mom to apologize for some of the antics she'd done as a kid.

"I didn't realize how much kids could make their parents worry," she'd said as she'd sat on the porch with her mom and aunt the night before.

"You never stop worrying. You and Cora would get into some things, but thankfully you were never too bad. At least I didn't have to worry about you being in a gang or anything."

Sheri had nothing to say to that. Deandre hadn't confirmed the rumor about DJ being in a gang. But that hadn't stopped Cora from making sure everyone in the family knew. Sheri was so done with her cousin and her antics. But she'd deal with that later.

When Deandre texted her at work and asked if he could come by after she got off, she'd quickly agreed. She missed him. And even though DJ wasn't her son, she wanted him to be okay. She worried that she was the reason for his acting out. She was falling hard for Deandre, but she didn't want to be the reason he and his son grew further apart.

Deandre looked tired when he got to her place. She cut him a huge slice of the lemon pound cake she'd baked and set it in front of him at the table. Despite the weariness in his eyes, his face lit up at the sight of the cake.

"When did you have time to bake this?"

"Don't worry about all that." She'd baked the cake during the day at work. "Just eat. You probably skipped lunch again today."

"I ate lunch. It just wasn't as good as your fried chicken."

"You should have come by the restaurant."

He shook his head. "Busy day. We're looking into the suspected gang activity in the south end."

She sat next to him. "There really is a gang problem?"

"Some kids are grouping up. It started with two separate groups fighting during the football season and the problem's escalating. We're figuring out a plan with the school district to see if we can curb it before things turn violent."

"Is DJ…?"

He sighed and shrugged. "I can't prove anything. I drug-tested him. It came back negative. Thankfully. But he's hanging with some kids that I do think are a part of the problem."

"What can we do?"

He looked up from the cake and raised a brow. "We?"

"If I can help in any way, I want to. I know I'm not family, but I care about you. Which means I care about DJ."

He took her hand in his. "You don't know how much I appreciate that. I wish DJ would give you a chance."

The words iced her heart. She pulled on her hand. "He doesn't like me."

Deandre didn't let her go. "He doesn't know you."

"But he doesn't want to try and know me. If I'm the problem…"

"You're not." He squeezed her hand.

"I'm part of the problem. Or you dating me is making it worse. Do you think we should—"

"No," he said firmly. "Let's give it some time."

"We've given it time. I don't want to end things, but maybe we do need to take a step back. Let you focus on DJ and whatever is going on with the kids he's hanging around. I know it's not ideal, but it's probably the right thing for now."

He sat up straight. "You want to break up?"

She shook her head and her hands. "No, hell no! We're just chilling for a while. If you're not available or have family and work stuff, I understand. Right now, DJ is your priority and I respect that."

Deandre put down the fork. He placed his hand on the back of her head and pulled her forward for a kiss. It was quick and hard and made Sheri want to climb on his lap and take him deep. When he pulled back, she was breathless.

"Thank you for being great," he said.

Sheri's cheeks tingled as she grinned. "You just like my pound cake."

"No. I like you. And hopefully, we'll get through this."

Chapter Eighteen

Sheri walked into the alley behind her restaurant and froze. The space was darker than usual. The overhead lights that illuminated the back doors of the businesses were out. It wasn't unusual for one or two to go out. They weren't the LED lights that lasted forever, but for them all to be out wasn't normal. She'd decided to go into the restaurant early to work on the schedule for the following week before everyone else came in and things got busy. She hadn't seen Deandre in two weeks, and when he'd texted her last night asking if they could meet up when she got off, she'd immediately said yes.

She missed him. Way more than she'd thought she would. So, getting up earlier than usual so she could get out of there as soon as possible after closing was an easy decision. They hadn't had problems with break-ins since the Connecting the Community event, so she also hadn't worried that whoever had tried to rob the place weeks ago would be back.

What little light came from the streetlights and waning glow from the moon glinted off broken glass on the ground behind the building. The lights weren't out because the bulbs were old. They were out because someone had vandalized the building.

She pulled out her cell phone and turned on the flashlight. The light from her phone seemed bright as the sun when she used it at home, but in the dark alley it felt inadequate. She studied the area but there weren't any signs that anyone was still there. She just needed to unlock the door, get in and then she'd call the police. The business owners had gone in together to purchase cameras to monitor the alley as part of the recommendations to have better surveillance in the area. The police could pull the footage and they'd quickly find out who'd done it. Probably just some bored kids, and no one who meant any real harm.

She pulled her keys out of her purse and then quickly walked to the back door. The hairs on the back of her neck stood up as soon as she put the key into the lock and turned. A second later, the sound of footsteps hurrying down the alley echoed off the building.

Sheri turned to see two figures approaching her fast. She didn't wait to find out what was going on. She opened the door and rushed inside, her heart pounding. She tried to turn and slam the door, but the people behind her were already there. One of them slammed into the door. The impact was so sudden and unexpected that Sheri stumbled back.

The person came inside, followed by another figure. They wore masks over their faces and were dressed in all black. She guessed based on their size that they were male, but from what she could see of the first one, she immediately assumed teenager or young adult.

"What do you want?" She tried not to sound intimidated despite her racing heart and the cold sweat breaking out over her body.

"The money in the safe. All of it," the guy said. Definitely a teenager.

Sheri frowned. "I don't have money in a safe."

"You've got money in here. I know you do. Now get it."

Sheri held up her hand and shook her head. "Look, I

don't keep cash in here like that. I'm not a bank or a convenience store. If you're looking for money, you came to the wrong place."

She did have money in the safe in the office, but there was no way she'd let on that there was anything there. She needed them to leave as soon as possible. And preferably without damage to her or the restaurant.

"That's a lie. Now give me the money." He reached into his pocket and pulled out a gun.

Sheri's heart dropped to her stomach. The room spun and she took a step back, arms raised. "I swear I don't have anything."

The other kid stepped forward. "Hey, J, you said you were just going to scare her."

The first one looked at the second. "And if she doesn't give us the money, I'm really going to scare her."

Sheri blinked. She had to be hearing this wrong. "DJ?"

The second kid's eyes swung to her. Her stomach twisted into a tight knot. She shook her head. No, not DJ. Why in the world would he be robbing her?

The first kid, J, stepped into her line of sight. Gun still pointed straight at Sheri. "To hell with that. I'm not playing. Give me the money or I'm going to shoot your ass."

"Yo, J, hold up," DJ said, his voice panicked and tight. "That's not what we talked about."

"I don't care what we talked about. This place is always busy. I know there's money up in here."

"Nah, I'm not down for this," DJ said, taking a step back.

"You want to be a part of us, then you have to be down." J looked back at Sheri. "And if she knows who you are, then she'll snitch." He focused on DJ. "So we can't leave her to tell."

"What? Nah, man! No." DJ moved back toward the door.

J turned his back to Sheri. That was all she needed. She grabbed a bowl off the counter and tossed it straight for J's head. She missed and hit his hand instead. The gun went off. The sound of the shot was like a crack of thunder in the small space.

J cursed as the gun fell from his hand. Sheri grabbed a rolling pin and ran toward J. Kid or not, she was going to clock him. He was going to shoot her! Which meant she felt no guilt about trying to defend herself. She swung, but he was fast. He ducked out of the way. Then his hand shot out as he punched the side of her face. Pain exploded through her head. Sheri stumbled and fell to the floor.

"The cops!" DJ yelled.

"Shit!" J ran toward the back door, shoving DJ out of the way as he hurried out.

Sheri placed a hand to the side of her head. Pain throbbed with every heartbeat and her vision was blurry. She'd never been punched in the face. The experience was new—and horrible. DJ rushed over. Sheri flinched when he reached for her.

"Sheri, damn, I'm sorry. It wasn't supposed to go down like this. I was just trying to..."

She scowled. "Scare me! Well, it worked!"

"Lil Bit!" JD's voice echoed as he burst in the back door. His frantic eyes searched the room, landed on DJ standing above her and fury filled his face. "You little punk." He rushed forward and grabbed DJ by the back of the neck.

Sheri jumped up, the room spun and she shook her head to clear the fog. Not a good idea. That just made everything hurt worse. "Hold up. It wasn't him."

DJ struggled against JD's hold, but he didn't let go. "Then why's he struggling? I'm holding his behind right there until the cops come."

Sheri stared at DJ. He didn't struggle against JD's grip.

If anything, the fear in his eyes said he knew he'd messed up. Sheri wished she didn't have to make the call, but what he'd done? What his friend had done? It couldn't be ignored. She nodded slowly to not make the pain in her head worse.

"You call the cops, and I'll call his dad."

"I told you to stay away from him."

Sheri sighed before dropping the ice pack pressed to the side of her face. She glared at Cora standing at the base of the stairs leading up to the porch. Sheri had wanted to spend a few minutes alone to process everything that happened that day. The day felt like a blur. The police coming. DJ getting arrested. Her mom insisting Sheri go to the hospital to get checked out, and Sheri compromising with a trip to urgent care instead. Followed by going to the police station to give a statement.

In all of that she'd only seen Deandre in passing. He'd been dealing with the fallout with DJ. Their eyes met as they crossed paths in the station. He'd taken one look at her face, scowled and stalked away. She wasn't sure if she should call him or leave well enough alone.

She had enough to deal with and wasn't in the mood to deal with Cora's smug attitude. She narrowed her eyes at Cora. "Did you come here to gloat?"

Cora held up her hands in surrender before coming up the stairs. "I came to check on you."

"And to say I told you so."

Cora leaned against the porch rail. She sucked her teeth and shook her head. "Your eye is swollen."

"I already knew that. If you came to point out the obvious, you can go." Sheri picked up the ice pack and put it back on her face.

Cora sighed and crossed her arms. They sat there in

silence for several minutes. Sheri refused to break the silence. She was mad. Mad that DJ would go so far to scare her. Mad that Deandre could barely look at her. Mad that she'd had to shut the restaurant down for the day because of this foolishness. And, especially mad that Cora had been right about DJ all along.

"Look," Cora finally said. "I didn't come to say I told you so. I was worried about you."

"I'm fine. You've checked on me. Now you can go."

"Lil Bit, don't be like that. I didn't want things to turn out like this. Deandre *is* a nice guy."

She looked at her cousin. "You're ready to finally admit that."

Cora huffed out a breath before flicking her bang out of her face. "I never said he wasn't. I just knew his son was a problem, and you got all mad at me."

"I got all mad because you seemed to love telling me how things weren't going to work out with him. You know how hard it's been for me to move on since that mess with Tyrone. Why couldn't you at least be supportive?"

"Because I was jealous."

Sheri blinked. "What?" That was not what she expected.

Cora rolled her eyes. "Don't act like you didn't know. Why do you always end up with the good ones and I get the bustas?"

"Good ones?" Sheri dropped the ice pack to point at her chest. "Since when do I get the good ones?"

"You do okay. The nice guys like you and the sorry ones come my way. So, yes, I was jealous. But I wouldn't try to intentionally hurt you. Not after you got in trouble back then."

"Did you intentionally try to hurt me then?"

Cora met her gaze. "No."

Sheri believed her. Plus, her mom was right. Cora had egged her on, but ultimately, the decision to take her revenge on Tyrone for hurting her was her own. "Were you glad to see my heart broken?"

Cora's shoulders straightened. "No! I knew he was going to hurt you. That's why I was down when you wanted to mess up his car after he did. Not because I was happy about how it went down. Just like I'm not happy about what happened today. You really think I want to see you robbed and beat?"

Sheri slumped back in her chair. "No. And I didn't get beat. I got hit once." Despite everything, she knew Cora wouldn't wish bad on her. Her cousin was messy, and gossipy, and an instigator, but when push came to shove, she'd always been there for Sheri. Even when she was doing dumb things or making foolish decisions.

"I told you about DJ because you thought Deandre was perfect. Well, girl, he's not. When I heard his son might be in a gang, then I knew that was going to be trouble. I was just trying to give you a heads-up. That's all."

Sheri closed her eyes and dropped her head back. "I wanted this to work out."

"I don't see how it can. Not when this happened. DJ doesn't like you and I'm not going to be cool with watching him try to hurt you."

"I know. But..." She looked at her cousin. "Cora, I really like Deandre. Like, I think I love him."

Cora's eyes widened. She quickly moved and sat in the chair next to Sheri. "Lil Bit? You serious?"

She nodded, tears welling in her eyes as the anger from the day turned into pain. "I do. But if his son hates me enough to do this..."

"Then how can you make it work?"

"I don't know. Even if I want to try, Deandre might not. He barely looked at me today."

"Because his son tried to rob you and you almost got shot. If he did look you in the eye without a problem, then I'd say that's a problem. Don't you take on any responsibility for this one. This is on Deandre and his son. Not you."

"I know." Sheri sat up and swiped at her eyes. "I just really hate that when I finally find a guy that I can love, it has to end like this."

Cora sighed. "You know what?"

Sheri put the ice pack back on her face. "What?"

She waited for Cora to tell her to move on. That she didn't need to waste tears for a man. That she was better off without him.

"Maybe things will work out."

Sheri swung her head toward Cora so fast that her headache throbbed. "Come again?"

Cora shrugged. "I'm just saying. You've been through a lot. Deandre is a good guy. Maybe, and that's a big *maybe*, he feels the same and ya'll can make this work."

Sheri grinned before reaching over to lightly push her cousin's shoulder. "That's the nicest thing you've ever said to me."

Cora rolled her eyes and pushed Sheri's hand away. "I've been around you too long. Got me hoping in fairy tales. But who knows. Maybe the little bit of love you're feeling for him will work out."

Sheri grinned even though in her heart she wasn't sure how they would make it all work. She looked at the sky and sent up a silent prayer. "Maybe so."

Chapter Nineteen

DJ knocked on Deandre's door after midnight. Deandre stared at his closed bedroom door. He was angry, frustrated and disappointed. But mostly, he was tired. It had taken calling in every favor he had and pulling his position with the police department to keep DJ from spending the night in jail. At first his plan was to let his son spend the night in jail. Maybe two. If he wanted to be a damn thug, then he'd see what life was like for one. But Rose had cried and Cliff had begged, so Deandre had pleaded with the judge and the chief and pulled money out of his savings account to get his son out on bail.

He hated that he had to do that. Hated that he was using an advantage that so many other people didn't have in this situation. Hated that DJ had put him in this situation in the first place. That he'd *missed* it. That missing this had damn near cost Sheri everything.

DJ knocked again. "Dad, you up?"

Deandre wanted to ignore him. Wanted to turn off his light, pull the covers over his head and forget this horrible day. But he couldn't. When he signed up for parenthood it hadn't been just for birthdays, holidays and special occasions at school.

"Come on in, DJ," he called back.

A second passed, then another before his son opened

the bedroom door. He'd showered and changed into pajamas, a pair of basketball shorts and a T-shirt. His shoulders were slumped, and he looked wary as he entered Deandre's bedroom.

"I just want to say I'm sorry. About today."

Deandre narrowed his eyes. "You're sorry? Do you even realize how much of a privilege it is for you to even be here, in my room, saying you're sorry? You should still be in jail right now with your friend J. But I had to pull strings to get you here to even tell me you're sorry."

DJ flinched and crossed his arms in front of his chest. For the first time in months, he looked like a kid. No defiance and frustration in his eyes. Just sadness and fear.

"I know. I messed up. Things got out of hand. It wasn't supposed to go down like that."

"Then how was it supposed to go down? What did you want to happen?"

"Just to scare her a little," he said in a small voice.

"For what? Do you hate her that much? Is the idea of me dating her so bad that you want to scare her off? Scare her so bad that you get a kid who's trying to recruit you into his gang to come at her with a gun? You hate her enough to risk this armed robbery charge?"

That part had come out in the aftermath. DJ wasn't officially in J's gang, but he'd started hanging with them and showing interest. Deandre had been shocked, hurt, but mostly he'd been disappointed in himself. He hadn't been there for his son. He hadn't noticed what was going on. He should have pushed for more information. He should have made DJ tell him what was going on. Instead, he'd gotten lost in work and missed all the signs.

"No, I mean…" DJ paused, then sighed and held out his

hands helplessly. "I don't know. I just... She was getting all your attention."

"What?"

"You've been busy. With the switch in your job and you're always worried about fixing the south end of the beach. You're never around. And then, all of a sudden, she was there. You already weren't paying attention to me and then you had her. It was like you didn't care about me anymore."

Deandre frowned. He got up from the bed and crossed the room. "DJ, I will always care about you. You're my son. I love you. No matter what's going on."

"I didn't mean to join them. It was just hanging around. I was losing on the wrestling team and the other guys started teasing me. But when I started hanging with J, they left me alone. It got out of hand. I didn't know how to get out." His voice cracked. "They wouldn't let me out."

Deandre put his hands on his son's shoulders. "That's when you come to me." He moved his face until DJ finally met his eyes. "There is always a way out, understand? I'll fight this entire damn world to help you. No one is going to take advantage of my son. You hear me?"

DJ nodded. He hastily wiped his face and looked away. Deandre's own eyes burned. "But, DJ, even if you felt that way, you should have told me. I asked you over and over to talk to me. Why didn't you?"

"I thought you'd be upset."

"Yeah, I would have been, but I would have helped you figure a way out."

"Then she told you what I said that day when I was with J."

"She told me because she cared about you. She didn't want you to get in trouble."

He used *cared* because he wasn't sure how Sheri felt

now. He hadn't had the chance to talk to her. He didn't even know what he would say. How could he approach her after what DJ had done? He couldn't blame her if she never wanted to see either of them again.

"I know, but… You told me that you'd always love Mom."

The softly spoken words tore a hole in Deandre's heart. He squeezed DJ's shoulder. "I will always love your mom. The way I feel about Sheri is different. It won't replace that love or make me forget your mom."

"I don't want you to forget her."

"I won't. Just like I won't stop trying to be there for you. If you need me to be around more, or to be more available, I will. We'll start over. We'll get through this and figure out the best way forward. Even if it means without Sheri in my life."

The last words burned like acid as he spoke them. He didn't want to give her up, but this crisis showed him one thing. His son needed him, and he'd missed the signs. He wouldn't blame it on his relationship with Sheri. DJ had started acting differently before they'd come together. But he wouldn't put her in harm's way again.

"For real?" DJ asked.

Deandre nodded slowly. "If that's what it takes to make things right with us, then I will."

DJ looked at the floor. "I didn't think you'd do that for me."

Deandre gently shook DJ's shoulder until he looked back up. "Son, I love you. You're the most important thing in my life. You're in a world of trouble for this. But that doesn't take away that I want to help you."

DJ's eyes glistened. He quickly wiped them and Deandre pulled him into his arms. For the first time in months, DJ hugged him back.

"I love you, too, Dad."

Chapter Twenty

Sheri was in the back going over the sales receipts for the day when her mom came into the office.

"Lil Bit, that boy is out there to see you."

Sheri looked up from her calculator and frowned at her mom. "What boy?"

Her mom crossed her arms and twisted her lips. "Deandre's son."

Sheri's jaw dropped. She never expected DJ to come see her. "What for? I said everything I needed to say in court earlier."

Sheri had gone to his bond hearing and told the judge she was not pressing charges against DJ. His friend J, on the other hand, was not getting his charges dropped. Though she hadn't forgiven DJ for agreeing to go along with this, he at least hadn't come with the intention of trying to shoot her. He also didn't have to stick around and help her even though he was going to be arrested. J hadn't bothered to show any signs of remorse, where DJ had apologized to her. Something she was sure Deandre had a hand in, but knowing he wasn't a bad kid, she'd given him a second chance just like she'd been given.

"He says he wants to say something to you. You want me to kick him out?" her mom asked a little too eagerly.

"Is his dad with him?"

"Nope. Just him."

Intrigued, Sheri stood. She wasn't afraid that he'd hurt her. Not after what happened and not with the workers in the restaurant still there. "I'll go see what he wants."

She left the office and went out into the dining area. The restaurant had closed an hour earlier and most of the waitstaff had finished up cleaning their areas and were finalizing end-of-the-day prep in the kitchen. DJ stood by the hostess's stand, his head bent as he kicked at the floor. He was still dressed in the suit and tie he'd worn for court earlier that day, but now the tie was loose.

"You wanted to see me?"

DJ's head jerked up. He glanced around nervously, as if he wasn't sure why he'd come, before finally meeting her eye. "Um…yeah. I mean, yes, ma'am."

Sheri pointed to one of the tables. "Want something to eat?" She couldn't help it, food always made difficult talks a little easier.

He shook his head. "Nah, I'm good." He pulled out a chair and sat.

Sheri sat opposite him. He scratched at the table for several seconds before Sheri asked, "What's up?"

"Why did you drop the charges?" he blurted out.

Sheri took a long breath before crossing her arms and sitting back in her chair. "Because you stuck around to help me."

His brows drew together. "That's it?"

"That, and you're not a bad kid. Everyone deserves a second chance. I got one."

"When you messed up that guy's car?" he asked.

She let out a dry chuckle before shaking her head. She would never live that down. "No, before that. When I was your age. Hanging out down here on the south end of the beach. Me and my friends thought it would be cool to steal key chains from the gift shop. We would try to see who could get the most. Well, one day I had the most and I was the one the security guard caught."

DJ sat forward in his chair. "You were stealing key chains? Why?" he asked as if that were the most asinine thing he'd ever heard.

She shook her head and laughed. Looking back, it was an asinine decision. "No good reason other than the key chains had dirty phrases and we wanted them."

He nodded as if that made sense, then leaned forward and asked, "What happened?"

"The security guard called the police, but the store owner, Mr. Lee, got there at the same time. He told the cops he'd given me permission to take them. Later, he told me that I was a good kid and didn't need to mess up my life trying to steal his key chains. He gave me a second chance when he didn't have to. All because he saw potential in me even when I wanted to be dumb with my friends. I don't know why you decided to run with J and his crew, or why you decided that scaring me was what you needed to do, but I've seen you with your dad, your grandparents and around other adults. You're not bad. So, this is my second chance for you. What you do with it is up to you."

DJ chewed on his lower lip. His eyes studied the table for several seconds before he sat up and met her eye. "I didn't want you with my dad."

Sheri shrugged. "I figured that much."

"I thought you'd be drama. That you'd get mad at him and mess up his car. That's what I heard anyway."

"Rumors aren't always the truth. But I will give you that. I made some bad decisions before."

"And you and my dad, y'all broke up…because of me?"

"He wants to focus on being there for you because he loves you. I want to make sure your dad is okay because I care about him. And, believe it or not, I care about you, too."

DJ nodded slowly. "I meant what I said earlier today. About being sorry. My dad didn't make me say that. I just wanted to play a prank. I didn't think J would…" He trailed off and drummed his fingers on the table.

Sheri reached over and placed her hand over his. "Thankfully, nothing bad happened. But, DJ, if this happens again, things may not turn out okay. For your dad's sake, try not to run with that crowd."

She pulled her hand back. DJ looked down at his hand before focusing on her again. "If I said I never wanted you with my dad, would you walk away?"

She sucked in a breath. Stepping back from Deandre had already been difficult to do. She loved him and missed him. The realization that she loved him made her chest ache. She wanted to see him smile, bring him lunch so she knew he would eat on a busy day, and listen to him talk. But she knew how much he loved his son. If being with her would damage his relationship with DJ, then, yes, he might still choose to be with her, but at what cost? She didn't want to put him in that situation and find out.

"I don't want to come between you and your dad," she said honestly.

"I don't want to come between you and my dad," DJ said. "Not anymore."

Sheri sat up straight, surprised by his words. "What?"

"Look, I don't know how this works. My dad didn't really date like that after Mom passed. I don't want him alone forever, I just didn't want him with…excuse me for what I'm about to say, someone I thought was kind of rachet."

Sheri blinked, then laughed. She wasn't offended. It wasn't the first time someone had tried to label her, and it wouldn't be the last time. "I don't think your dad would be into me if I was."

He smiled. It was the first time he'd smiled at her. "True."

She raised a brow. "So… You're good with me and him together?"

He nodded. "Yeah. If you'll give him a second chance. And, if you're cool with me."

Sheri's mom came from the back into the dining area. "Sheri, his dad is here to see you."

Sheri and DJ swung toward her mom. "Deandre's here?"

Her mom nodded. "He came to the back door and knocked. He's lucky JD didn't hit him with a rolling pin. He scared us knocking on the door like the damn police. You want to see him?"

Sheri and DJ exchanged a look. Deandre was, in fact, the police. But they wouldn't point that out.

"Yes, send him in here." Her mom went back toward the kitchen and Sheri turned to DJ. "Does he know you're here?"

DJ shook his head. "Nah. He left me at home while he went out. I came here on my own."

"Are you going to get in trouble for being here?"

DJ shrugged. "I don't know. Maybe."

Sheri rolled her eyes and sighed. Teenagers. She and Deandre would have a time with him.

Deandre came from the back. He looked at Sheri, then DJ and back at her. Her heart ached with the need to cross the room and wrap her arms around him. She missed being with him so much.

His focus finally settled on his son. "DJ, what are you doing here?"

DJ stood. "I came to thank Ms. Thomas for not pressing charges."

Deandre's worried expression morphed to one of surprise. He clearly hadn't expected that answer. "Oh."

"And, to tell her that I'm good with you two being together." He walked to his dad. "I'll let ya'll talk." DJ placed a hand on his dad's shoulder. He looked back at Sheri, smiled, then went toward the kitchen.

Deandre watched with a slack jaw as his son disappeared into the kitchen. He swung back to Sheri several seconds after DJ disappeared "What did I miss?"

Sheri stood. "I don't think he thought I would give him a second chance. He wanted to know why."

"And when you told him why?"

"Then he understood that I wasn't doing it just because I love you, but because I was given a second chance. I didn't expect him to give us his blessing."

Deandre held up a finger. "Hold up, go back. What did you say?"

"I said I was given a second chance."

He shook his head. "Nah, before that. That you weren't doing it because why?"

Sheri's heart jumped and her palms turned slick. She'd said she loved him. Just blurted it out as if they'd been saying it to each other for years. When she may have jumped the gun. She could brush over it. Take the words back or pretend as if she hadn't said them. But she wasn't the type of person to back down from what she said or lie.

"I said, I didn't just do it because I love you."

Deandre was across the room with his arms around her in two steps. His mouth covered hers and he kissed her as if he'd learned the secret to everlasting happiness and that secret was in her arms. Sheri didn't hesitate. Her arms wrapped around his neck, and she lifted to her toes, pressing her body against his as she kissed him just as desperately. When he broke off the kiss, their breathing was ragged.

"I love you so much," he said in a tight voice. "I missed you. I thought you wouldn't want to be with me after what happened. That's why I came here."

She pulled back and frowned. "You came here to break up with me?"

"No. I came here to convince you that somehow, we'll make this work. That I believed DJ had learned his lesson and, if you were willing, we could start over."

"How did you know DJ would be good with us?"

"He was floored when you dropped the charges. His grandparents got on him about how wrong he'd been when you'd been nothing but nice to him. He admitted he messed up. I didn't know he would come here."

"I'm glad he came. We needed to talk and air things out. I want to start over with you, too, but I gotta admit, knowing that DJ is okay makes this even better."

"Does that mean you agree? That we'll give this another shot? Even though I once arrested you and my son made a horrible decision that nearly ruined your life?"

Sheri considered everything. What she was agreeing to. To try and heal the rift between her and DJ. To try and make a relationship work with Deandre. To, maybe not be a step-mom right away, but be there for both Deandre and DJ as they figured everything out. All things she never thought she'd want to do. Things she wouldn't have considered if she hadn't met and fallen for the last guy on earth she ever thought she'd be with.

She met his eyes and said with her entire heart, "Yes.

Let's give this a shot and see if we've got enough love to make this work."

Deandre grinned and placed his forehead on her. "Lil Bit, we've got more than enough."

* * * * *

ABOUT LAST NIGHT

Chapter One

"What do you mean you're not coming?"

Joanne Wilson placed one hand on her hip while the other gripped the cell phone against her ear. She looked around at the multiple boxes filling what would be the lobby of her new beauty salon. A beauty salon she'd waited two decades to finally turn from previously failed dream into reality. The boxes contained the decorative tables and accent chairs she'd ordered online with the hope of giving the place a polished, sophisticated look. Stacks of framed prints by Black artists leaned against one wall waiting to be hung, along with the strings of lights she'd gotten to add just a small touch of whimsicality to the space. Her brother had agreed to meet her bright and early to help put together the furniture, hang the pictures and the lights. Now he was giving her some excuse about another job.

She wanted to scream. Or cry. Maybe both.

"Kalen, you know my grand-opening party is next Saturday before I officially open for clients on Tuesday. I need to get this stuff together today." Which meant she had a week to get the space cleaned up and ready before the party that weekend.

"I know, I know," he said, not sounding the least bit repentant about bailing on her.

"Then why are you on my phone telling me that you can't come?" She tried and failed to keep her voice even. Snapping at her younger brother typically got her the opposite of what her goal was, but today she didn't care about sweet-talking to get what she wanted. "I've got to help Mom with Bible study at her church tomorrow night and if we wait until Thursday or Friday there's a chance we won't get everything done before Saturday. I need all day Friday to finalize any last-minute details."

"Jo, chill, all right—I've got you." She could hear the smile in Kalen's voice. How dare he smile right now? This was serious.

"How do you have me? Because you just said you're driving to Augusta for a job. Is it money? Okay, I'll pay you to help me."

"It's not about the money. This is about my reputation. I promised to do this job but forgot to put it on my schedule." Kalen did home inspections for new home buyers and was constantly forgetting to add an inspection to his calendar, despite the hundreds of times Joanne reminded him to use an actual scheduler instead of sticky notes and napkins.

"So I've got to suffer? Seriously, Kalen, how could you leave me hanging like this?" she snapped, no longer caring about irritating him as panic twisted her stomach. She needed this grand opening to be perfect. She didn't want to wait until the last minute only to have something go wrong.

Joanne paced back and forth in the small area between the boxes and other decorations waiting to fill her space. The space she'd saved up for so she could finally afford a prime spot in the revitalized downtown commercial district of her hometown of Peachtree Cove, Georgia. The storefront in the refurbished building had been coveted by other business owners in the area, but Joanne had managed to snatch it up before anyone else, thanks to a client casually mentioning the property would be listed the next morning.

A few people around town doubted she'd be able to afford the rent, much less keep her business open. After giving birth to her son when she was eighteen, she'd spent years doing hair in her mother's kitchen. When she'd first tried opening her own salon at twenty-five, she'd had to quickly scale back to doing hair in her home. The same people she knew doubted her now had received invitations to her opening celebration on Saturday, but thanks to Kalen and his inability to use a calendar correctly, there might not be any furniture to sit on if she couldn't get everything assembled that day.

"If you'll let me talk, you'll understand I didn't leave you hanging. I got you some help."

Joanne rolled her eyes. She turned away from the boxes to look at the large pane windows that would provide a view of Main Street. Brown paper covered them from the inside to prevent people from looking in. The sign that read Joanne's Day Spa and Salon would be installed the next morning. She walked to the door, which wasn't covered, and looked out. Only a few people were downtown at 7:00 a.m. on a Saturday. The boutiques and restaurants that had returned to downtown as part of Peachtree Cove's revitalization effort wouldn't open for a few more hours. The streets would be bustling with activity then.

A dark burgundy pickup truck pulled into the space next to her small SUV. Joanne sucked in a breath. She recognized that truck.

"Who did you get to help me, Kalen?" she asked in a low voice.

The driver's-side door opened right as she asked the question. She spun away, hoping her hunch was wrong.

That maybe someone else with a similar pickup had parked next to her. That she wasn't about to come face-to-face with a temptation she had no business feeling.

"Devante should be there by now." Her brother dashed her hopes with one sentence spoken in a look-at-me-saving-the-day tone of voice.

"Why did you call Devante?" Joanne asked, trying not to reveal the wild emotions bouncing through her.

She spun back toward the door and looked out. Sure enough, the tall, dark-skinned man getting out of the truck was Devante Thompson. Instead of heading her way, he rummaged through the storage container in the bed of his truck.

"Because he's my boy and he's better than me at this stuff. We were out last night and when I realized I mixed up the dates, he offered to help you out. Why you acting all irritated? Devante is like family. I thought you'd be happier having him there than me."

Joanne suppressed a sigh. Of course, he would think that. Everyone would think that. Devante and her brother were best friends. They'd bonded over a mutual love of anime and comic books when they were in middle school and the bond had grown ever since. Devante had just been another kid in the house full of family and friends at every cookout, holiday and birthday party. He was like family.

Her problem was that in the last year or so, she'd had a hard time viewing him as her kid brother's homeboy and could only see him as the very handsome, very sexy man he'd grown to become. Had to be the post-forty hormone fluctuation. At least that was what she tried to tell herself.

"Nothing's wrong," she said to her brother. If she continued to panic, he'd get suspicious. Then she'd have to try and find an excuse to explain why she didn't want Devante's help. Something other than spending the day in her new salon with him was going to be difficult because his smile made her heart race and anytime they accidentally touched, her body went into a lay-me-down-and-make-sweet-love-to-me tailspin. She was not going to admit to that.

"As a matter of fact, he just pulled up," she said. "Go do your inspection and I'll talk with him."

"Good," he said, sounding relieved. "You're welcome."

"Mmm-hmm...thanks." She ended the call before he could complain about her lukewarm thanks.

She turned back to the door. Her eyes met Devante's. On cue, her stomach did a little clench. Full, thick lips creased up in a heart-stopping grin as he raised a big hand to wave. Joanne pressed one hand to her heart, which was currently doing backflips, and waved the other.

Down, girl! He probably sees you as a big sister. Or worse...an auntie. She fought not to cringe with the idea of that moniker and unlocked the door.

She forced her gaze not to linger on his broad shoulders, or the gray joggers clinging to his butt and thighs as he walked toward her. She didn't know when Devante had grown into his looks. She'd been so busy trying to get her son through college and saving enough to open her own salon, that one day she'd looked up and the scrawny kid who also liked building things was a successful contractor with half the women in town fawning over him. Some of whom had once rejected him.

She used to just wave a hand and laugh when ladies in the salon gossiped about how fine he was, or wondered whom he might be sleeping with, because like her brother he got around. Now she fought not to join in to get more information, and in the last few years, there had been a lot of information about the various women Devante was with.

He wasn't considered a playboy because there were never rumors of him treating anyone badly, but no one doubted he enjoyed the single life. Last she heard, he was fooling around with some woman named Mandy from the other side of town.

She pushed open the door as he neared. He stopped at the threshold and grinned down at her. "Hey, Jo, did Kalen tell you I was coming?"

She met dark, cocoa-brown eyes set in a chocolate-brown face. He didn't have facial hair, like many guys wore today, but the dark shadow of a beard and mustache on his chin and cheeks made her wonder if he hadn't shaved this morning. He was several inches taller than her, with a compact, muscled body that even the plainest of outfits, like he was wearing today, couldn't hide the strength beneath. Back when she'd had to babysit him and her brother, he'd been awkward and intelligent. That awkwardness had smoothed out into a comfortable sex appeal and the intelligence still lingered beneath his confident smile.

"Yeah… I just got off the phone with him. You sure you want to help me? I know you've got to be busy."

Devante lifted a shoulder. "For you? Of course. You know I'll do anything for you, Jo." He cocked his chin slightly with the words. His eyes narrowed slightly as he looked at her as if he really would do anything she asked.

Jo sucked in a breath and pressed a hand to her head. She fought the urge to tug on her microlocs in embarrassment. Oh, no, what she wouldn't—couldn't—do was spend today hearing innuendos in every damn word he said. Otherwise, this was going to be a long, frustrating day.

His smile deepened and he bit the corner of his lip. Joanne swallowed hard. Jesus be a fence! This young man was going to make her embarrass herself today.

Chapter Two

Devante tightened the last screw in a small, round accent table Joanne had taken out of one of the many boxes in her new salon. He liked putting things together, so helping her wasn't a problem and he'd finish up in no time. He completed the last turn just as she came back through the door carrying a tray with two cups of coffee and a bag.

"Breakfast is ready," she said. She smiled as she crossed the room to him.

Devante dropped the Allen wrench. It clattered against the underside of the table. Heat filled his cheeks, and he ran sweaty palms across his sweats. Damn, he was pitiful. It was as if he was still the teenager struck speechless whenever she walked into a room. He'd had a crush on Joanne since he was thirteen. A crush that had waned as he'd gotten older and accepted that she had absolutely no interest in him, but had never completely gone away.

Not crushing on Joanne was next to impossible. Not just because she was beautiful. Her caramel skin, thick hips and ass, bright smile and small, shoulder-length, blond locs typically got attention, but it was her never-give-up attitude encased in a giving heart that made him want to stick around for a while.

She put down the bag with the Books and Vibes logo on the side. Joanne slid out one of the cups of coffee. "Sumatra blend, black." She held out the coffee to him. "Here you go, young man."

Devante scowled as he took the coffee from her. In the last year she'd taken to calling him "young man." He didn't know why, and the words weren't really an insult, but every time they spilled from her lips his neck and shoulders tightened. He was thirty-five. Ten years younger than her. He wasn't that damn young.

She responded with a cute smile that made his insides twist, then she pulled out the second cup. "And a caramel latte for me. I'm so glad Patricia and Van opened the bookstore and coffee shop around the corner. It'll be nice having quality caffeine nearby."

"Yeah, they're cool. They've even got a small manga section. Peachtree Cove is really coming up."

"And my day spa is going to be a big part of that come up." Confidence filled her voice. Her eyes left his and looked over the table. "You're done with that already?"

Devante nodded. He set down the coffee, then flipped over the table. "Yep. I told you it wouldn't take long."

She had five chairs for her waiting area and four of the round accent tables. They only required attaching the legs and tightening a few screws to make it work. He'd hoped she'd have more stuff so he could extend his time with her.

"I was upset when Kalen bailed on me, but maybe sending you was a good idea. You've already got the tables and chairs put together." She took a tentative sip of her latte then licked her lips.

He licked his own in response, then looked away before she noticed his longing. He remained seated on the floor and bent one knee to rest his arm on. "All you needed was to add the legs to the chairs. It really wasn't that hard."

She sighed and sat in one of the chairs he'd just put together that had a dark blue plush seat with silver buttons along the arms and back. "I was so worried it would take a long time. When Kalen called, all I could think of was a terrible opening next Saturday."

"Terrible opening? Woman, don't you know everyone in Peachtree Cove is waiting for your grand-opening party? This space could be empty, and it would still be a hit."

He wasn't lying. Joanne had been doing hair in Peachtree Cove since high school. He remembered her styling her friends' hair in her parents' kitchen back when he'd be over playing video games with Kalen. Later, she'd done hair at her apartment and eventually in her own home, not missing a beat when she'd become a single mom at eighteen. Everybody in town knew Joanne was the best stylist in Peachtree Cove and only haters wouldn't be happy for her new success.

"Maybe so, but I want it to be perfect." The conviction in her voice mingled with doubt. "You know how many people in this town didn't think I would be able to do this after I failed the first time. They'll show up, too. I don't want to give anyone a reason to talk badly about my new shop."

"That first time was a learning experience. Owning a business is difficult and now you know what to expect. You're more prepared now."

"I wasn't at all prepared before. I really didn't have a clue about what I was doing. I just wanted to make money and get out of my mom's house."

He remembered the arguments she used to have with her mom about finding a stable job and doing more for her son. One day Joanne was there and the next day she'd moved out and was opening a business. When things hadn't worked out, her family expected her to move back in with her mom, but instead, she'd gotten a job, kept her place and styled hair on the side. Giving up wasn't in Joanne's vocabulary and it was one of the reasons why he admired her.

"I want everyone to see my place as *the* place to get your hair done in town," she said.

"You're already *the* place. Even in high school you had a list of people waiting for you to style their hair. That hasn't changed no matter where you set up shop."

She laughed and raised her brows. "You remember that?"

He grinned and leaned back against the wall. "Yeah, I remember. I used to watch you and be in awe at the way you would whip up those styles in no time. All you'd talk about is how you were going to have your own shop one day and how it would be the fanciest place this town ever saw."

She placed a hand to her cheek and shook her head. "Wow! I can't believe you remember the way I'd brag to anyone who'd listen. I was full of so many dreams."

"And, despite some bumps on the road, you made those dreams come true. You know, you are part of the reason why I became a contractor."

Her brows drew together. "Now you're messing with me."

"I'm serious."

"How in the world did me doing hair make you want to be a contractor?" She leaned against the armrest and smirked. Despite the skeptical look in her eyes, his body heated from the cute way her lips pursed with the movement.

He took another sip of the coffee. The burn of the liquid was a welcome distraction from the other burn growing in his midsection. "Everyone said I needed to go into gaming or computers or something just because I liked comic books and anime, but I always wanted to do stuff with my hands. I liked building things, taking stuff apart and putting it back together. You know my dad was a handyman… if you could catch him sober."

Joanne's smirk dissolved and compassion filled her face. Part of the reason he spent so much time at her place was because whenever his dad came home drunk, his mom yelled and fussed about him being no good and then turned that same anger on her kids. She'd dump her disappointment on them right before she'd storm out of the house to spend time with her married boyfriend. He and his sister, Tracey, took every opportunity to escape their house. Tracey escaped to hang out with her two best friends, Imani and Halle. Devante found the stability of Kalen's home as his place of solace. Kalen's family became his second family, and his friendship with Kalen was something he'd always appreciate.

Pushing aside the old memories, he continued, "When I helped him fix stuff, I enjoyed it. My mom didn't think there was any money in being a handyman. I didn't, either, until one day Dad brought me with him to help fix the cabinet at Ms. Baker's house. You remember Ms. Baker?" Joanne nodded and he continued. "Well, Dad wasn't sober that day and hadn't been the day before when he'd messed up her cabinet. When we got there, she'd hired a contractor. This white guy with the name Richards Contracting on the side of a fancy black truck. He was nice and all, but Dad was pissed about losing another job. I asked what a contractor was, and he said nothing but a fancy handyman."

Joanne cocked her head to the side. "It's a little more than that."

He chuckled. "I had that same look. I looked up his business, then learned about what contractors did, and made up my mind that I'd be a fancy handyman. Make real money fixing things and not be like my dad."

Confusion remained in her eyes. "That sounds like you were inspired by something other than me."

He leaned forward. "You probably don't remember, but one day when you were talking about your dream, I said I would own a fancy truck with Thompson Contracting on the side. You gave me a high five, and the biggest smile, before looking me in the eye and saying 'hell yes, you will.'"

She stared at him for several long seconds before blinking. "Really? I'd forgotten all about that," she said with a slight laugh. "I didn't know that inspired you. I meant what I said, but you were always so smart and determined. You kept Kalen in line half the time. When you started a business I just assumed it was because that's what you wanted to do."

He wasn't surprised she didn't know. He'd never told anyone how much Joanne's words affected him. Admitting that meant also admitting the reason why. His crush was obvious when he was younger, but most assumed it had gone away with time. Despite how Joanne might view her failures, he'd always considered her out of his league. Older, wiser and interested in men who seemed completely the opposite of him. He'd never believed he'd have a chance.

"I never forgot," he said. "I watched you never give up on your dream even after your first try didn't work out. That inspired me to never give up on mine."

She took another sip of her coffee. Her brows knitted as his words sunk in. "I mean… I never thought you, much less anyone, would look at me as any type of inspiration or role model."

"Why not?"

She shrugged before waving a hand. "I don't know." She stood and pointed at the pictures propped against the wall next to him. "Help me hang these."

He got up from the floor and stretched. "Nah, tell me. Why didn't you think you'd be considered a role model?"

He wasn't the only one who looked up to Joanne. Kalen was proud of her. He'd begged Devante to help because he didn't want his sister's grand opening to be ruined. Everyone Devante knew who got their hair styled by Joanne sang her praises. Not only did people love her styling abilities, but they also talked about feeling comfortable in her chair. She didn't judge, spread anyone's business to other clients, or give unsolicited advice. Her time with a client was about relaxation. After failing to open a successful salon, she'd joined the town's business guild and became an active member in the organization. Joanne was a part of the Peachtree Cove community. So many people in town liked and respected her.

"A lot of folks supported me before and I failed," she admitted. "After I had Julian, my family and some friends really thought I wouldn't be able to start my own business. That first shop was a way to prove them wrong. When I had to close down, everyone I cared about was supportive, but I remember the comments about all the things I should have done differently to make it work, or that I was trying to do too much and should focus on raising Julian. Then there were the few people who outright said they knew I wouldn't amount to much after having Julian."

"People brought that back up?"

She scoffed and cocked a brow. "You were a kid when I had Julian, so you don't remember the things people said."

He hated that she said it as if he'd been absolutely clueless about her situation. "Because of his father?"

She cleared her throat. "Mmm-hmm." She sipped from her cup and avoided his eyes.

"Well, despite being a kid, I remembered the way you

cried. He lied to you and then didn't treat you right. I never did like that guy."

Joanne's eyes widened. "Excuse me? You were too young to be judging who I dated."

He stared her dead in the eye. "I was right not to like him."

He remembered the guy. Flashy college student from Atlanta, in designer clothes and driving an expensive car. Joanne's family hadn't struggled as much as Devante's, but they'd struggled enough for her to also talk about wanting to one day meet and marry a rich man who could give her a fancy life. He remembered how much Joanne had liked that guy because his name brands and slick style had shown Devante just how far he was from being on Joanne's radar. So, yeah, a part of him had hated the guy just on principle, but he and her brother had thought he was shady.

Turns out they were right. He'd also gotten someone else pregnant while dating Jo. After Joanne got pregnant, they'd never seen him in Peachtree Cove again.

Joanne sighed and nodded. "You were right not to like him. The only good thing I got from him was Julian."

"And look how you raised him. He graduated, right?"

The smile that spread across her face was like sunshine on a Sunday morning. "Yes, he did. Dean's list and summa cum laude. He got a job with the engineering firm he had the internship with last year."

The pride in her voice rang clear and strong. The radiant smile on her face drew him to her side. Her eyes, a clear espresso-brown, sparkled with the joy of talking about her son.

"That's why people look up to you. Why I look up to you. You worked hard to get Julian through college and graduate school and to grow your business. You're awesome and you know it."

"Hell yes, I am." She snapped her finger and did a quick shimmy of her hips. "Sometimes I have to remind myself of that." She put her latte on one of the tables then flipped through the framed art. "Now, Momma plans to enjoy her life. Julian's settled and able to support himself. I'm ready to figure out how to start living again."

He froze. "What do you mean?"

"My life has been work and Julian. After my grand opening, I'll have achieved the work goal. Figuring out the personal goals...well, that's a little bit harder."

"What kind of personal goals?"

Devante's heart thumped heavily. This was what he'd wanted to confirm. A few weeks ago, Kalen mentioned Joanne wanted to start dating again. Devante had less than a tenth of a chance, but he damn sure was going to try. He was sure there'd be competition. She'd had no problem with boyfriends and admirers over the years. Her personality and charm was a natural draw. After she'd had Julian, she'd only openly dated a few people. He only knew that because of his friendship with Kalen.

"Just personal." Her smile was sly and secretive as she glanced at him out of the corner of her eye.

His heart pounded. No way in hell was she going to look at him like that and he wouldn't shoot his shot. "If you're looking for a man you shouldn't have any problem with that." His eyes dipped, traced over her ample curves, jumped back to her face. "Any man would jump at the chance."

Her lips parted as she sucked in a breath. In an instant, the comfortable, easy atmosphere between them shifted. An electric current that he'd felt plenty of times in her presence kicked to life. He was used to feeling this way around her only for her to look back at him with no hint of attraction or interest. This time was different. This time, her eyes widened ever so slightly. She quickly licked her lips and glanced away.

She lifted a hand and lightly pushed his shoulder. "Stop before you make an old woman feel good."

Devante took a step closer. Their bodies didn't touch, but the heat of her, tempting and reassuring, pressed against him. She smelled like coconut and lemongrass, a body butter mixture she'd used before. A smell that automatically sent his body on alert, made him want to pull her close, lose himself in her.

"I don't see an old woman." His voice came out lower than he'd planned.

She swallowed and stared down at the pictures, though her fingers were no longer flipping through them. "What do you see?"

The rasp in her voice was as tantalizing as the scratch of nails across his back, igniting a primal response in him he wasn't ready to control.

"I see," he said slowly and took a half step closer, as his chest brushed her arm and her body shivered, "a smart, capable and sexy woman."

For several agonizing seconds the only sound in the space was of her choppy breaths. Had he gone too far? Said too much? She'd only looked at him as her kid brother's friend. Hell, she'd once wiped his tears when he'd broken his arm on the swing set in their backyard. He never would have dreamed she'd feel a fraction of what he felt, but if she did, he damn sure wouldn't let the opportunity pass him by.

Slowly, she turned and faced him. Her eyes were lowered, and she ran her tongue over her bottom lip. Rejoicing that she hadn't scolded him, stepped away, or worse, broke out in laughter, he followed his instincts. He brushed a hand over her arm. Her skin was soft and smooth. He wanted to touch more.

His fingers trailed up her arm then back down. Her eyes raised to his and his heart slammed against his rib cage. Desire simmered in the depths of her gaze. He leaned in, ready to kiss her.

The door to the shop opened. "Hello!"

Devante and Joanne both jumped back. Disappointment rushed through him. He looked up and spotted Joanne's best friend, Kayce.

"Oh, my God, Jo, this place looks great!" Kayce exclaimed, oblivious to the scene she'd interrupted. "I knew you were working and decided to come over and help."

Joanne hurried over to her friend. "Great, I'm glad you came. Kalen couldn't make it, so Devante agreed to help out. Isn't he great? Such a nice young man." She glanced at him then looked away quickly.

Devante gritted his teeth as the words *young man* punched him in the jaw. The urge to cross the room, pull her into his arms and show her exactly what this *young man* could do made his feet twitch. Somehow, he managed to raise a hand and give Kayce a semblance of a smile. There was plenty of time for that later.

Joanne glanced at him, then away. She quickly went into details with Kayce about how she wanted the room set up.

That's all right, Jo, he thought as he tried to cool the adrenaline and desire pumping through his veins at a hundred beats per minute. *I've got your young man.*

Chapter Three

"Joanne, this place is amazing!"

Joanne grinned and accepted the hug from Octavia, one of Joanne's teammates on the recreational tennis team. She'd decided to join after one of her clients mentioned needing a new player for their beginners' team. Joanne needed exercise and a way to socialize with other adults, so she'd joined. Two years later and she now was a member of two teams.

Octavia and many of her other teammates had shown up for the grand-opening celebration, which, thanks to Devante's help, had arrived with everything in place. Tonight was about showing off her new space, giving information on the services that would be offered besides just hairstyling and thanking the clients and friends who'd supported her over the years. She wanted—needed—everything to be perfect. Tonight was her night to prove she belonged with the other respected members of Peachtree Cove's business owners.

"Thank you so much, Octavia," Joanne said after pulling back. "I'm glad you were able to make it out."

"I wouldn't miss it for the world." Octavia's broad smile revealed her dimples and her short, natural hair was cut so low to her scalp that if Joanne hadn't bleached it platinum-blond, people might've thought she'd shaved it all off.

"Nobody does hair like you and I'm so glad that you were finally able to open your own place."

"It's been a lifelong dream." That was the only response she had. She'd received so many congratulations in the first hour of the grand opening that she was overwhelmed with the outpouring of support for her second chance at being a business owner.

Someone called her name and Joanne turned to see Kayce waving her over. She nodded and turned back to Octavia. "Be sure to get a chair massage and sign up for the drawing for a free facial."

Octavia's eyes lit up. "I will."

Joanne urged her in the direction of the room where the masseuse was set up. Massages weren't going to be a staple at her salon, but for her grand opening she decided to offer free chair massages. Tonight was going to be a night people would remember as celebrating the opening of more than a traditional beauty salon. That's one of the reasons it had taken her so long to save up and finally get to this point. She'd hired colleagues she'd known from beauty school, a nail technician to offer manicures and pedicures and an esthetician for facials. There were also three other stylists in her salon. Each one was there tonight discussing their services and giving mini-tutorials on hair, skin and nail care. The sound of smooth jazz played over the speakers inserted in the ceiling and she'd gotten a local restaurant to cater the appetizers.

She'd worried things wouldn't go well, but it had all been for nothing. The grand opening was going much better than she'd planned and the people who'd come out to celebrate with her filled the space.

When she reached Kayce, she asked, "Is everything okay?"

Her best friend since high school was tall and wore six-inch heels that added to her height. Her braids were pulled back and a simple black wrap dress hugged her slim frame. "It is. I just wanted you to meet Jackson Cooper." Kayce indicated the man standing next to her. "He's rented the space next to yours and will be opening an art studio."

Kayce wiggled her brows as she looked at Joanne and she immediately understood the real reason she'd been summoned. Jackson was a handsome white guy who looked to be around the same age as Joanne. A dusting of white at his temples and glasses gave him the air of a sexy professor and his gray eyes were kind as they met hers.

"Hello, Jackson. I think I've seen you around. You've been renovating your space as well."

Jackson nodded. "I have. I hope you don't mind that I've joined your grand opening. When I heard about it, I was curious to see how you'd set up the place. That and I was hoping for a reason to introduce myself. Since we're neighbors."

Kayce grinned and bumped her elbow to Joanne's. Joanne smiled and tried not to bump her friend back. Kayce was on a mission to hook up Joanne with an eligible guy. She'd gotten married the year before and because she was blissfully wed, she wanted her best friend to join her.

For years, Joanne had given up hopes of joining the married squad. At one point she thought she was too set in her ways to change for any man. Now that her son was officially out of her pocket and she'd reached her professional goal, the spark of hope that maybe she'd also find someone to spend her life with had reignited.

The memory of Devante looking into her eyes filled her mind. *I see a smart, capable and sexy woman.* Those words in his rumbling voice made her suck in a breath. She pushed them aside for the hundredth time since that day. She reminded herself that Devante was supposedly dating a girl named Mandy. If he wasn't dating, then she was pretty sure he was sleeping with her. He was just being nice, not insinuating that he wanted anything to do with her romantically.

"Well, neighbor, I don't mind at all," she said, focusing on the man in front of her. "Just know I'll be coming to your grand opening as well."

Jackson leaned forward and winked. "You'll get a special invitation."

The back of Joanne's neck tingled a second before Devante's broad shoulders butted into the small space separating Joanne and Jackson. "Special invitation to what?"

Joanne's face heated as Devante stared down at her. She didn't know why she felt guilty—she hadn't done anything, and Devante wasn't her man. She had to be projecting again. One compliment when he'd helped her with the furniture had her spending too much time dissecting every word, facial expression and nuance since that day. She was overreacting, and he had not been seriously flirting. The fact that a few words from Devante had her fantasizing about a guy who was not thinking of her in that way proved she needed to start dating again and quick.

She pushed aside the feelings of guilt. "Devante, this is Jackson. He's opening the art gallery in the space next to me. We were talking about his grand opening. Jackson, this is Devante. This young man is my little brother's best friend."

She added the "young man" and "little brother" after she noticed the curiosity in Jackson's eyes as he'd looked between her and Devante. As much as her body may react to Devante, it didn't mean she would ruin the possibility of starting something with a nice guy. Jackson was new in town, but the rumor mill had already supplied that he was a nice, single and not screwing around with the women in town.

Jackson's eyes lit up. "Ah, nice to meet you, Devante. I saw you helping the other day." He held out his hand.

Devante took his hand. "Jo knows I'm willing to help her. Anytime and with anything she needs." He stared back at Jackson.

Jackson's smile wavered and he pulled back on his hand. Devante let him go and Jackson flexed his fingers. "Umm… good to know. I guess you would look out for a friend of the family."

Joanne nodded. "He does. He's like a part of the family. My son looks up to him almost as if he's another uncle."

Devante narrowed his eyes at her. "He doesn't view me as an uncle."

She tried to laugh but Devante's frown made her feel awkward. She looked from Devante back to Jackson. "Yes, he does. I always tell him that he should model himself to be like Kalen. You both are young men who serve as good role models."

Devante's nostrils flared. He rubbed the back of his neck. "Oh, really."

His jaw and shoulders were tense and there was a glint in his eye. He couldn't possibly be mad? She'd complimented him. "Really. You are a very nice young man."

"Can I talk to you somewhere for a second," he said quickly.

Joanne blinked. She looked at Kayce, who appeared just as confused as she felt. "Sure."

"In private," he said.

Nodding, she pointed to the storage room in the back. "We can go over there."

"Aight, let's go." He put his hand on her elbow and led her toward the storage area.

Joanne smiled and nodded at the patrons as Devante pushed through the crowd. She had no idea why he seemed angry, but whatever the reason was, it didn't give him the right to be rude to her guests. She frowned after they were in the storage room. "What is wrong with you?"

He let her go and placed his hands on his waist. "What's wrong with you?"

Joanne's head snapped back. Oh, he was angry. Her own frustration jumped up in response. She'd done nothing wrong. He was acting foolish. "What are you talking about?"

"This *young-man* mess. Why do you keep calling me that?"

Joanne blinked, surprised and embarrassed that he'd called her out. "Because you are a young man… I mean… what do you want me to call you?"

"You say it like I'm some kid. I'm not a kid, Jo."

"Nobody said you were a kid. I didn't mean anything by it."

"I think you do mean something." He took a step closer. "I think you're trying to make it seem like I'm too young."

"Too young for what?" Damn, she sounded breathless. She tried to focus on slowing her breathing, but he stood too close. His cologne was too intoxicating. The fire in his eyes too intense.

"Too young for you. I'm not a young man. I'm a grown man. A grown man who wants to be your man."

Joanne's jaw dropped. Her heart stuttered before beating frantically. She tried to come up with words. To formulate an appropriate response, but she had nothing. She'd never really prepared to have a fantasy come to life. Unease crept up her spine. Fantasies too often turned into heartbreak.

Devante closed the distance between them and cupped the back of her neck. Joanne leaned into him, stunned but automatically reacting to his embrace. "If you'll let me." Seconds ticked by like hours as he lowered his head and brushed his lips across hers. "Will you let me be your man, Jo?"

Chapter Four

She couldn't believe he kissed her. The brush of his lips over hers and the whispered "Will you let me be your man, Jo?" was so surreal she wondered if she was daydreaming. This wouldn't be the first time she'd pictured Devante's lips on her, his hands pulling her tight against his body or his arms embracing her. This wasn't a daydream, this was very real.

The heat of his body ignited her desire. The feel of his lips, soft but confident, turned her thoughts into bubbles. This was no dream. The first brush of his lips gave way to a full-on press of his mouth against hers. Shock held her still momentarily. Desire shoved shock out of the way. Before she could overthink what was happening, and why, her hands clutched his wide shoulders and her lips parted.

Devante kissed her deeply. His tongue slipped past her lips and boldly explored her mouth. There was no hesitancy, no timidness, no testing the waters. He kissed her as if he was her man, and he finally had her in his arms after a long separation. The last time she'd been held like this, kissed this thoroughly, was longer ago than she cared to remember. The passage of time didn't matter, because her body responded as if she always belonged in Devante's embrace.

His strong hands roamed over her back, down to her ass,

which he palmed and kneaded. He squeezed her curves and tugged her forward until the hard press of his growing erection dug into her lower abdomen. A delicious shiver went through her body. Her mind filled with images of everything she'd ever imagined him doing to her. She wanted him to back her against the wall, craved for him to tug up her shirt, to kiss and caress her all over, jerk up her skirt, rip off her panties and touch her there.

The mental playlist shot fire through her veins. She squirmed against him, wanting more but knowing just kissing him wouldn't put out this fire. He gripped a handful of her skirt in his hands and pulled it up until the hem brushed the top of her thighs. In the back of her mind, she remembered they were in the storage room. That multiple people had watched them enter together, and that if Devante did all the things running through her mind, everyone out there would know because she wouldn't be able to suppress any cries of ecstasy. She started to pull back, but his hand slid under her hemline and the heat of his palm against her thigh seared away all worries about being caught in a compromising position.

"Devante," she breathed out shakily when he quickly broke the kiss.

"Damn, I love the way you say my name." His low voice rumbled through her body. He kissed her again.

"We should..." His fingers dug into the tender flesh of her behind and her voice trailed off.

"Should what?" he murmured against her mouth.

His voice, so daring and delicious. Why in the world would she break this magical spell? "Keep going." She lifted her chin and kissed him deeper.

He took a step forward and she moved with him. They didn't break the kiss as he guided her farther into the storage room. With ease, he lifted then sat her down on top of the plastic storage bins stacked against the wall. Her legs spread and his hips fit right in the junction of her thighs. His hands gripped her thighs before easing up her skirt until the tips of his fingers traced the seam of her panties. Joanne's soft moan echoed with his in the small space.

"Joanne?" The question in his gruff voice was one she didn't hesitate to answer.

"Keep going." No part of her wanted to stop now. Now when they were so close, and she'd fantasized about this for so long.

Devante quickly pulled aside her panties and touched her. The soft brush across her sex sent waves of pleasure through her body.

She felt his lips rise with a smile. "You're wet for me."

The fire in her veins combusted into a full-body inferno as his fingers dipped into her folds. Her head fell back, but he cupped the back of her head and pulled her forward, their lips and tongues once again coming together in a wave of passion. His other hand glided across her sex casually, back and forth in a rhythm that had her hips gyrating and pressing forward for more.

The door to the storage room flew open. "I'll get more from back here. Oh, my God!"

Joanne pushed against Devante's chest. He jerked back. They both looked over his shoulder into the shocked eyes of Robin, the nail technician. Behind her stood Octavia. Behind Octavia stood Kayce, and behind Kayce, every other guest in the party stared at the open doors of the storage room to see the cause of the exclamation.

Kayce moved first. She hurried forward, jerked back Octavia and the other guest, then threw Joanne a what-the-hell look and slammed the door shut.

* * *

"What the hell were you thinking? And with Devante, of all people? You ain't got no business fooling around with that boy!"

Joanne leaned against the counter in her mom's kitchen and pinched the bridge of her nose. She shouldn't have come over here. She should have stayed home, in bed, hiding from the embarrassment of getting caught with Devante's hand up her skirt by practically everyone in town. But, no, she had to be a "good daughter" and come over when her mom said she needed Joanne to take her to the pharmacy because her car was in the shop and none of her other kids could make it.

Joanne had hoped word hadn't gotten back to her mom yet. Had almost believed she'd been lucky when they'd gotten through Joanne's arrival and the trip to the pharmacy with no mention of what happened. She should have known her mom would blindside her and bring it up as soon as Joanne's guard was down. Right as Joanne was heading to the door and trying to escape to the safety of her home.

She dropped her hand from her face and looked at her mom. Doris Wilson was an older version of Joanne. Her golden-brown skin was now lined with age and her short, styled hair was fully gray. Her mom had never been short of opinions. Opinions she loved to share whether her kids wanted to hear it or not.

"Momma, I'm not fooling around with Devante and he's a man, not a boy." She didn't even ask how word had gotten back to her mom. There were very few secrets in Peachtree Cove. Not to mention everyone loved to mind other people's business.

Doris crossed her arms and legs from where she sat at the table, watching Joanne. Her brows drawn together. A mask of frustration on her face. Joanne was used to that look of frustration. She'd received that same look when she'd come home from work only to find Joanne styling someone's hair at her kitchen table. Then again, when Joanne said she was keeping the baby after the guy she thought loved her said he didn't want anything to do with either of them. And the look resurfaced later when Joanne had announced she was moving out and starting her own business because she wouldn't raise Julian under her mom's thumb. Almost every move Joanne made resulted in frustration from her mom.

"What do you call it then? Is it true you two were doing it in the storage room?"

"No! We weren't doing anything. He kissed me. That's all." At least, that was all she was going to admit to with her mom.

"Why are you *kissing* that boy?" Doris said *kissing* as if kissing was just as bad as being caught *doing it*. "He's way too young for you."

"He's thirty-five, Momma. Please stop calling him a boy," Joanne said, exasperated.

"He's the same age as Kalen, who will always be my baby, which makes him a baby to me. I thought you got all that foolishness out of your system. First you come home pregnant by that stuck-up college boy and then a few years ago you go and date that married guy, and now this."

Her mom never called Julian's father by his real name. He was always "that stuck-up college boy." Joanne agreed— Orlando had been stuck-up. Her impressionable heart had viewed his personality as sophisticated at the time. She'd realized just how wrong she'd been after he told her to get rid of the baby. That he was having a baby with someone else, a law student who would be accustomed to the lifestyle he planned to live. He never said the words "you aren't good enough" but his actions more than implied his true feelings.

Believing Orlando loved her had been all her mistake. The lies told to her by the men she'd dated after him, however, were not her fault. She'd learned to forgive herself for the mistakes she made in the past. She'd entered each relationship with honesty and an open heart. Which is why she wouldn't stand here and let her mother make her feel bad, or accuse her of being the deceptive one in those relationships.

"I came home pregnant over twenty-five years ago," she said. "And you know Douglas was not married but lied to me about being engaged. Why you gotta bring up those situations now?"

Doris looked at Joanne as if her question was out of line. "Because apparently I need to remind you how the last time you were acting fast you derailed your life. Here you are, opening your own business again and finally getting your life together, and now you want to throw it all away messing with some young man. And not just any young man, but Devante Thompson, of all people?"

Joanne's shoulders tensed. "How am I throwing anything away? And what's wrong with Devante? You like him."

Her mom threw up a hand and shrugged. "Devante's nice and all, but you don't need to be messing around with someone who can't lift you up. He's too young and you know he's still out there acting wild. Just like his mom. Always out in the street. You know he was screwing Gwendolyn's granddaughter, Mandy, just last month. Now he's trying to add you as a notch on his bedpost."

"I'm not a notch," she said with conviction. In her heart, she wavered. She'd known about the rumors surrounding Devante and Mandy. Rumors she'd completely forgotten about the moment he kissed her. Was she really just lining up to be another name in a string of names of people he'd slept with? That had been the main reason why she'd talked herself out of ever acting on the attraction she'd developed for Devante. He was single and was obviously enjoying being single. She, on the other hand, wanted to be special to someone. She hadn't been special to Julian's father. Hadn't been worth commitment from the men she'd dated after. She'd always refused to settle for anything less in a relationship and she wouldn't start now.

"You don't have the best track record with men," her mom said, as if she could read the direction of Joanne's thoughts. "Devante's been drooling over you since he was a boy. Now he's getting to live out a fantasy. Don't go messing up your life because some young man got you thinking you can play a cougar. You ain't built for that."

"I'm not playing cougar. Ten years isn't that big of an age difference. Daddy was eight years older than you."

Her mom grunted before waving a hand. "Then are you playing dumb? Because you ruined your grand-opening celebration following behind that boy. You ought to know better than that, Jo. I helped you out as much as I could when you got pregnant with Julian. I let you live here and do hair out of my kitchen. I helped you out when the first store didn't work out because I understood you were trying to do better. I'm old now. If your business tanks because of this thing I can't help you out of this hole. Find you a nice man. I don't care if he's your age, older or younger, but he needs to be about the same things you're about. Quit being stupid behind some guy. You know better than that."

Her mother's phone rang before Joanne could reply. She didn't need to hear any more. As much as she hated the lecture, she also couldn't deny the truth and good intentions behind her mom's words. Joanne was a romantic. Had believed in love and happily-ever-afters and that the sweet words men whispered during lovemaking were true. She'd learned the hard way they weren't. She'd been tossed aside enough when she was younger to finally stop dating and focus on raising her son and saving to open a salon ten times better than the one she first tried. Now that she was ready to start dating again, was she just falling into the same habits that had hurt her in the past?

Despite years of being a stylist and having a business, she never felt she belonged in the circles of other business owners working to make Peachtree Cove thrive again. She'd struggled to make a dream that seemed as reachable as the moon a reality. It had taken this long to get her life on track. Her grand opening had been a success until that embarrassing moment. She wasn't sure if clients would show up on Tuesday and, if they did, she'd lost any respect or semblance of class she'd wanted her place to have the second she'd followed Devante into that storage room. She had to think carefully about what she was doing before she let Devante, and the possibility of being a fantasy notch on his bedpost, upset and ruin everything she'd worked for.

Chapter Five

"Yo, man, my sister?"

Devante froze in the middle of adding a twenty-five-pound weight to the bar on the weight bench in his garage. Suppressing a sigh, he turned and faced his friend. Kalen stood at the garage's entrance. He was a few inches shorter than Devante with a low-cut fade and an athletic build that came from continuing to play recreational flag football. He stood with his legs spread, and hands planted firmly on his hips. Disbelief filled his dark eyes as he stared at Devante like a stranger. Devante slid the twenty-five-pound weight on the bar before facing what he'd known was coming.

"It's not what you think," Devante said.

Kalen raised his brows. "Then you better get to talking because what I'm thinking is not what I want for my sister."

The words stopped Devante in his tracks. He could understand Kalen being surprised even though he knew about Devante's crush on Joanne. He hadn't expected his friend to take Devante being in a relationship with Joanne as something he wouldn't want for his sister.

Devante pressed a hand to his chest. "Come on, Kalen, you know me. I wouldn't treat your sister wrong."

Kalen wagged a finger at Devante. "You say that, but I also don't know what's going on in your head. You aren't looking for anything serious. Jo may talk a lot of junk about being ready to be out there and start dating again, but she's not looking for one-night stands and hookups. She's not like that despite what people say about her after that mess with Douglas Stone."

"You think I listen to what people say about her?" Devante replied, annoyed. "I know Jo better than that. I know what she's really looking for."

Devante knew about the rumors, but that situation with Douglas lying about being engaged was over two years ago. He knew better than most that rumors were spread by simpleminded people who only found happiness in spreading the misery of others. His family had been the source of much of the gossip and rumors in town back when his parents were still together. Kalen was the very one who'd talked him down whenever he'd wanted to blow up and get into a fight after someone called his mom a whore, his dad a drunk, or claimed he and his sister, Tracey, would be just like them. Kalen, more than anyone, should know Devante didn't judge people based on the town gossips.

"After the way people talked about me and my family, you actually think I believe what people say about her?"

Some of the fight in Kalen's eyes evaporated. He ran a hand over his face. "But what are you looking for? 'Cause if it's just another hookup I can't be cool with that. Not for Jo. She's been through a lot and worked hard to get where she is. I don't want you messing around or playing around with her just as she's finally getting what she wants."

He wished he could fault Kalen for thinking Devante would only want to sleep with his sister. He hadn't been interested in much more than hookups and superficial dating. He'd been more focused on building his contracting company than settling down. But to think he'd play around with Joanne, his best friend's sister and someone he'd not only liked for years, but also respected, made him want to defend himself.

"Playing around...really, Kalen? You think I would do that to your sister? Forget you kicking my ass, I know she wouldn't stand for it."

Kalen cocked his head to the side. "So you're not fucking Mandy right now?"

Leave it to Kalen to be blunt. "I'm not. I cut things off with Mandy the day you told me Jo was ready to date again and asked you to hook her up."

He and Mandy had been hooking up, but neither had been interested in making the move to turn their fling into a full-fledged relationship. He always held out on getting serious. The moment Kalen said his sister wanted to start dating again he'd immediately known that he hadn't held out on relationships because he wanted to grow his business. A part of him had always been waiting for a chance with Jo.

Kalen narrowed his eyes. "For real?"

Devante raised a brow. "Have you seen me with anyone since that day? Have I mentioned Mandy or anyone else since then?" When Kalen frowned and his gaze drifted away, Devante waited.

Kalen's eyes focused back on him with a look of shock. He waved a hand. "Hold up, hold up, hold up...is that really why you broke things off with Mandy?"

Devante nodded. "Pretty much."

"Wait...you're for real?" This time only shock coated Kalen's voice. No hints of disapproval or an underlying threat of bodily harm to anyone who dared to break his sister's heart.

"Yes. I'm for real. I want to be with Jo. You know I like her."

Kalen came farther into the garage. "I know you've crushed on her since we were teens, but… I mean I never thought you were holding on to it this long. Or that you were serious."

"Well, I did and I am."

"You know people are gonna talk if ya'll hook up. They're going to think that you're just playing around with her."

Devante shrugged. He didn't give a damn about what anyone would have to say. He doubted anyone would doubt the reasons why he was interested in her. More people respected and appreciated her in the community than didn't. He, on the other hand, still walked in the shadow of his family being social pariahs in their town. More people would probably talk about Joanne lowering her standards to date him. Despite the small group of people who might hate on anything he started with Joanne, all that mattered was what she thought.

"It took this long for her to finally see me as a real option. I don't care what other people say—as long as she's okay with this then I'm okay."

He meant that. Joanne never cared about his screwed-up family dynamics. She always judged him for himself. Her willingness to give them a try was all that mattered.

"Oh, really?"

"Really. I'm going to marry your sister." He knew the words as surely as he knew he could bench the two hundred and fifty pounds on his weight bench. Joanne was the woman he wanted to spend the rest of his life with. If she would have him.

Kalen leaned back and grinned. "Oh, it's like that?"

"Yes. It's been like that. I was just waiting on my time."

Kalen studied him for several long seconds before grinning and holding out his hand. Devante slapped hands with his friend and didn't resist when Kalen pulled him in for a hug.

"You trying to be my brother for real, huh," Kalen said with a half grin.

"God willing and the creek don't rise," Devante said, grinning back. That's one of the things he appreciated about Kalen. When he was convinced, he was all in. His best friend readily accepting him as his brother spread warmth through his chest.

"Then as my potential brother, let me give you some advice," Kalen said, looking serious again.

"What advice?"

"Joanne wants her new salon to be successful. She planned for the grand opening forever and what happened? You two are caught in her storage room. Now people are talking, and my mom is going to give her a hard time about ruining her life over a man again. I don't know why you decided to finally make a play for her at the party, but that's also going to make people talk about her and her business."

Devante stepped back. Guilt twisted his insides. He'd overheard Kayce mention introducing Joanne to that guy Jackson and he'd felt his chance at being with her slipping away with each passing second. He hadn't thought about ruining her big night, but in the end he had.

Devante pinched the bridge of his nose. "Shit. I ruined everything."

Kalen put a hand on Devante's shoulder. "I wouldn't say you ruined everything. Joanne's too good at her job and people like her too much for me to say her business is ruined. This is me throwing you a lifeline. Jo's also looking for someone who can support her as she grows her dream. The next time you want to show her how you feel…maybe don't do it at her shop."

Devante sighed and nodded. "I'll apologize to Jo."

Kalen chuckled and shook his head. "You don't have to look so dejected. I just had to say something."

"I understand. Believe me when I say this, I only want what's best for her. I'll do better the next time."

"I can't believe you waited this long to make a move, but if you're serious and you really want to make my sister happy then I'm all for it. She deserves to be happy."

"She does, and if she believes me when I say I only want to make her happy, being with her will have been worth waiting for."

After leaving her mom's house, Joanne settled on the couch in her bathrobe for an afternoon of watching Lifetime. There had to be someone whose day was going worse than hers, even if it was a fictional character. Her mother's warnings stuck to her like glue. Even though she wanted to reach out to Devante and ask what their moment in her storage room meant, she also wasn't going to be clingy with a guy she wasn't dating. She didn't know if he was still seeing Mandy or anyone else. He could've just kissed her because she'd called him young man and he wanted to prove a point.

He didn't have to kiss you to prove that particular point. Her hopeful thoughts cut through the doubt. She wanted to cling to that, but hopeful thoughts had led her astray in the past.

Julian called her halfway through a movie about a woman discovering her landlord was a serial killer. Definitely a worse day than hers. Joanne happily accepted his call. She listened as Julian updated her on his new job and how he was getting acclimated to living in his new apartment.

"Let me know if you need anything," she said. "I'll be sure to send it to you."

Julian groaned then laughed. "Mom, seriously, you don't have to send me anything. I'm making good money now and it's my time to help you out."

"You don't have to help me with anything. I've got me. I just need to make sure my baby is doing well and is comfortable."

Even though she'd counted down the days until he graduated high school, then college and finally graduate school, she still missed having her only child close by. Now that he was truly out of the nest and living life as a responsible adult, she still wanted to take care of him in some way. To know that despite him being a grown man, a part of him still needed her. Maybe this was what most empty nesters felt.

"I'm doing well. You did a good job with me." Pride filled his voice, and she could imagine his handsome face smiling the same way he used to whenever he brought home a good grade on a test in elementary school. "I hope to be settled enough to have you come and stay with me this summer."

"I'd love to come visit you. Just say when and I'll buy the ticket."

"I'll buy your ticket." She didn't have to see him to know he was shaking his head. She didn't care. After sacrificing so much for him for the last twenty-five years she was also having a hard time imagining him being able to take care of her.

"We'll see when you're settled," she offered as a truce.

"Good." There was a brief pause before he spoke again. This time his voice hesitant. "So, Mom... I've got a question."

"What is it, baby?" Joanne asked, distracted by the

woman on screen fighting off her serial-killer landlord with a baseball bat. She'd have to remember to buy a bat to put beside her front door.

"Um...you and Devante."

All thoughts of bats and the TV movie flew out of her head with those simple words. She knew the Peachtree Cove gossip mill was fast, but not fast enough to reach Julian in Chicago in less than twenty-four hours. He did keep up with his high-school friends, some of whom had returned to town after college and would have heard what happened. Which meant she was even a hot topic with Peachtree Cove's young crowd. Julian kept talking before she could reply.

"I mean, I don't typically get in your business, but when one of my old friends called and said you and Devante were...you know. Well, I decided to check for myself."

She'd hoped word about what had happened wouldn't have ever gotten to Julian. She should have known better than to underestimate the Peachtree Cove gossips.

Her immediate urge was to tell Julian to mind his business. She didn't talk about her dating life with her son, but she also didn't want lies or exaggerations about what happened to reach him and make him worry. "What did you hear?"

"Just that you two were kissing at your grand opening. Is it true? Are you and he...?"

She looked skyward and pressed a hand to her temple. Thank goodness, he'd only heard they were kissing. If he'd heard more, she doubted he'd tell her, and she wasn't about to push to hear any additional details he may have gotten.

"Do you have a problem with Devante?" She cared about that more than him hearing the gossip. Did he disapprove just like her mom? She had no clue what was going on with her and Devante, or if it would amount to anything, but whatever happened she didn't want Julian to worry about her.

"Nah, in fact, I'm not really surprised. I've always known he had a crush on you. I just never thought you'd go for him."

"You knew he had a crush on me?"

"Yeah, me and Uncle Kalen tease him about it sometimes."

"Say what?" she said louder than she'd intended.

Julian laughed. "We tease him about it. I thought you knew he had a crush on you?"

She'd known he'd had a crush when he was a teenager, because Kalen would sometimes tease him in front of her. She'd thought it was cute and hadn't given it much thought. Her life was on another path with working and raising Julian. As she'd gotten older, she'd hadn't considered Devante as anything other than Kalen's friend until the last year or so, when her body and brain registered an attraction for him.

"And you're okay if I date him?"

"I am. I like Devante. He's got his own business and I think he's a good guy. Besides, I don't want you to be lonely."

"Who says I'm lonely," she said defensively.

"I didn't say you were lonely. I'm saying I don't want you to *get* lonely. I worry about you, Mom. I know you did a lot for me while I was growing up. I appreciate all that you did, and I want you to finally find someone who can do that for you. Be happy. You deserve it."

The doorbell rang and Joanne got up from the couch. "You don't think he's not right for me?"

"Ma, Devante would do anything for you. I can't believe you didn't realize he's been crushing on you this long," Julian said, as if Devante's feelings had been stitched across his forehead for years.

Joanne shook her head as she walked to the front door. Maybe they had been and she'd been too oblivious to notice. Her track record with men hadn't allowed her to think of Devante's actions as anything but him being nice. "He's ten years younger than me."

"As if that matters. You're forty-five. That's not that old," he replied.

"Who said forty-five is any kind of old?"

"That's not what I meant. I'm messing this up. What I'm trying to say is you're still good-looking and I've got friends from college who thought you were fine. I'm not surprised that guys your age and younger are interested. So go for who you like."

"You never stop finding ways to make your momma feel special," she said. She looked out the window next to her front door and gulped in air. "Devante!"

"What?" Julian asked. "Are you saying that you like him, too?"

"No, he's at the door. Um… I've got to call you back."

"Good luck!" he said with a laugh.

Joanne ended the call then quickly unlocked the door. After she opened the door, she remembered she was in her lounging-at-home attire: a fluffy bathrobe with nothing but a tank top and underwear underneath and a satin bonnet over her locs. Changing wasn't an option since she'd been too shocked to think before answering.

"Devante? Why are you here?"

She tried to sound casual despite her heart impersonating a jackrabbit in her chest. He would show up looking absolutely divine in a long-sleeved, dark T-shirt and gray sweats that paid homage to every line and curve of his strong body.

How was she supposed to behave and think rationally when she wanted to toss off her robe and let him prop her up on a table and pick up where they'd left off the night before?

"We need to talk," he said. "Can I come in?"

She stepped back and waved him in. "Sure."

He crossed the threshold and followed her from the foyer to the living area. The sound of gunshots followed by a man's scream came from the television. Guessing the woman in the movie finally eliminated her landlord, Joanne picked up the remote and muted the television.

"About last night," Devante said.

She met his gaze. "Did you mean what you said?"

His brows drew together. "What I said?"

"When you asked if you could be my man. Did you mean it?"

The confusion on his face cleared up. He took two steps toward her. His face was serious as he stared into her eyes. "I meant it."

"But what does that mean? What's your definition of being my man? Does that mean you want to sleep with me for a little bit? That you want to date exclusively? That you want to date me and other people like Mandy? I need to know because I'm not making assumptions only to end up hurt later."

Maybe tossing out all these questions up front was too much, but she didn't have the patience or the energy for a wait-and-see situation. She needed to know where they stood. She needed to know if she was heading toward a mistake or if this was a chance she needed to take.

"It means I want to date you. Exclusively you. Mandy and I are through. It also means I want to be there to support you. That I laugh with you on good days and hold you on bad days. That I stand next to you as you continue to grow and become even more amazing. That I can take care of you without smothering you. That I hold you in my arms and make love to you. That's what I mean when I say I want to be your man." He stepped close enough for the smell of his cologne to swirl around her. "Is that okay with you?"

Chapter Six

Devante held his breath as he watched Joanne. A multitude of emotions skittered across her face. He'd surprised her, that was clear by the widening of her eyes as he spoke. Skepticism made her lips purse and one brow raise. Then there was the wary hope in her expression. A hesitancy in her gaze that spoke to the previous hurts that pushed her to question if he meant what he said. He hated the hesitancy. Not because he wanted her immediate answer. He hated it because lies from others caused her to doubt his word. All he wanted to do was prove to her that she could put her trust in him.

"I'm okay with that," she finally said in a soft, but firm, voice.

Devante exhaled and grinned. The relief that hit him was so satisfying and exhilarating that he couldn't stop himself from placing a hand on her hip and pulling her forward until the soft material of her robe rested against his chest.

He wondered what was beneath the robe, then tried to push aside the thought. He hadn't come over here for sex. He'd come to clear the air. To let her know how he felt, but when she put her hands on his shoulders and leaned into him, not thinking about what was beneath the robe was nearly impossible.

"Are you sure?" he asked.

She cocked her head to the side "Are you sure?"

"You're still asking after everything I just said?" Couldn't she see how much he wanted her?

Her eyes were serious as they stared back into his. "History has taught me to check and double-check. I don't want to be surprised later because I didn't ask."

He gently tugged her hips. "Jo, can you remember one thing for me?"

"What?"

"I'm not like those other brothas."

He lowered his head and kissed her. She gasped and for a half a second, he worried she'd pull back. That maybe she wanted to talk more instead of kiss, but a moment later her body relaxed, and she softened into his embrace. Devante didn't need any other encouragement. His tongue slipped between her sweet lips and deepened the kiss.

Joanne let out the softest of whimpers and his heart rate jumped up a thousandfold. His hand moved from her hip to grip the fullness of her ass. He squeezed and pressed her forward. She was so soft, but the thick material of her robe was in the way. He jerked the loose knot free and pushed back the sides of the robe. His hands slid beneath the material to the warmth beneath, where his fingertips brushed over soft curves. His hand explored, only encountering a thin shirt and underwear blocking his fingers from her naked body. His breathing stuttered as desire swelled within him.

"Where are your clothes, Jo?" he said in a low, gruff voice as he brushed his lips over her cheeks.

"Do I need clothes for what we're doing?" Her snarky reply set his body on fire.

"No, the hell we don't."

Need drove him and he pushed his hands beneath her

shirt and cupped the heavy weight of her breasts. Her nipples were so damn hard his mouth watered the second his fingers brushed over them. He wanted to taste them, roll them over his tongue and pull them deep into his mouth, hear every damn moan and catch of her breath as he sucked to his heart's content.

Devante's entire body shook. If he didn't calm down, he'd barely make it to the bedroom. All his fantasies of having Joanne in his arms were coming true and they were better than he imagined. Her softness, her scent and her sighs all invaded his senses and would be forever imprinted into his memory. He didn't know how to process or handle all the feelings bouncing through him.

He shoved the robe off her shoulders. It pooled in a heap at her feet. Joanne's hands jerked on the edge of his shirt. He stepped back long enough to pull it over his head and toss it to the side. Her eyes widened appreciatively as she took in his bare chest. They both rushed forward, and their mouths met in an urgent, hungry kiss.

He didn't know how they got to the bedroom without breaking something. Their lips barely left each other. Their clothes created a messy trail behind them. Their hands explored every inch of skin exposed to the other.

When they finally made their way to her queen-size bed, they were both naked except for his socks and the bonnet on Joanne's head. She sat on the edge of the bed, legs spread, and more tempting than anything he'd ever experienced in life. Devante stood between her legs. He leaned forward and kissed her. His hands gripped the soft skin of her thighs. Joanne gasped and her hips pushed forward. He ran his hands to where her hips and thighs met. Pushing her legs wider, he brushed his thumbs over the damp curls covering her sex. She was so soft and warm that he worried he'd lose control in that moment.

Joanne stared at him between lowered lids. "What's that smile for?"

Devante's grin grew hearing the desire thick in her voice. He ran his fingers over her sweet heat. "Because I can't wait to feel you against my tongue."

Joanne thought her body would erupt in flames after Devante's words. She was so close to the edge. No one had touched her like this in so long she was afraid she'd shatter just from imagining his tongue against her most sensitive spot. She didn't want to shatter. She wanted to savor.

Her hand wrapped around the hard length of his erection. Devante shuddered and when he straightened, she didn't hesitate to take him deep into her mouth.

He gasped. "Jo…damn, Jo."

The way he said her name, his tone reverent and throaty, sent a thrill down her spine. She relished in every tremble of his body. The way he snatched the bonnet off her head to bury his fingers into her hair and pull. The erratic tensing of his muscles. How he sucked air through his teeth and his head fell back, then forward.

When his eyes opened and met hers, the raw desire there made her sex clench. And the tender emotion she saw reflected also made her heart ache. She wanted to believe every word he said.

He pulled back quickly. "Not yet, Jo."

She bit her lips to try and suppress her cocky grin. "Are you that close?"

The lift of his lips made her heart flip. "Don't get it twisted. No matter how close I am, you come before me. And best believe, we're going multiple rounds."

Her eyes widened. The promise in his voice made her want to clap in delight. A delighted smile brushed her lips just as he dropped to his knees. She barely registered his intention before his mouth was there, and pleasure became her best friend.

Joanne cried out. The delicious feelings acute and wonderful. She leaned back on the bed, using her forearms for support. Her hands clutched the sheets in fists and she was gone, so lost in a whirlwind of pleasure that when his long fingers joined his mouth, she exploded. Devante rode the wave with her, slowly easing her back down with soft kisses and until she was lying sated and spent on the bed.

Joanne pointed to the nightstand. "Condoms are there." He reached for the drawer. "And lube." If he really was going to give her the multiple rounds he promised then they were going to need it.

He grinned as he pulled them both out. "My girl."

He quickly slid on the condom and added the extra lube before pulling her into his embrace and filling her completely. Afterward, he pulled her against his chest and kissed her softly. The delicious ache in her body from their lovemaking told her one very important thing. If this was what a relationship with Devante was like she was going to be a very happy woman.

Chapter Seven

Later that night, Devante leaned against Jo's headboard. She sat between his legs, her back against his chest. He lazily ran his hands up and down her arms as they listened to the jazz playing through the Bluetooth speaker on her nightstand. They'd spent the time between lovemaking talking, and when she mentioned Gregory Porter was one of her favorite musicians, he'd pulled up the latest album on his streaming service so they could listen together.

That moment, the entire afternoon, was surreal. He'd fantasized and dreamed about spending a day with Joanne in his arms, but never really thought it would happen. They were really together. His lips lifted and he grinned.

"You know what surprised me?" Joanne said quietly.

He stopped trailing his fingers over her stomach. "What surprised you?"

Her head tilted to the side. "All of the people saying you had a crush on me. My mom, Kayce, even Julian. They all said the same thing."

Devante wrapped his arms around her and gently squeezed her soft curves close. "I'm surprised you couldn't tell. I've had a crush on you since I was a teenager. I thought you were the finest, coolest girl out there."

Joanne chuckled and shook her head. "I mean... I noticed a little when you were younger, but I always viewed your crush as puppy love or something. After I got pregnant and had Julian, I focused so much on taking care of him while also trying to make money that I forgot all about your crush." She sighed and stared at the wall. "Not to mention, I haven't been really good at reading signals from men."

"What I said at your shop the other day is true. I've not only liked you, but respected and admired your drive. You never gave up on your dream and you supported Julian's dreams. Of course, I still crushed on you." He leaned down and kissed her cheek.

Her resulting smile was what he wanted. He didn't like the self-doubt in her eyes or the worry about how her past relationships played out when they were together. He only wanted her to look forward to the bright future he would work hard as hell to give her.

"I'm sorry about your grand opening."

She twisted in his arms so she could frown at him over her shoulder. "Sorry for what?"

"For what happened. I didn't mean to ruin your night. I knew you wanted everything to be perfect. I swear I didn't come with the intention of trying to have sex with you in the storage room."

"Then why did you take me in the storage room?"

"When I saw you and that guy...what was his name?"

"Jackson?" The pitch of her voice and her brows both rose.

"Yeah, Jackson. It wasn't just seeing you flirt with him. It was you calling me *young man*. All I knew was that I didn't want you to think of me like that anymore. I wanted you to know how I felt. I don't regret letting you know my feelings, but I do regret that it ruined your night. I'm sorry."

Joanne took a long breath before settling back into her

original position. "Thank you for saying that, but I played a part in what happened, too."

"Do you regret it?"

She placed her arms over his, which were encircling her waist, and squeezed. "No. Not really. Do I regret getting caught? Yes. Do I regret kissing you back? No. I am nervous about Tuesday. I was worried about clients canceling on me, but honestly, I've been caught up in worse scandals than this and people still came to me and that was when I was doing hair at home. This won't be the first time people talk about me and it won't be the last. Whatever happens on Tuesday, I'll deal with it."

"But that's the thing. I don't want you to have to deal with gossip because you're with me. I don't want to make your life harder."

Joanne chuckled. "Devante, people are going to talk about us regardless."

He stiffened, expecting her to say because of his family's reputation. That she was dating a guy from a less-than-stellar family who could do nothing for her.

"Until you kissed me, I would've kept thinking of you as off-limits. Why do you think I called you 'young man' so much? So I could remind myself that my little brother's best friend who was out here, let's be honest, hooking up with different people, wasn't seriously interested in me."

Devante only slightly relaxed. "I wasn't out here hooking up with different people. I've dated, but I haven't been with anyone I wanted to start anything long-term or serious with."

"What makes this different?" The unsureness in her voice made him wish he could chase away all her doubts. That would come with time. When he consistently showed her his feelings were real, then she'd never doubt his feelings, and he planned to be consistent.

"Because you're the only person I've liked and wanted to be with for most of my life. You're the woman I compare other women to. You're the woman whose smile makes me smile. You're the woman I not only desire, but admire. The way I feel about you isn't how I feel about other people."

She smiled at him over her shoulder. "You are really good with the words."

"They're nothing but the truth." He leaned down and kissed her. "I know it'll take time for you to believe everything I say. I'm not going to rush you. I'm going to show you. Every day we're together."

She was quiet for a few seconds, then asked in a hesitant voice, "Does my age bother you at all? It may not seem like much now, but I am ten years older. I can have kids but I'm not really in the mood to start over after getting Julian through college."

Devante considered her words before answering. "I haven't thought a lot about having kids. I'm not in a big rush. There's also adoption or being a foster parent if that particular urge ever comes up."

She pursed her lips as if considering before nodding slowly and smiling. "I might be okay with being a foster parent. Believe it or not, I considered that when Julian first went to college. The house was so quiet, and I wanted someone to take care of, but was struggling so hard just to save up and cover his expenses that I let the idea go."

"Well, then we'll think about that later. I want to be with you. Let's figure this out one day at a time. Can we do that?"

She sat up and shifted until she faced him. "What if you change your mind?"

Her blond locs hung loose around her shoulders. She looked beautiful, and vulnerable, and all he wanted to do was pull her back into his arms and make love to her until she never questioned his feelings. He'd do that, but first he needed her to understand that the way he felt about her went deeper than just sexual attraction.

Devante took her hands in his and pulled. She repositioned her legs until they were on either side of his waist. He wrapped his arms around her waist, and she put hers loosely around his neck. He stared deep into her eyes when he spoke.

"Jo, I won't change my mind anytime soon, if ever. What if you change your mind?"

She laughed. "Sir, we've officially been together for a few hours, and you've already made me happier than I've been in any other relationship. If you keep this up, you might be stuck with me."

He hoped that was the case. Joanne was a smart, hardworking woman who wanted a bit of glamour in her life. While he was trying to get to a point where he could give her all of that, he wasn't there yet. His earnest feelings might have gotten him here, but would they keep him by her side?

He wouldn't bring up his insecurities today. Today was too great to cast a shadow over. He only wanted to show her confidence. Confidence and assurance of his commitment to making this work.

Grinning, he leaned forward and kissed her. "Oh, really? I kind of like the idea of you being stuck to me." He moved his hands to squeeze her hips and tugged her forward until the softness between her thighs brushed against his thickening erection.

Joanne gasped and her eyes widened. "Are you seriously ready to go again? Are you trying to wear me out?"

Honestly, he couldn't get enough of her. "I asked you before if you could hang. But if you'd rather do something else, I'm down for whatever you want."

The warmth of her body seeped into his as she tightened her arms around his neck and pressed her forehead against his. "Oh, I can hang. I'm just making sure you can keep up with me."

Devante grabbed a handful of her locs and lightly pulled. "Don't doubt that I can keep up. I'll follow you to the ends of the earth, Jo." Emotion filled his voice. An emotion he hadn't planned to let slip through so soon. He was afraid to let her know how much he cared, because he didn't want to scare her off. Maybe he was offering too much too soon.

For a second, she seemed unsure, doubtful. Devante kissed her before those thoughts could take root. He may not be the best match for her, but he'd use every weapon in his arsenal to keep her until he was the perfect man for her. Her body softened and a moment later they were both lost in the kiss. Devante's insecurities drifted away. Right now, they were together and that's all that mattered.

Chapter Eight

Despite being caught nearly making love to Devante in her storage room during her grand-opening celebration, Joanne's first day officially open was going extremely well. She'd been worried no one would show up, or worse, everyone who did show up would only come to shame her for what happened. Her clients hadn't canceled, and even though there were the occasional smirks or questions about if it was true that she and Devante were dating, no one threw shade or gave her a hard time about her new relationship.

Emily Coleman, president of the business guild, and its secretary, Cyril Dash, who also owned a brewery downtown, came by to wish Joanne well on her opening day. Jackson smiled and waved as he passed by to go to his studio next door. Her mom and brother came through to drop off lunch because they knew she would be busy and not have time to go eat anything. And several of the other business owners in the downtown area dropped by to wish her luck while many residents shopping in the area waved or gave a thumbs-up as they passed by.

If anyone did try to bring up her relationship with Devante, she was quick to say yes they were dating and deflect. As she worked with her various clients, she deftly changed the conversation to her clients' children, what was happening with their jobs, the upcoming St. Patrick's Day Festival, or the latest antics on the soaps that Joanne had playing in the background. She diverted the conversation from other town gossip. All in all, her first day was going perfectly. The two nail technicians kept busy, and Joanne and the three other stylists managed to convince a few clients to fill in the two open spots on the esthetician's schedule for a facial.

"Joanne, this place is fantastic. I am so proud of you," Latasha Baker, Joanne's latest client, said as Joanne removed the plastic cape around her neck. Latasha looked in the mirror and did one last pat of her hair, a braided updo, before following Joanne to the front desk.

There wasn't a receptionist there yet, but Joanne planned to eventually have someone sitting at the front desk to greet clients as they walked in the door. Latasha stopped before the desk and grinned at Joanne. "Who would have thought you'd have all this when you were doing hair out of your kitchen?"

"I imagined all of this back when I was doing hair in my momma's kitchen. I'm just blessed to finally get here." Joanne handed Latasha a brochure with the various services now offered at her salon. She made sure to give one to every client she'd worked with today.

Latasha pursed her lips then wagged a finger. "You did imagine all this and made it a reality. Good for you."

"Nothing wrong with going after big dreams," Joanne replied confidently.

The door to the salon opened. Joanne looked up, prepared to greet the next customer. "Hey, how can I help—" Her eyes met those of the woman who entered, and her smile hardened around the edges. "Mattie? I didn't know you had an appointment today?"

Mattie Bryant was the sister of Peachtree Cove's mayor, Miriam Parker. While most people in town adored and got along well with Miriam, Mattie was an entirely different story. *Bougie* was the nicest word Joanne could use to describe her, because Mattie didn't mind letting everyone in town know that she had the best taste and the most class of any of them around there.

She was of average height and wore a curly, auburn-colored wig that flattered her sienna complexion and round face. She tugged on the stylish houndstooth blazer she'd matched with a denim shirt and tan pants as she glanced round the entryway with a critical eye. Her inspection ended with a sniff after she scanned the back of the salon, where the stylists and their customers were chatting and laughing. She crinkled her nose before giving Joanne a fake smile. "Well, I heard today was opening day for your little salon and as a board member for the downtown revitalization committee I had to come by and show my support. I have a brow-waxing appointment with Keisha."

Joanne ignored the "little salon" comment. Mattie loved getting a rise out of people and Joanne wasn't about to give her the satisfaction. Instead, she glanced back at Keisha, who'd just finished a silk press for the client in her seat. "She'll be with you in a moment. Please have a seat." Joanne pointed to one of the plush blue chairs in the waiting area.

"I see timeliness isn't at the forefront here," Mattie mumbled before sitting on the edge of the chair.

Joanne stopped herself from rolling her eyes and looked back at Latasha. "Have a good day, Latasha. I'll see you at your next appointment."

Latasha glanced over at Mattie, then back at Joanne. She looked as if she wanted to hover. Not surprising—when Mattie showed up there was usually drama and Latasha, who was also the editor of the *Peachtree Cove Gazette,* enjoyed drama.

"Um…okay. Thanks, Joanne," she murmured, then was off with a wiggle of her fingers.

Thankfully, Keisha came to the front with her client just as Latasha walked out. She turned a pleasant smile Mattie's way, but Joanne knew the young stylist well enough to recognize a fake smile from a sincere one.

"I'm ready for you, Ms. Bryant," Keisha said.

Mattie stood slowly and sniffed. "I'm glad I didn't have to wait too long."

Keisha's smile didn't waver. "You're actually here early. But I'm ready for you now. You can come on back."

Keisha headed toward her chair. Mattie followed and Joanne took up the rear. Since Mattie was only there for a brow waxing, Joanne hoped she would be in and out with no problem. Joanne had thirty minutes before her next client, so she swept up the hair around her chair.

"So, Joanne, I hear you're sleeping around with Devante Thompson," Mattie said loudly, not two seconds after she was settled back in the chair and Keisha had slathered wax on her right brow.

A hush fell over the salon as everyone turned to eye Mattie with varying levels of curiosity and disbelief. Not surprising, since that was what Mattie hoped for. Publicly calling out other people had to be one of her kinks.

Taking a calming breath, Joanne stopped sweeping and turned toward Mattie. She gave the woman a pointed stare. "Not that it's any of your business, but yes, we are dating. If that's what you're getting at."

Mattie laughed as if she'd made some great joke. "I never expected you to be the next notch on his bedpost. Really, Joanne, I'm surprised," she said as if she was lecturing a misbehaving child. She tilted her head to the side and pressed a finger to the corner of her mouth. "Though honestly, you were always one to walk on the wild side. Remember when you were messing around with Douglas Stone. Wasn't he married to someone one town over?"

Keisha ripped off the paper on Mattie's brow. Her gasp matched the ones from the other women in the salon. Joanne gripped the broom. Douglas was the last guy she'd openly dated. He hadn't been married, but he'd apparently been hiding a fiancée in Augusta. Mattie knew the other woman and had happily spread the word far and wide. When the other woman found out about Joanne, she'd publicly confronted Joanne when she was out with Julian at the town's Peach Festival and accused her of intentionally going after Douglas. One thing Joanne didn't do was fight over a man. She'd told the woman Douglas was all hers and she wouldn't have to worry about Joanne knocking on his door ever again. Everyone heard and talked about the scene for weeks.

That had been years ago. And while Joanne had never forgotten that Mattie was the one who'd initiated the embarrassing scene, she'd been glad to discover Douglas's true colors before she'd gotten further involved. She'd long since moved on, but, of course, today would be the day Mattie decided to remind everyone in town.

"Do you have a point, Mattie? Or do you get off coming into someone's place of business to spread negativity and lies."

There was no way she was about to show how much Mattie's petty dig had gotten to her. If she let the memory take hold, she would begin to question her decision to date Devante. She wouldn't let the pain of her past relationships have a seat at the table now and ruin her happiness.

Mattie blinked, but her coy smile didn't go away. The door to the salon opened, but Joanne was too focused on the rattlesnake in Keisha's chair to greet the newcomer.

"I'm just saying you have a history. Now you're trying to get your groove back or something. Not that I blame you, but with Devante Thompson, of all people?"

Joanne placed a hand on her hip and glared. "What are you trying to say about Devante?"

Mattie shrugged. "I mean… I give it to him and his sister for trying to dig themselves out of the gutter by starting businesses, but everyone knows their entire family is ghetto." Mattie chuckled as if she'd made a joke, ignoring the fact that no one joined in her laughter. "I wonder what his sister thinks. Knowing a woman older than her is messing with her baby brother."

A woman's angry voice came from the front of the salon. "How about you keep my name and my brother's name out your mouth before you catch these hands. That's what you can wonder about."

A collective gasp went through the room. Joanne spun around and froze. Devante's older sister, Tracey, was standing there, legs spread, hands on her full hips and her normally thick wavy hair braided back. She wore a navy blue polo shirt with the logo of the bed-and-breakfast she'd opened three years before, and she was glaring like a prize-fighter. She was flanked by two other women: one tall and curvy, wearing black slacks and a green button-up blouse, and the other of average height and thinner, wearing jeans and a T-shirt with her hair in a messy ponytail. Tracey's two best friends, Halle and Imani.

Joanne's surprise at seeing the trio lasted a second before she focused on the rage simmering in Tracey's eyes.

She'd seen that look before. The last thing she needed on her first day open was a fight.

She spun back toward Mattie. "I think it's time for you to go."

Mattie's shock morphed into disbelief. "But she only finished one brow."

Joanne waved off her words. She did not care about Mattie's half-done wax job. "And you started something knowing you were in the middle of a service. You should have saved your comments until after you were done."

Keisha smirked as she put down the waxing stick and stepped back. She crossed her arms and leaned against the counter. Joanne cocked her head to the side and gave Mattie a hurry-up look.

"What? I can't believe you would do this. Kicking out a client without even finishing the work. All I'm trying to do is look out and give a fellow business owner some advice. Do you really think your little shop is going to make it if you don't try to clean up appearances?"

Tracey spoke up again. "My brother is happy. Joanne is happy. Everyone in here is happy except for your hateful ass. Maybe if you met a guy who could give it to you on the regular you wouldn't be here minding other people's business."

Mattie scoffed and jumped up from her seat. Tracey took a step forward. Joanne moved between them. She turned to Mattie. "You really don't want to go there. You've done what you came to do. Stir up trouble. Get out now before you make things worse."

Sputtering, Mattie jerked off the cape and threw it on the floor. "I didn't want anything from your silly little shop, anyway." She raised her chin and stormed out.

The women in the shop burst out laughing and clapped as she left. Joanne's relief at her being gone was palpable, but other concerns wouldn't let her celebrate. More drama, and more stuff for people to talk about. Her perfect opening day would forever be tainted by Mattie's hatefulness.

She met Tracey's eyes, which still simmered from the encounter. Joanne wondered if any of the lingering anger was directed at her. Though Tracey was older than Devante, she was still several years younger than Joanne. She was also fiercely loyal and ready to fight anyone who did her family wrong. And she'd shown up with her friends.

"Can we talk?" Tracey asked.

Joanne nodded. "Sure. We can go outside."

Tracey nodded and turned to walk out. Imani and Halle gave Joanne small, reassuring smiles before they followed. Outside they moved away from the door to stand by Tracey's burgundy minivan. Despite her ride-or-die personality, Tracey had done a good job of separating herself from the wild child she'd once been. Occasional appearances from her fiery temper wouldn't let her completely live it down.

"Is this about Devante?" Joanne asked.

Tracey shook her head. "Not really, but kinda. I was over at the bookstore when I heard Mattie talking on her cell to a friend about coming by your shop. She was saying it was probably a crappy hole-in-the-wall and that she was going to give you a hard time. Especially since you're screwing around with my brother. Well, that made me mad."

Imani nodded and chuckled. "So she called us."

Halle looked at her friends with affection. "And we came to make sure she didn't start any trouble."

Joanne stared at the three women and then shook her head. "Don't tell me The Get Fresh Crew showed up to help me out?" Joanne said, using the nickname the women had used to describe their group when they were teens who picked peaches around town during the summers.

The three friends laughed. "I haven't heard that in forever," Imani said.

"That's because you don't come to town enough," Tracey replied. "They still talk about us."

The three had been best friends growing up. Seeing one usually meant the other two weren't far behind and they always had each other's backs. Imani worked as a doctor in Florida, but was in town for her mother's upcoming wedding, which had been the talk of the town pre-Joanne's scene with Devante. Halle was Peachtree Cove Middle School's vice principal.

"I appreciate you all rolling up," Joanne said. "But I could handle Mattie."

Tracey shrugged again. "I know that, but you're dating Devante. He's been in love with you since forever. Now that you're together, you're family. No one talks about or messes with my family."

Joanne grinned, touched by Tracey's words and the emotions they swirled in her. She'd been prepared to face all of the claims that she was being a fool in love again, or that maybe she was just another notch on Devante's bedpost, because she believed in the emotion in Devante's voice when he spoke to her, and the trust in his eyes when they stared into hers. But having the support of his sister, though—that unexpected action made her throat tighten.

Joanne stepped forward and hugged Tracey. "I'm more than happy to be a part of the family."

Chapter Nine

Devante took one last look at the setup in the living area of his two-bedroom apartment and wondered if it was too much or not enough. He'd seen a picture online of someone who'd turned their living room into a home theater for a romantic date night and decided to give it a try. He'd blown up an air mattress and laid it before his sofa for plenty of lounging space, hooked up a projector that would display the movie on a screen he'd set up in front of the television and decorated the screen with Christmas lights he'd gotten from his sister. Bowls of popcorn, candy and a meat-and-cheese tray he'd put together himself sat waiting on a platter next to the air mattress.

He thought the setup was nice, but he couldn't get some of the comments on the picture out of his mind. He shouldn't have read the comments. That was his first mistake. There'd been a lot of people who called the idea cheap and stupid. Others said if your partner couldn't afford movie tickets then why date them in the first place. Those comments made him doubt if his idea was a romantic as he'd originally thought, or just tacky.

All he could do now was hope Joanne liked the idea. He'd already invited her to his place to celebrate ending her first full week open, and he didn't want to change their plans. The men she'd dated before him might have turned out to be jerks, but they'd all had one thing in common: class. They'd been college guys or professionals. The type of guys Joanne used to say she wanted to be with. He was proud of being a contractor, but no one would say he was classy. His contracting business was successful, but small. The call for bids on a new state project he'd gone after would help him grow. It was the biggest contract he'd ever sought, but even if he was selected, that wouldn't take away his past or the way people in town, like Mattie, might view him.

A knock on the door broke him from his thoughts. He took a deep breath. The time to change was too late. If she didn't like it, then he'd do what he could to impress her the next time.

He opened the door and Joanne greeted him on the other side with a big smile. "I hope I'm not too early." Her locs were twisted up into a cute style and she was dressed casually in a pair of jeans and a red sweater.

Devante grinned and pulled her into his arms for a huge hug. "You're never too early." He breathed in the lemongrass-and-coconut scent of her lotion and kissed her. He still couldn't believe she was dating him, but he damn sure wouldn't take their time for granted.

"Good, because I was getting ready and could have hung around the house longer, but I was ready to see you."

Her words warmed him faster than a blazing fire. "Same for me. I hope you're ready for a fun night."

"What do you have planned?"

He pulled her in and waved his hand toward the living room. "Ta da! A romantic indoor movie experience."

Joanne's eyes widened and she took in the space. Devante held his breath as she looked over his attempt to be romantic. His anxiety rose with each second she examined the room. Now he couldn't overlook how the Christmas lights drooped a little on one side. The crackers he'd put on the plate weren't arranged perfectly, and he'd gotten the first box of butter crackers he'd seen. Maybe he should have gone for the fancier brand. In fact, maybe he should have ordered a tray from the natural-foods store. Didn't she enjoy natural foods?

"I love this!" Joanne clamped a hand to her heart.

Devante let out a breath. He worried his knees would buckle from his relief. "Really?"

She beamed up at him. "Yes. I saw something like this online a while back. I thought it would be fun to do, but I never got around to setting it up. I wasn't sure if my girl-friends were interested, and well… Julian isn't coming home just to watch movies on an air mattress with his momma."

"Anything you see that you want to try, let me know. I'm always willing to do something new."

Her eyes sparkled. "Don't tease me, because I see a lot of stuff I want to try." She left him to settle onto the air mat-tress. He'd set it up so they could lean against the couch for support, and he'd put several pillows out to also make the space more comfortable. "What are we watching?"

"*The Photograph*. I heard it was a good romantic movie. Have you seen it?"

She nodded but frowned. "I went to the theater to see it but didn't get to finish."

"Why not?"

She sighed and shrugged. "The person I was with said it was boring and wanted to go. I just never got back to watching it."

"Did you think it was boring?" He grabbed the wine chilling in a bucket off the dinette table that separated the kitchen from the living area and came back to her.

"Nope. I was enjoying the story."

"And they wanted to leave even though you liked it?"

She rolled her eyes and reached for the popcorn. "He was like that. I didn't see him anymore after that."

Devante frowned as he poured wine into the glasses already on the tray table on the air mattress. "Was that that investment guy?"

"You remember him?"

He handed her a glass and met her eye. "Yeah. I remember most of the guys you dated."

She blinked then lowered her eyes. "Keeping a tally?"

He placed a finger under her chin, so she'd meet his eyes again. "Nah, checking out the competition."

That made her smile, and she shook her head. "There is no competition."

"It felt a little like that to me. On the real, the types of guys you dated is one of the reasons I didn't think I stood a chance with you."

"Why? Those guys weren't great. You, on the other hand, are pretty amazing." She leaned forward and kissed him.

Devante wanted to follow her when she pulled back, but instead he sipped his wine. There would be plenty of time to kiss and do all the things he wanted to do with Joanne. He hadn't brought the air mattress out just for lounging.

"Yeah, but those guys were professional, suit-and-tie guys," he said. "I knew you wanted someone who could help take care of you and Julian. You wanted someone stable who would lift you up, not hold you back. I never knew if I'd live up to that."

She scrunched up her nose. "You make me sound a little stuck-up."

He shook his head. "I always understood what you meant. You had enough on your plate taking care of Julian. I knew you didn't want a man who was just going to be like another person to raise."

She sighed and leaned back against his sofa. "I did think I could only get support from a certain type of guy," she said in a considering tone. "I know all successful men aren't jerks. I just happened to end up with a few who were. They thought I should be thankful if they showed me the slightest bit of interest because I wouldn't be able to do better. Those guys, I quickly tossed aside."

Devante sat next to her on the mattress. He rested an arm on the seat of the sofa and met her eyes. "I want to be a partner to you. I don't want to hold you back. I'm going after this new contract in Augusta. If I get it, I'll finally be the lead contractor on a project and not just a sub. Which means, this will be the most money my business has made. It'll help me be able to give you nice things."

Joanne placed a hand on his cheek. "Devante, I'll be the first one to celebrate if you get the new contract. But only because I'd be proud of you. I'm not looking for someone who can give me nice things. I'm looking for someone who treats me well and who's kind. You've already proven to be both."

Tracey and Joanne had told him about what happened on her opening day. The way Mattie had talked about their family. He didn't expect anything less of Joanne or his sister than for them to stand up for him. But, once again, he'd caused a scene at her shop.

"You mean that?" he asked, hating the uncertainty in his voice.

"More than anything. I'm not chasing money or status. The other day you said you want to be my partner as I grow. Let's be partners as we grow together."

The sincerity in her voice and the affection in her eyes

calmed the worry in his heart. "I can't help but think about what Mattie Bryant said at your shop."

She sighed and rolled her eyes. "Mattie's got her own problems and everyone in town knows she's hateful."

"She is, but Mattie isn't the only one in town who still thinks of us as nobodies. That we're pretending to be something we're not."

"Mattie and the people like her are unhappy with their own lives for whatever reason and try to make other people unhappy. I've never judged you or your family. Lord knows I am not a model of virtuous behavior."

"Hearing people still think like that…it makes me mad that people only see me for where I started and not what I've accomplished. My parents didn't have it easy, and they didn't always know how to make things better, but they loved us…in their own way. I guess those feelings of not being good enough still sit with me sometimes. Makes me want to be more, do more. Makes me want to become so successful they can't say a damn thing about me or my past."

"I get it. I felt that way at first about my new salon. I wanted to be a success with no drama. I worried that people would only see the bad and not my hard work. But guess what, opening day was great, despite Mattie. Everyone who matters supports me. And my work speaks for itself. It did when I was doing hair at a kitchen table, and it matters now. I do what makes me happy. Always have and always will. What makes you happy? Are you only going to be happy if you get this contract and can show people you're worthy? Or will you go after the next contract and the next one?"

He shook his head. "Even if I don't get it, I won't give up. Worked my butt off to one day become the lead contractor. I'm proud of my business."

She patted his chest. "Then that's what matters. Not

Mattie, or even me if I were looking for someone to buy me stuff. I like you, Devante. Your kindness, your drive and your determination. Let's do what we both want and grow together."

Devante stared down into Joanne's dark eyes and emotion swelled in his chest. He loved her. Not just the puppy love from before, not the infatuation he'd carried for years. He was in love with this strong, supportive, amazing woman. He wanted to tell her, but knew the time wasn't right. They were just getting started, and she was still learning to trust what they had. Instead of saying what he felt, he kissed her. The kiss was deep, and before long they were both lost.

When he finally pulled back, her moan made him want to forget the romantic evening he planned and spend the rest of the night making love to her. "The movie," he said in a rumbling voice.

Joanne's wicked smile made his body burn. "Can wait," she whispered against his lips.

That's all he needed to hear.

Chapter Ten

Joanne swayed to the sounds of the Gregory Porter album as part of her last round of cleaning the shop when someone knocked on the glass door. Although the other stylists and technicians did a good job keeping their areas clean, she always did one final walk-through to check everything and make sure the shop was in top shape before opening the next day. In the month since she'd opened, business had been great. So great she might even be able to reduce the number of heads she styled a day and rent out her booth space to another stylist. Then she could focus solely on running the business, but that was a dream and a thought for another day.

She leaned the broom against her styling chair and sashayed to the door. As expected, Devante stood on the other side of the glass on the sidewalk. It was dark outside, and the streetlights along Main Street, along with the lights from the other shops, cast a golden glow against his skin. She quickly unlocked the door and let him in.

A burst of cool spring air accompanied him as he hurried inside. "Ready to leave?"

She nodded but didn't move to get her stuff. "I am." She raised her brows and excitedly patted his chest. "So…what happened at the bid opening?"

She was anxious to know the answer. For the last few

days he'd been nervous about the bid he submitted. She'd overheard him talking to the people he worked with about their capacity to take on the project. Watched as he'd gone over the list of his equipment and the quantities of materials needed to do the job. He'd put together a competitive bid that wouldn't stretch him and would allow him to do a good job.

He took in a deep breath before placing his hands on her shoulders. "Well, it looks like I'm…"

Joanne raised her brows and waited. When he continued to stare at her without revealing if the news was good or bad, she thought she would burst with anticipation. She gripped his shirt and tried to shake him.

"Looks like you're what? Quit playing with me?"

He laughed and pulled her into his arms for a tight hug. "It looks like I'm the low bidder."

Joanne screamed in excitement and jumped up and down. "See, I told you that you'd get it. I knew you didn't have anything to worry about."

His hands looped around her waist and stopped her celebratory hopping. "I know, but they still have to do a full review of the bids. Make sure I didn't miss anything."

"You didn't. You spent so much time making sure you met all the requirements for the project. I'm not surprised at all."

"It's amazing and kind of unbelievable. I always dreamed of this, but it's still kind of hard to believe, if that makes sense."

"It makes sense. I still have to look around my shop and pinch myself to believe it's real. That something I've dreamed of for so long is actually real."

She pulled away from him and went back to her station. Devante followed her as she took the broom and put it in the storage room.

"You know you don't have to stay here after everyone else leaves and clean up," he said evenly.

Joanne suppressed a chuckle. He didn't like her staying later than everyone else and often came to walk her out whenever he didn't have another job. "I know, but I still like doing it. Cleaning up after the last client was one of my favorite things to do when I was doing hair out of my kitchen."

"Why?" There wasn't any judgment in his voice, just curiosity.

"One, I don't mind cleaning. I enjoy putting things back in order. Two, because when I cleaned up by myself, I could think back on the day and my accomplishments. Back then that was the only way I could make myself feel as if I'd done something worthwhile."

"Do you still need to feel that way?"

She looked around her salon. Clean and ready for the next day. Thought about earlier, with all of the seats filled with clients, the nail technicians busy with manicures and pedicures all day, and the esthetician working on facials and making product recommendations. Her dream was a reality and she'd done that. Something she never thought she'd accomplish back when she was struggling to buy formula and diapers for Julian. When she had to fight his father in court for child-support payments. When people who were supposed to be close to her said her dream was cool and all, but didn't look at her as if she'd really accomplish it.

She looked back at Devante and smiled. "No. Now I like to stick around and just bask in what I've built. I'm so damn proud of this shop. So humbled to see it be successful. I just like being here."

He stood, crossed over to her and wrapped her in his embrace. "Then I won't bother you about sticking around after everyone leaves. You should enjoy and bask in what you've accomplished."

"I'm not just happy about what I did here with the salon. I'm also happy when I'm with you."

"You are?" The way he asked, as if he still couldn't believe she was excited about being with him, was another humbling thing. She never would have believed a man would feel blessed to be with her. She'd internalized the rejections so much she'd lost sight of just how precious she was. That's why it had taken her so long to admit that she wanted to start dating again. She'd been afraid of being rejected and once again shown she wasn't enough. She was deserving of love and affection. She wasn't afraid to admit that anymore, and she wasn't going to let the past stop her from accepting every bit of affection Devante was willing to give.

"I am. I know it's early and we're just starting…but I think I love you." She said the words she'd promised never to say to another man. Every time she said the words, disaster struck. A small part of her heart worried that this would be the breaking point. That Devante would look at her and realize he could find someone younger, prettier, sexier.

Instead, Devante's face filled with such joy it made her heart ache. "I know I love you, Joanne. It started with puppy love, turned into something else. Something I never thought I'd see returned by you, and it's grown into a feeling I can't call anything but love. I love you and I can't believe someone as amazing as you loves me, too."

She lifted on her toes and pressed her lips to his. "Believe it. Otherwise, I'll have to find ways to constantly show you."

"Ways like what?"

She looked at him and grinned. Slipping out of his arms,

she went to the front door and flipped the lock. His brows raised as she came back to him and took his hand in hers.

"What are you doing?"

She gave him a wicked smile. "Taking you to the storage room. I'm going to show you just how much I love you as we finish what we started the night of my grand opening."

* * * * *

Acknowledgments

Thank you to all the family and friends who encouraged me, supported me, and put up with me as I worked on this book during ladies' trips, family trips, and coffee meet ups. Thank you to Ashley, Toya, Tori, KD, Dren, Cheris, Yasmin, Eric, EJ, Sam, Mom, Dad, James, Jayden, Jacob and Timmy. I appreciate each and every one of you.

HARLEQUIN
Reader Service

Enjoyed your book?

Try the perfect subscription for Romance readers and get more great books like this delivered right to your door.

See why over 10+ million readers have tried Harlequin Reader Service.

Start with a Free Welcome Collection with free books and a gift—valued over $20.

Choose any series in print or ebook. See website for details and order today:

TryReaderService.com/subscriptions